Mack Bolan leaned around the door and fired the Desert Eagle

He was driven back once more by return fire. Behind him, he heard the steady release of .223 rounds from Seven's M-16, and the constant pounding from the roof across the alley hadn't let up since the sniper had climbed the ladder to a better position.

Sooner or later, the sniper behind them was going to find his groove. He'd get Seven first, then Bolan. Allowing his partner across the hall to have full access to Luiza Polyakova.

Bolan checked his extra ammo. He had enough to keep the stalemate going at least a little longer. The bottom line was that if something drastic didn't happen soon, they were going to die.

MACK BOLAN ®
The Executioner

The Executioner

Don Pendleton's®

SOVIET SPECTER

A GOLD EAGLE BOOK FROM

W☉RLDWIDE®

TORONTO • NEW YORK • LONDON
AMSTERDAM • PARIS • SYDNEY • HAMBURG
STOCKHOLM • ATHENS • TOKYO • MILAN
MADRID • WARSAW • BUDAPEST • AUCKLAND

First edition March 2004

ISBN 0-373-64304-7

Special thanks and acknowledgment to
Jerry VanCook for his contribution to this work.

SOVIET SPECTER

Say not thou, What is *the cause* that the former days were better than these? for thou dost not inquire wisely concerning this.

—*Ecclesiastes* VII, 10

The best prophet of the future is the past.
—John Sherman, speech in the Senate,
June 5, 1890

Stop evil in one way and it just comes back in another. My job is to eliminate evil men and delay its return.

—Mack Bolan

For Bob Smith

Prologue

With trembling fingers Luiza Polyakova pulled the bottle of antacid tablets from her purse and dumped four into her palm. The same shaking hand somehow got them to her mouth without dropping them.

She placed the bottle back into her handbag, chewed and tried to swallow. The tiny flakes of powder felt like fire-dipped cannonballs burning her throat and threatening to choke off her air. She covered her mouth with both hands and coughed, silently praying no one around her would notice the state she was in. Finally her throat relaxed and she could breathe again.

Polyakova felt the medicine enter her stomach and hoped it would bring relief from the terror that was centered there. But there were no pills for her quivering hands or the anxiety that encompassed her entire body and made her skin prickle. She closed her eyes.

What she really wanted to do was turn and run out of the building, but she knew she couldn't. Instead she crossed her arms tightly beneath her breasts and dug her fingernails into her ribs. The sharp nails in her flesh brought their own pain. But it was better than the horror that flooded her soul.

Polyakova stared through the huge glass windows at the runway a quarter of a mile from the terminal, across an open field. She watched the cargo plane with the Russian markings touch down on the tarmac and slow, its flaps fighting the air resistance of the plane's own creation. The sight sent her fingers even deeper into her sides, and a moan threatened to escape her lips. But she didn't dare make a sound or loosen her grip. She couldn't do anything that might draw the attention of the men in uniform.

"It is always like this," the Russian said under her breath. "Every time. And I will never get used to it." Tears threatened to form in her eyes but she blinked them away. In her mind, she heard her father's voice say, "You must be strong, Luiza."

For a moment she was transported back in time and was suddenly five years old again. She was about to leave for her first year at the Soviet training school for girls. She would be away from her family for months before seeing them again, and then only for a short visit. At five, there was no blinking away tears no matter how she tried, and she was crying openly in her father's arms.

Her mind jerked back to the present as she watched the plane taxi toward the U.S. Customs hangar. In the back of her brain, she still heard her father's voice—the voice she had heard that day so long ago. "Luiza, my darling," her father had said as he wiped away her tears with his handkerchief. "What cannot be overcome or escaped must be endured."

The Russian woman continued to watch the plane. "And there is no overcoming this," she whispered. "From this, there is no escape."

"Pardon me?" A deep voice just to her side broke into Polyakova's terror-induced half dream. She turned stiffly to see exactly what she had most feared—a U.S. Customs officer. He had stepped up next to her while her eyes were on the runway and her mind had been in the Soviet Union of thirty years ago.

But the man was smiling, and as she turned she saw his eyes fall briefly to her breasts before shooting back up to meet her eyes. Polyakova almost gasped out a breath of relief. He wasn't there to arrest her. He was only hoping to strike up a conversation that would eventually lead her into his bedroom. She caught the breath and forced a smile, hoping it didn't look as false as it felt. "Oh," she said coyly. "Did I say something?"

"Something," the officer said. "But I couldn't make out what it was." He had short-cropped blond hair and was actually quite handsome. Under other circumstances, with less grievous problems to occupy her mind, she might even have been interested. But such was not the case at the moment.

"It must not have been important," Polyakova said, keeping the smile frozen in place. "Because I can't remember what it was myself."

The man with the short blond hair laughed. "They say it's okay," he said.

She frowned. "What is okay?"

"It's okay if you talk to yourself. They say it's only crazy when you start answering."

Polyakova kept the smile in place and even managed a soft laugh. "I will remember that," she said. She turned back to face the window. In her peripheral vision, she saw the Customs man start to say something else. Then he stopped. His face betrayed the fact that he had given her up for a lost cause. He turned and walked away.

The Russian cargo plane reached the customs dock and ground to a halt. Polyakova saw more men in uniform come out onto the loading area with clipboards in their hands. She turned and began making her way down the concourse toward the office where she would be required to fill out forms. On them, she would swear under oath that she was receiving a shipment of oil paintings for sale at her Greenwich Village art gallery. As always, Nestor Rabashka, who had accompanied the shipment from Moscow, would meet her there to do his own paperwork before turning the consignment over to her.

Her high heels clicked along the tile as she thought of Rabashka. Even thinking about the short, portly man with the single gray eyebrow stretching across his forehead made her shudder. And when she was actually forced to *see* Rabashka it was all she could do to keep from screaming.

As she neared the door below the U.S. Customs sign, Polyakova thought of the cargo she was about to take into her possession. There would be the oil paintings, of course—paintings that she had purchased at bargain prices because they hadn't sold well in her native Moscow's depressed economy. But mixed in randomly among these paintings would be other stolen works of art. And hidden in all of the frames, regardless of whether the pictures were legitimate or not, would be the white powder.

What was it? Polyakova wondered as she continued on along the tile toward the door. Cocaine? Heroin? She had never seen either drug, and wouldn't recognize either if she did. And she had never asked Rabashka, not wanting to know. Agafonka Ontomanov—who she suspected had once been KGB or Soviet military—would then meet her at her art gallery in Greenwich Village. There, Ontomanov would collect the stolen paintings, then go through the frames, retrieving the small, tightly wrapped plastic bags.

Pushing her way through the glass door into the office, Polyakova was somewhat comforted to see a familiar face behind the counter. Henry Something. She didn't know his last name and never had. He looked up as she entered and smiled.

"Hello, Luiza," he said. "Good to see you again." Like the other customs man earlier, Henry couldn't resist a quick downward glance at her chest. Another time, another place, Polyakova might have found it irritating. But again, at this moment, she had far more important matters to consider than the fact that she had been well gifted in that department.

Henry turned and searched through a wall of small wooden shelves, finally picking out three forms and turning back to hand them to her. "Need something to write with?" he asked, his hand moving automatically to the pocket of his uniform.

The Russian shook her head. She took the forms, then retired across the room to take a seat at one of the small classroom-like desks against the opposite wall. She pulled a gold pen from her purse and began filling in the blanks. She had done so enough times in the past that she suspected she could have completed the forms blindfolded.

Which didn't seem like such a bad idea when Nestor Rabashka pushed through the glass door a moment later. Had she

been blindfolded she wouldn't have had to see him or feel the
inevitable tingling of horror his presence sent surging down her
spine. As always Rabashka's brown suit appeared to have been
slept in. His black-turning-white hair looked as if he had combed
it with a wrench, and that lone eyebrow seemed to wiggle across
the top of his face like a hairy worm. He wasn't close enough
yet but Polyakova knew she would soon be assaulted by the
stench of garlic and cabbage. She had never seen Rabashka when
he wasn't wearing both the brown suit and the odor.

Henry greeted the Russian with the same smile he'd given
Polyakova. The customs man didn't seem to mind Rabashka as
much as she did. But he had no reason to loathe Nestor Rabashka.
Henry didn't know that the dowdy man in the brown suit would
show or feel no more emotion plunging a dagger into his heart
than he showed filling out the customs forms. Turning his back
again, Henry picked out several other pages and handed them
across the counter. The Russian took them and made his way
across the room.

The garlic-cabbage scent was mixed with a whiff of pepper-
mint, and the combination was especially noxious. Rabashka sat
in the desk next to Polyakova without a word and pulled a pen
from somewhere inside the brown jacket.

Polyakova had just signed her name when the phone on the
counter suddenly rang. The shrill sound in the formerly quiet office caused her to jerk. She glanced up but Henry hadn't seen her.
He already had the receiver at his ear.

A moment later the smile on the customs man's face flickered
down into a frown. Then, almost as quickly, it returned to a
smile. But it was a different kind of smile than he'd worn before.
Fake. It reminded Polyakova of the false expressions of humor
and friendliness into which she'd contorted her own face when
talking to the handsome blond customs officer.

The phone still against his ear, Henry glanced up for an in-
stant and Polyakova saw the wooden grin of a marionette. "All
right," the customs man said into the phone. He paused, then nodded his head. "I'll tell them." He dropped the receiver back into

the cradle. "Seems to be some delay, Luiza. No big deal—they're probably just backed up on the docks. You know how it is these days after 9/11."

Polyakova nodded. The explanation was logical. Still, she couldn't help wondering if Henry's excuse for the delay was as phony as his smile. The possibility brought on a whole new flood of ice water in her veins. Was she just being paranoid? She didn't know, and it didn't really matter at this point. It was too late to run. What would happen, would happen.

The Russian art dealer dropped her pen back in her purse and pulled out a small compact to keep her hands busy while she waited. Flipping the lid, she looked into the small mirror and saw the terror in her eyes. Calm yourself, she ordered. You have done this countless times before. You are always frightened but everything always turns out all right.

You are a well-respected art importer, and you never receive more than a cursory check at customs. There is never any problem.

But from somewhere deep in her soul Polyakova heard a voice that reminded her that there was a first time for everything. Her hands started to shake again, and she gripped the sides of her purse.

A quick glance upward, through the glass walls leading to the hallway outside, did nothing to ease her fear. When she had come into the office, the hallway had been deserted. But now, close to a dozen men—all dressed in dark suits—stood along the corridor. They appeared to be trying just a little too hard to look casual. Trying a little too hard not to appear to be together when their suits were as telltale as uniforms.

Her eyes darted toward Rabashka. Maybe she was just being paranoid. But if so, so was the ugly Russian. He had fidgeted slightly when Henry announced the delay. But now Polyakova saw the huge beetle brow drop toward his nose. "I must go to the men's room," Rabashka said in his gravelly Russian accent. He stood. "I will be back." He turned and started out of the office.

The men outside saw him coming through the glass and all turned toward the door. They began to converge on the office as

Rabashka pushed through into the hallway. Their hands disappeared beneath their jackets.

Rabashka's own hand went into the side pocket of the brown suit coat and came out holding a small handgun. He raised his arm before any of the men could draw their weapons.

Two explosions roared through the still open glass door, and the man closest to the Russian went down. Then what sounded like a symphony from hell broke out in the hallway as the men in the suits poured round after round into Nestor Rabashka.

Polyakova sat frozen to her desk. It was as if she were in a theater, watching a movie she wished she hadn't come to see. But she no longer doubted her fears.

This wasn't her imagination. It wasn't paranoia.

This was real.

Two of the men knelt next to Rabashka's body. One of them grabbed the pistol and pried it from the Russian's hand. The other held a finger to the prostrate man's throat, then looked up and shook his head. Four more of the suits came crashing into the office, their guns still drawn and aimed at Polyakova. As they closed in on her, one of them held up a black wallet with a badge pinned to it. "Luiza Polyakova?" the man asked.

Polyakova wasn't sure whether she had nodded or not, but it didn't seem to matter. The man continued.

"Luiza Polyakova. United States Customs. You're under arrest."

As she was handcuffed behind her back and led out of the office, Polyakova heard the same man saying something about her having the right to remain silent.

The big man in the dark gray suit held a briefcase in his hand. He was staring through the one-way glass. Inside the small interrogation room he saw the woman seated on one side of the steel table bolted to the floor. She was unusually attractive with high Slavic cheekbones, sensuous lips and a smooth, fair complexion. Even in the loose-fitting jailhouse coveralls, it was impossible to avoid noticing her breasts. They appeared to have been meant for a much larger woman.

Tears streaked down her face, smearing the woman's makeup as she stared across the table. Across from her sat a middle-aged man with a balding scalp. He was overweight—but with the "hard fat" of someone who still remained active. His short-sleeved shirt was tucked into his navy blue slacks. A holster was visible on his belt. Although empty, the open-top friction retention leather showed the clear profile of a SIG-Sauer semiautomatic pistol.

The man's given name was John Jameson. But watching him through the one-way glass, Mack Bolan knew Jameson was more often referred to as "Johnny Seven."

An intercom connected the two rooms and Bolan stood near it. Not that he would have had to. Johnny Seven's voice boomed as he lambasted the woman. "No, Ms. Polyakova," the interrogator said sarcastically. "It's not just smuggling drugs. It would have been just smuggling drugs—heroin, to be exact—but two men got killed during the takedown. One of ours—Fred Kiley—who I knew, and that skell you worked with, Rabashka. That makes it two counts of murder during the commission of a felony, lady." He leaned in across the table and stuck his face into the woman's. "Which, in turn, means if you don't start answering my questions you're going to find yourself strapped down to a table with a needle in your arm!"

Johnny Seven's threat brought on a fresh flow of tears from the woman.

"Hope you like potassium," Seven said, moving back away again. "Big doses of it. 'Cause that's what they kill you with here in New York."

"I have already told you all I know!" the woman sobbed. Her eyes searched the table for something. Tissues, Bolan guessed, because he had seen her do so several times already before finally resorting to her hands to wipe her eyes. As she did so again now, repulsion contorted her face. She was obviously a woman not used to the slovenly conditions of a Rikers Island interrogation room.

Bolan shook his head behind the one-way glass. He could readily see that Drug Enforcement Administration Agent John "Johnny Seven" Jameson was taking the wrong approach with Luiza Polyakova. Johnny Seven was right on one count—the woman wasn't telling all she knew. Bolan could sense she was lying. But his instincts also told him she would continue to lie as long as these hardline tactics continued.

He glanced down at his watch in the dimly lit room. He would give the DEA agent another five minutes as a professional courtesy, then he would intercede.

As he listened to Johnny Seven continue to harangue Luiza Polyakova, Bolan thought back over the past few hours. He had just completed a mission in the Caribbean and been on his way back to the U.S. when Hal Brognola phoned him in the plane. Brognola, the director of the ultracovert Stony Man Farm and also a top-level Department of Justice administrator, had filled him in on the bust. U.S. Customs had called in the DEA. But word of the huge seizure had also reached the ears of the President of the United States. And the President had decided he wanted Stony Man Farm—the top secret counter-terrorist institution—involved. He suspected there was more to it than met the eye.

So did Mack Bolan.

When the five minutes had expired and nothing had changed in the interrogation room, Bolan opened the door and stepped out into the hall. As he entered the room he'd been watching, both the woman and man looked up. "Who the hell are you?" Seven demanded. "Get outta here."

Bolan had no official commission with the Justice Department, but that didn't mean he didn't have credentials. He pulled out the badge case holding the DOJ badge Brognola had finessed for him and held it up. "Matt Cooper," he said. "Justice."

"Justice?" Seven said, standing up behind the table. "What business does Justice have here?"

Bolan shrugged. "That's what I'm here to find out," he said.

"I'm Jameson, DEA," Seven practically spat. "And I don't need you."

"I know who you are," Bolan said. "And the President seems to think you do need me."

Johnny Seven scowled in puzzlement. "The president of *what?*"

"The United States."

"Right," he answered sarcastically. "He probably called you personally."

"No," Bolan said. "But I can get him on the phone right now if that's what it'll take to convince you."

Seven looked at Bolan as if he might have two heads. "Are you nuts? What, you expect me to believe all that? And I suppose you and the Man have a round of golf set up for later in the day, too."

Bolan reached into the inside pocket of his coat and pulled out his cellular phone. Tapping in a number, he handed the instrument to Seven. "Ask him yourself," he said. He smiled pleasantly. "And tell him I may have to cancel on the golf."

Johnny Seven snorted through his nose and took the phone,

holding it to his ear. But a second later, all the smugness left him. Bolan repressed a smile as he watched the shock come over the agent's face. The President's voice was still the most easily recognized voice in the world.

"Uh, excuse me, sir," Johnny Seven said uncomfortably. "I wasn't really expecting it to be you." He paused a few seconds while the President spoke, then said, "Yes, sir. My name's John Jameson. DEA. And yes, that's what it's about." After a few more seconds, he said, "Yes, sir," again. Then, "Thank you, sir. It was a pleasure talking to you." Pressing the button to end the call, he looked up at Bolan as he handed back the phone. "Sounds like you're for real."

"Sometimes too real," Bolan said as he stuck the phone back in his pocket.

"Good man, that guy," Seven said. "At least one hell of an improvement over the scumbag we had in the White House last go-around." The shock of talking to the President suddenly wore off and Seven remembered Polyakova. His head snapped back her way.

Before the agent could say anything further, Bolan cleared his throat. "I'd like to see you outside for a minute before we go on," he said. Without waiting for an answer, he turned and exited the room. Johnny Seven followed.

As soon as the door was closed behind them, Bolan asked, "How about letting me have a go at her?"

Seven's bristle was instinctive. He glanced at the observation room next door. "You've already been watching?"

Bolan nodded. He had read Seven's file during the flight to New York and knew enough about the man to respect his abilities. "You've hit a stone wall," Bolan said. "It can happen to anybody. Sometimes a fresh face behind the questions can change everything."

Johnny Seven didn't like it—his face showed that—but Bolan's low-key approach hadn't backed him into a corner in which his pride took over. Slowly, he nodded. "Want me in there?"

"Definitely," Bolan said. "But later. Let's throw her off stride with me by myself for now." He nodded to the observation room. "Why don't you watch from there?"

Seven hesitated, and for a moment it looked as if he might be angry. Then his entire body visibly relaxed and a thin grin curled his upper lip. "Well, hell. At least you're polite about stealing my case."

"Nobody's stealing your case," Bolan said. Then, before the conversation could get started again, he pushed back into the room and took the seat across from the Russian woman. He set his big briefcase down on the floor as he studied the frightened green eyes and smeared makeup on the other side of the table. Then, pulling a clean handkerchief from his pocket, he handed it to Luiza Polyakova.

Taking the cloth, she gently wiped her face. "I must look a mess," she said.

"You look fine," Bolan replied. He let a gentle smile spread across his face as Polyakova tried to return the handkerchief. Her eyes were still wet and he said, "Keep it."

The woman looked surprised, her hand freezing over the table. But already, Bolan could see, she was responding to his softer approach.

So he would continue it. There would be no more talk of dead men or murder charges or trials or executions. At least not from Mack Bolan. Even though he was better by his other name.

The Executioner.

WHILE LUIZA POLYAKOVA continued to compose herself from the crying jag, the Executioner glanced over at another table against the wall. A black purse rested on top of the otherwise bare surface. When the Russian saw him looking that way he asked, "Yours?"

She nodded.

The soldier rose to his feet, walked to the table and lifted the purse. He assumed it had already been searched for weapons and other contraband before his arrival. But he glanced through it quickly as he walked back to the woman and set it before her. "Go ahead," he told her as he resumed his seat. "You'll feel better."

Polyakova stared at him as if he'd just told her she'd won the lottery, then opened her purse and pulled out a small package of tissues, a compact and a lipstick. Bolan watched her as she went to work on her face. She really was an attractive woman, and a classiness emanated from her that even the seediness of the bright orange jail coveralls couldn't disguise. Bolan had noted that prisoners he'd seen in other cells on the way in also wore bright orange. The trustees, who moved through the runs and cell blocks with far more freedom, wore white.

Finally she snapped her compact closed again. She had redone her makeup, and her eyes were now dry. Her lips glistened wetly with a ruby-red hue, and her mascara was back in place on her eyelids rather than running down her cheeks.

Bolan reevaluated his opinion of her. She wasn't just attractive. She was stunning.

"I look better?" Polyakova asked.

"You look better," Bolan agreed. "Now, I know this is difficult, but we still need to talk."

Slowly, losing a little of her composure again, the woman nodded.

The soldier lifted the oversize briefcase to the top of the table. Leaving the clasps that secured the large main compartment in place, he unzipped a side pocket and pulled out two manila files. Dropping them on the table in front of him, he returned the briefcase to the floor. Opening the top file, he looked down at an Immigration and Naturalization Service photograph paper-clipped to the first page. It showed the smiling face of a ten-years-younger Luiza Polyakova. The face he saw before him now didn't look nearly as happy. But if there was any change at all, it had gotten even more lovely since she had become a U.S. citizen.

"Tell me what happened, Luiza," Bolan said in a calm voice.

"I don't know," the woman across from him said. "I have done business with these people many times in the past. This is the first time we have ever had any trouble." She stopped talking for a moment, gazing with hope at Bolan. Her eyes told him she was praying that he, unlike the DEA agent, would believe her.

And he did. At least partially. "I believe you've done business with them before," Bolan said. "But I can't believe the part about you not knowing what was going on."

She fidgeted in her seat. "They may have smuggled things in my paintings," she said. "If they did, I didn't know it."

It was the same story Bolan had heard her tell Johnny Seven as he watched through the one-way mirror. Seven didn't buy it. Neither did Bolan. "That would all make sense," he said calmly. "Except for one thing. You take possession of the shipments upon their arrival in the country. Straight from the customs department. I assume you then have them taken to your gallery?"

"Yes," Polyakova said. "Straight there. To sell."

"Then explain how Rabashka, or whoever was working with him, got to the drugs and stolen artwork without you knowing about it?"

Tears threatened to ruin her face again and Bolan held up a hand. "Relax," he said quietly. "Don't answer yet. I'm going to tell you how I think it happened, and then you can tell me if I'm wrong." He paused. "That's not the usual approach. But it beats having to wait while you do your makeup all over again."

A nervous giggle escaped her lips and she covered her mouth with long slender fingers. For the first time since he'd laid eyes upon her, Bolan saw a hint of a smile play at the corners of her sensuous lips. Hardly an expression of total relief, it was rather the look of a person who felt she had just bought herself a little more time.

Bolan opened the second file and saw a surveillance photo. In it, a man wearing a wrinkled brown suit was getting out of a car. The soldier glanced up at Polyakova. "We knew who Nestor Rabashka was before today," he said. "He's a former midlevel Soviet KGB official. Since the downfall of the Soviet Union, he's been hooked up with one of the organized crime syndicates operating out of Moscow. You know what I'm talking about."

Polyakova's eyes widened. But rather than a look of surprise, Bolan saw more the expression of a woman who had just had her worst fears confirmed. She had to have suspected Rabashka's mob connections all along.

Bolan leaned back against his chair and clasped his hands behind his head. "Here's what I'd guess happened. I think you knew all along that they were bringing in dope and stolen paintings. You didn't know the details but you knew something illegal was going on."

The woman started to protest but Bolan held up his hand again. "Let me finish. Even though you knew it, I don't think you wanted it done. I don't think you wanted to help them." He paused to watch her face soften again before going on. "I think they have some kind of hammer on you, Luiza."

The Russian woman's eyebrows lowered slightly. "They have a hammer? What does this mean, they have a hammer?"

The Executioner smiled. Leaning in across the table, he clasped his hands in front of him. His face was now only a foot from hers. But rather than draw back as she had when Seven had pressed her that way, she now leaned in slightly. "It's an American police expression," Bolan said softly. "It means they have some kind of leverage on you. Something they could hold over your head in order to make you do what they want." He stopped. Luiza Polyakova was, yet again, about to burst into tears.

"What I'm saying," Bolan went on, "is that I don't think you're guilty, Luiza. Technically, yes. But I don't think you wanted to do what you did. I think you felt like you had to. And I think we may be able to work this out so that you help us and you don't end up doing any time in prison or even have a felony record."

A glimmer of hope now sparked in the beautiful green eyes. And this time there was no holding back the tears—they flooded out as if the gates of a great aqueduct had sprung open. But now they were tears of joy rather than terror.

Bolan stood. She needed time to think, time to relax. He suppressed a smile. And to redo her makeup again. Luiza Polyakova was obviously a woman who took pride in her appearance, and she'd feel even better once they got her out of the coveralls and back into her own clothes. "I'm going outside for a moment," he told her. "I'll be back."

Polyakova was reaching into her purse as he headed into the hallway.

Turning the corner, Bolan saw a white-clad woman pushing a broom down the run. The stub of a cigarette hung from the corner of her mouth. He entered the observation room where Johnny Seven stood staring through the mirror as Polyakova went to work again on her face. He turned to Bolan as the door opened.

"Congratulations," the DEA man said, a slight smirk on his face. "You got her to stop crying. But beyond that, you haven't gotten a thing I didn't already have."

"We aren't finished yet," Bolan said. The female trustee pushed the broom past the door as it swung closed behind him. "Before I could talk to her—or get her to talk to me—I had to get her to trust me." He refrained from adding, *And undo the damage you already did.*

Seven snorted. "Okay," he said. "We'll see." He glanced back into the interrogation room before his eyes returned to look up at the Executioner. "What've you got planned next? Wine and cheese tasting, maybe? Or you might want to take her to the opera?"

Bolan couldn't repress a short laugh. Seven was a pushy sort. But there was something about him that kept Bolan from getting mad. Maybe it was the fact that the soldier sensed that he was really a good cop, probably one of the best when interrogating suspects who were truly guilty rather than victims of circumstance. Or it could have been the fact that Bolan knew that any cop would get ticked off if some outsider came in and took over his case. "I'm going to give her a little time to think about it," he said. "Then I'm going in and offer her a deal."

"What kind of a deal?" Seven was suspicious.

"The best I can." Behind him, Bolan heard the swoosh of more brooms sweeping the hall. He turned to see two more female prisoners in orange coveralls pushing dust mops along the run. He looked back to Johnny Seven. "You heard us in there, didn't you?"

"Yeah, I heard you," the DEA agent answered.

"I meant what I said. I don't think she did this because she wanted to. I think she was coerced."

"Of course she was coerced," Seven said in exasperation. "Any rookie could see that. She's a successful self-made millionaire. She has art galleries here and in Europe, too, from what I hear. And she has no criminal record." He stared at the Executioner incredulously and repeated, "Of course she was coerced into this. A woman like that doesn't get into it on her own."

"You weren't treating her as if she was innocent," Bolan said.

"That's 'cause I want to know what she knows. And the threat of prison or a lethal injection is the best way I know to get it."

Bolan grinned at the DEA agent. "With some people it is. Not with her." More sounds in the hallway caused him to turn to the window in the door. Yet another pair of orange-clad women had entered the run outside the interrogation and observation rooms. One carried a mop, the other, a bucket filled with water.

An uneasy feeling spread through the Executioner's chest as he turned back around. He couldn't put his finger on exactly what it was, but something was out of place.

"Well, we'll see," Seven said. "What exactly is the deal you plan to offer her?"

"Immunity from prosecution," Bolan replied. "No record— not even of the arrest. As long as she helps us."

"You can't guarantee that," he said. "You'll never get the D.A.'s office to go for it."

Bolan pulled the cell phone halfway out of his inside pocket, reminding Seven of the phone call they'd made earlier to the White House.

Jameson shrugged in resignation. "Then again," he said, "maybe you will." He shook his head in disbelief. "Forget everything I've said so far and everything I say from now on. Suddenly the rule book has changed on me. It's like I've played baseball for twenty years and thought we were still playing baseball, then you walk in and suddenly I'm in the middle of a football game. When do you plan to—"

The DEA man stopped talking in midsentence. His eyes shot to Bolan's side—to the one-way mirror.

The Executioner turned to see that someone in a pair of orange coveralls had just entered the interrogation room, and suddenly realized why his battle senses had gone on alert a moment earlier. Trustees—who wore white—were the only women who walked the runs and cleaned up the hallways. Anyone clad in orange was not a trustee and should have been locked in a cell.

But before he could think about it further one of the woman carrying a broom let it fall to the floor. She jerked a kitchen knife from inside her orange coveralls.

The woman behind her lifted a knee and broke the broom handle over it, creating two long, sharp-pointed stakes.

The other pair of female prisoners appeared in the doorway.

And all four began closing in on a shrieking Luiza Polyakova.

THE SWORD HANGING on the wall had a thirty-two inch blade. The overall length was 37.5 inches and it weighed slightly under 2.5 pounds. A Nazi eagle had been cast into the brass pommel on the end of the hardwood grip, a brass bolster separated the blade from that grip.

The sword had been used to kill his father.

From behind his desk, Anton Zdorovye studied the sword hanging on the opposite wall. It had been appropriated by Igor Golitsin, only seconds after Golitsin had shot the Cossack who'd used it on Zdorovye's father. At the time, Zdorovye's mother hadn't even known she was with child. That realization had come nearly a month later, and two weeks after learning that the father had been killed in Ukraine by one of the traitorous Don Cossacks. The Cossacks had joined the invading Germans early during World War II, and many such swords had been forged bearing the eagle and swastika. Later the Germans and Cossacks had parted ways, and the fragmentation of that union had played an instrumental part in changing the course of the war, and consequently, world history.

But the breakup had come too late to do Zdorovye's father,

or Zdorovye himself, any good. The Russian often wondered about the man who had sired him, and wished he could have known him. He had died an honorable death, which Zdorovye longed to do himself. But he knew that the road in life he had chosen made that highly unlikely.

Zdorovye heard the phone ring on his desk and dropped his eyes from the wall. He lifted the receiver and heard the voice of his secretary, Amalia. "You have an overseas call, Mr. Zdorovye," the woman said in Russian.

"From…?" he asked.

"Afghanistan. It is Ali."

"Put him through," Zdorovye said in a brisk voice.

A moment later a heavily accented Mideastern voice said, "Hello?"

"I am here, Ali," Zdorovye said. "Speak Arabic. I can understand it better than your fractured Russian."

The connection wasn't good and the line crackled. "I have a decision to make," Ali said in Arabic.

"Go on."

"As you may know, the Americans have offered us money to destroy the poppy crops," said the Afghan. "A substantial amount of money."

"Take it."

On the other end of the line, Zdorovye heard a cough. "Excuse me, the connection is not good. Can you repeat that please?"

"I said take the money."

"That is what I thought you said. But that will mean we can't do business."

"Why?" the Russian asked. "I see no problem."

"But Mr. Zdorovye," Ali said, "if we destroy the poppy crops, I will have no opium or heroin for you."

Zdorovye shook his head silently. He wondered briefly how such men had ever run a country. He wondered even more how they could have repelled the Soviet invasion and occupation years ago—an invasion and occupation of which he had been a part of as a tank crewman. He had always found Ali to be wretched, dirty, and not particularly bright. But the Afghan was cunning—he had to grant him that. Ali served his purpose, and Zdorovye was grateful for all of the contacts he had made in that godforsaken wasteland during his two years there. He hadn't gotten rich by any means, but he had made a decent living on the side, supplementing his army pay by dealing with local tribesmen in the black market. And the men he had dealt with then had gone on to bigger and better things after the Soviets had pulled out. The Taliban could boast as much as it wanted that it had curtailed the growth of poppies during its short and maniacal reign. Zdorovye knew different.

Ali cut into Zdorovye's thoughts. "Did you hear me?" he asked. "Did I hear *you?* You want me to destroy—"

"I want you to destroy nothing," the Russian said in the same voice he used when correcting his four-year-old niece. "Do what everyone always does to the Americans."

"What is that?"

"Screw them. Take their money, tell them you will destroy the crop, then harvest it and sell it to me as always."

"But what if they find out what I have done?"

"Then they will react the way the Americans always react. They will decide it was all their fault because they didn't pay you enough this year. So they will pay you even more money to destroy the next year's crops, and you can do it all over again."

A soft chuckle came over the other end of the line. "I should have thought of that myself," Ali said.

"You did think of it yourself," Zdorovye said. "You aren't stupid. The real purpose of this call was in the hopes that you could raise the price on me by pretending there was a shortage of product. There will not be, and the price will be the same." The Russian hung up the phone in Ali's ear.

Zdorovye's eyes shot back to the wall and the sword. He wondered, as he always did when he looked at the sword, what kind of man his father had been. Igor Golitsin and his mother had told tales of a fearless warrior when Zdorovye was growing up. But the former tank crewman knew such tales were always inflated when one died. The phone ringing again pulled him once more from his reverie.

"It is from America," Amalia said.

Zdorovye frowned as the call was transferred to him. He opened a large desk planner on his desk and looked at the week. Several shipments were planned for America that week, but the only one that should have already gone down was yesterday. A simple one—Moscow to New York. To the art gallery of the Russian woman in Greenwich Village.

The man who now said hello had little, if any, trace of the accent which had once dominated his speech. But he still spoke Russian perfectly and there was no need to decide on a common language as there had been with Ali. Zdorovye had known the man for over twenty years, and still used his code name, Gregor.

"We have trouble," Gregor stated.

Zdorovye's stomach tightened. "What kind of trouble?"

"A bust at the airport. Customs got the drugs and the paintings."

"Customs? American Customs? How could that happen?" Zdorovye felt his fingers tighten around the receiver. He glanced down and saw that his knuckles had turned white.

"Freak accident, the way I hear. Rat chewed through the cardboard containers and insulation, all the way into one of the pictures. They saw white powder on the floor and freaked. You know the Americans—guy's first thought was anthrax."

"How much money did we lose?"

"It wasn't gigantic. Just a little over a million."

Zdorovye's fingers relaxed slightly. It could have been worse. Much worse. "What is your man's name who accompanies those flights? Is he in custody?"

"Rabashka. But no, he's not in custody. He's dead. They shot him."

More blood drained back into Zdorovye's knuckles. At least the man couldn't talk. They had lost a million dollars, yes, but they could easily absorb such a loss, and it was one of the hazards of the profession he was in. The situation would be salvaged.

"But there's other bad news," said the voice from America.

Zdorovye waited.

"They got the woman. Luiza Polyakova."

The hand on the receiver gripped down so hard now that Zdorovye heard the plastic crack. "Where is she?" he demanded.

"Rikers Island."

The Russian suddenly realized he had been holding his breath, his teeth clenched. Now, he let it out. The woman would break under the pressure of even a lightweight American interrogation. But if she hadn't yet talked it was still not too late, and they couldn't have taken her to a better place than Rikers for Zdorovye's purposes.

"Take care of that problem," Zdorovye asked. "But don't put yourself at risk in so doing."

"Consider it done," Gregor said.

Zdorovye hesitated, then said, "Have you informed Ontomanov?"

"I just got off the phone with him," said the man in America. "He knows to stay away from the gallery."

"Good," Zdorovye said. "Keep me informed. I want to know as soon as…what is her name again?"

"Polyakova. Luiza Polyakova."

"I want to know as soon as she is dead." Zdorovye hung up the phone, stood, and walked to the wall. Reaching up, he grasped the sword with both hands and lowered it from the brackets on the wall. Slowly he ran his hand over the steel. Dark black splotches covered the blade—his father's blood had stained the steel permanently. Reverently he replaced the sword and turned back to his desk.

It was a minor setback. Business would go on as usual.

He had other calls to make. Some would be for the Zdorovye Russian Fur Company, which acted as his cover business. Other calls would concern the many drug shipments going out to America, Canada, Europe and other places. The situation in New York wasn't good but it would soon be under control and he forced a sigh of relief from between his clenched teeth.

Zdorovye glanced at his watch as he sat back down. There

were so many Russian mobsters locked up in Rikers Island that the Americans had doubled local police and even U.S. Coast Guard patrol of the area, fearing a major breakout would some day occur. No, the American police who had arrested Luiza Polyakova couldn't have taken her to a better place as far as he was concerned.

BOLAN BOLTED OUT THE DOOR of the observation room into the cell run. Dropping low, he pivoted like an offensive guard pulling on a trap play, and turned the corner into the interrogation room. His hand had already slapped the empty holster under his coat before he realized he had left his weapons secured in a locker before entering the holding area. Such was the usual procedure in jails and prisons around the world, and since he had been masquerading as a Justice Department agent he had followed the rules.

As he swung open the door to the interrogation room the Executioner heard Seven's rubber-soled shoes slapping the concrete behind him. He pushed inside just as the woman with the kitchen knife reached Polyakova.

He'd never get between them in time.

But the wealthy art gallery owner surprised the Executioner. Drawing back her fist, she sent a fairly respectable right hook into the eye of the woman in orange.

The prisoner screamed in both pain and rage as her free hand flew to her face, pressing the dirty blond hair that had fallen over her eyes into the socket. Bolan left his feet just as she recovered, diving through the air, his arm outstretched.

The butcher knife was halfway to Polyakova's chest when the Executioner grabbed the wrist holding it. He twisted hard as he fell onto his chest across the interrogation table.

The blonde screamed again. The clank, then rattle of steel against steel met Bolan's ears as the knife fell to the table then wobbled back and forth next to him. Brushing his arm across the surface, he swept the blade away and heard it thump against the wall.

Bolan rolled to his back and came up in a sitting position just in time to see a sharp object heading toward his face. He ducked, parrying upward at the same time and redirecting the broken broom handle away from him. The second woman—her hair dyed a bright and unnatural red—brought the sharp stick toward him. As he had done with the blonde, the Executioner reached up, grabbing the wrist that held the broken broom handle.

Bolan brought his other hand across his body. He slapped the heel of his palm against the inside of the woman's arm. The redhead howled even louder than her partner had as the makeshift spear went flying across the room. Before she knew what had happened, the Executioner had ripped the first stick from her other hand.

Reaching up with both hands, Bolan grabbed both females by the front of their coveralls. He threw them back toward the door. Both of the orange-clad females hit the wall and loud gasps echoed across the room as the air rushed from their lungs. They slid to sitting positions on the floor.

But another flicker of orange appeared in the Executioner's peripheral vision. He pushed himself off the table as a homemade knife stabbed through the air past his cheek. The woman holding it was big, maybe five foot ten, and weighed 250 pounds. Sweat poured from her forehead as she pulled the shank back, chambering it next to her side and preparing to thrust again.

As the crude weapon came forward, the Executioner twisted and stepped in, grabbing her hand and trapping the blade against the woman's chest with his own. Reaching out for her other forearm, he secured it by the wrist and twisted it behind her back, using his weight to spin her away from him. The pain shot up her contorted arm, causing her to cry out and drop the knife to the floor. The Executioner reached up and grabbed a handful of her sweaty black hair, pulling downward as he kept her arm twisted painfully behind her.

Looking up, Bolan saw that Johnny Seven was entangled with the fourth and final attacker. She, too, had a shank, but the DEA man had been less successful at disarming her. She wore her hair long and straight, and Seven had grabbed two handfuls of it. He now threw her back and forth in an attempt to keep her off balance as the knife flashed in front of his face.

"Drop it!" Seven shouted over and over.

Bolan's eyes flew to the wall where the two women sitting down were about to recover. Their weapons were still scattered across the room, and before long they would catch their breath and begin looking for them. In the meantime he had his hands full with the big woman who still wriggled and cursed in his arms.

So far, the Executioner hadn't seriously hurt any of the women. And he hoped he wouldn't have to do so. But if the DEA agent didn't take care of the woman with the shank soon, he was going to have to resort to more drastic action.

The problem was answered for Bolan as Johnny Seven, who obviously held no reservations about injuring women, suddenly had enough. Drawing back his fist, he held the woman still long enough to drive it into her face. There was a loud cracking sound as knuckles met jaw, then she dropped the shank and fell to the floor unconscious.

Bolan pushed the big woman in his hands away from him toward the other two he had disarmed. She stumbled, crashing down to sprawl across both of their laps. Before any of them could rise to their feet again, the Executioner circled the room, grabbing up the broken broom handles, the butcher knife and the two shanks. By that time the female prisoners who were still awake had started to get up. But when they saw their weapons in Bolan's hands they sank back to the floor in defeat.

By now the screaming and other noise had brought two uniformed male guards to the interrogation room. Bolan looked up as they entered the room, and the same feeling of unease he had experienced when he'd seen the orange-clad women spread over him. But this time, he had no doubt what caused it.

Several discrepancies caught the Executioner's eye immediately. First, the hair below the caps of the two guards was long, unkempt and greasy. Second, their uniforms didn't fit. But third, and most importantly, they not only had sidearms in their holsters, but also they were in the process of drawing them. And neither of them was looking at any of the female prisoners.

THE EXECUTIONER'S FOOT SHOT OUT, tapping Polyakova on
the back of the knee with the flat of his sole. The Russian
woman's legs buckled under her and she fell to the floor, behind
the table and out of the line of fire.

A split second later a loud explosion sounded within the con-
fines of the interrogation room. Bolan felt the air pressure change
as the bullet passed just over his head. It struck the wall, then ric-
ocheted off the concrete to zip around the room.

Johnny Seven reached out to grab the 9 mm Ruger in the hand
of the nearest guard, but the man in the uniform stepped back
and pumped a quick double-tap into the DEA agent's chest.
Seven groaned, backpedaled a half dozen steps, then hit the floor.

The guard's knuckles went white as his fingers tightened
around the pistol again. Bolan dropped farther, joining Polyakova
on the floor behind the table and shielding her with his body.

The next 9 mm round missed him by a wider margin but
again struck the wall and bounced off. What felt like a hard-
thrown rock struck Bolan in the back, and he knew it had to be
the deformed lead. But the bullet's lack of velocity meant it
failed to even penetrate his jacket.

Lucky. But such luck wouldn't last forever.

In any case, it wasn't ricochets that worried Bolan. Even now,
beneath the table, he could see the feet of both guards advanc-
ing toward him and the Russian woman. The men intended to
move forward to achieve a better angle—where they could shoot
down over the table at their targets. The old cliché about shooting fish in a barrel raced through the Executioner's mind as he
formed his battle plan. With Seven out of the way, he could expect no assistance.

Bolan still held the broken sticks, butcher knife and shanks
in his hands. He dropped the knife into the side pocket of his
jacket. Keeping one of the shanks in his right hand and the
longer piece of broom handle in his left, he let the rest fall to
the floor. Then, diving headfirst beneath the table, he lunged
out with his arm and sank the shank into the shin of the nearest guard.

A howl of anguish went up above the tabletop.

The Executioner's own momentum carried him out from under the table, and his shoulder caught his attacker at the knee. A sickening snap sounded as the vulnerable joint broke, and the man dressed as a guard screamed again. Rising to his knees, Bolan broke the shortened broom handle over the man's head. The end piece fell to the floor. He then caught the guard in the jaw with the stub in his hand as the man went down.

But the Executioner was on the floor, and a good eight feet away from the other uniformed man. He looked up as the same Ruger that had just shot Seven begin to turn his way. On his knees, there was no way he could close that gap before the 9 mm pistol roared again. He had only one chance.

Drawing back his arm, Bolan sent the shank flying through the air at the attacker's chest. But the poorly balanced weapon struck flat against the badge and bounced off harmlessly.

The man in the guard's uniform threw back his head to laugh.

His arrogance was his downfall.

Bolan transferred the broken broom handle stub to his right hand and brought it back over his shoulder like a spear. It was too short to fly well, and the balance wasn't any better than the shank. But it was all he had during the split second that the guard was laughing and exposing his throat. In a moment, the man would look back down at him and pull the trigger. The less than perfect javelin would have to do.

Putting all of the strength in his shoulder and arm behind the throw, the Executioner sent the broom handle streaking forward. The sharp broken end struck the uniformed man squarely in the throat, then flipped off to the side, end over end. But it had pierced the carotid artery just below the man's skin, and now a projectile stream of crimson shot forth.

The guard's head dropped down to his chest protectively, all humor now draining from his face as the blood drained from his body. His free hand went to his throat in a fruitless attempt to stop the flow.

The Executioner knew from experience that a severed carotid

brought on unconsciousness in roughly five seconds, and death seven seconds later. But five seconds was an eternity in a gunfight. As he rose to his feet, Bolan saw the guard wave the Ruger back in front of his blood-soaked chest, trying to steady it on the Executioner as his eyes filled with hatred.

Bolan lunged forward, his hand dropping into his pocket as he flew through the air. His fingers found the cracked wooden handle of the butcher knife and wrapped tightly around it. By that time, he was within arm's reach of the guard.

Grabbing the wrist that held the Ruger with his left hand, Bolan pushed the gun up and out of the way. The weapon discharged, and a 9 mm slug sailed into the air to strike the ceiling before rebounding around the interrogation room like an angry wasp. The Executioner felt nothing strike him this time, and he heard no moans or other indications that the others in the room had been struck.

The guard was fading now. The Executioner helped him go. Clutching the butcher knife against his side, he then plunged it into the man's sternum. The knife penetrated the thin uniform, and sank into the heart. Bolan twisted the blade, but little blood escaped the wound.

Most of the guard's blood had already left through his throat.

The Ruger clattered to the floor and the guard slid after it, dead before he hit the ground.

Spinning a quick 360 degrees to check for other threats, Bolan satisfied himself there were none. The woman Seven had knocked out had slept through the rest of the battle. The three other women sat perfectly still against the wall, no longer wanting any part of the action.

Bolan hurried to where Seven had fallen onto his face and knelt next to the DEA man. Turning the heavy body over, two things surprised the Executioner. First, there was no blood where the duo of 9 mm rounds had struck. And second, Seven's eyes were not only open, but he also looked alert.

Through the ripped cloth of Seven's shirt, Bolan saw the white ballistic nylon vest. It had been charred brown and black by the gunpowder and gases from the near contact shots, but the bullets hadn't penetrated the layers of resistant cloth.

"You okay?" the Executioner asked.

Seven looked up at him, still only half-aware of his surroundings. "Oh, yeah," he said. "Never been better."

Footsteps pounded down the run toward the interrogation area. Bolan turned to the door, Ruger in hand. But the men who entered the room, while wearing riot gear, had no guns. They were real guards. He looked down at the dead men in uniform on the ground. He didn't know who they were—probably prisoners who had been paid to back up the women.

Bolan helped Seven to his feet, then surveyed the carnage within the interrogation room once more. This had been a hit, pure and simple. An attempt to get Luiza Polyakova out of the way before she could talk. It involved at least six inmates, and it wouldn't have come cheap, which told him whoever had put it out had both money and connections into the prison system.

Bolan shoved the Ruger into his belt beneath his jacket. He didn't yet know who had that kind of power and financing.

But he intended to find out.

The glass outside the office read, Rutherford B. Kasparak, Deputy Commissioner, New York City Department Of Corrections. Bolan opened the door and ushered Luiza Polyakova, Johnny Seven and four other guards—genuine Rikers Island guards—into the outer office. A woman with coal-black, white-rooted hair and heavy makeup glanced up from her computer. "Go right on in," she said. "Deputy Commissioner Kasparak is expecting you." She indicated the door in a side wall with a nod.

Again Bolan performed door duties, letting one of the guards go first. Another walked Polyakova—still in her orange coveralls but now wearing handcuffs and a belly chain—past him. The rest followed.

Rutherford Kasparak stood waiting behind a desk covered with neatly arranged stacks of paper. He was nearing the end of middle age, painfully thin, and his face held the expression of a man who had just been diagnosed with an inoperable brain tumor. He wore old black horn-rimmed eyeglasses, and his blue pin-striped suit hung from his frame as if it might slide off at any moment. Like Johnny Seven the top of his head was bald but he had a thin ring of white hair that ran from one ear, around the back of his head, to the other ear. He coughed nervously, his hand making a strange little waving motion as he pointed them to seats around the room.

The guards started to sit but Kasparak said, "No, Bandy," as he nodded toward a guard wearing captain's bars on his epaulets. "You stay. The rest of you won't be needed." His hand jerked again as he glanced toward the door. The three guards left while the captain took a seat in a straight-backed chair against the wall.

Bolan and Seven found seats at the ends of a couch opposite Captain Bandy. The Executioner guided Luiza Polyakova between them. Kasparak leaned forward in his chair and folded his hands in front of him on the desk. His right hand continued to jerk, and Bolan now recognized the movement as a nervous twitch. An unusual tic, Kasparak kept bending his wrist back as if he were trying to touch the back of his hand to his forearm.

Bolan wasn't surprised that the man was bothered. The deaths on Rikers Island would bring about investigations from both state and federal authorities, and create the kind of accountability bureaucrats like Kasparak dreaded.

When the guards had closed the door behind them, Kasparak tightened his folded hands and the tic stopped momentarily. "Okay," he said. "Will someone please tell me what's going on in my institution? I have two male prisoners dead, and four women being treated for minor injuries. The men—both of whom are awaiting trial for murder and somehow got out of *maximum security*—were wearing guard's uniforms!" He had been looking down at the desk as he spoke, but now he threw up his hands and stared at Bandy. When he spoke next, it was with a sudden burst of anger and frustration. "Captain, I want to know how they got the uniforms!" he shouted. "And I want to know how they got out of max and into the women's building! And I want to know now!" Suddenly Kasparak blushed in embarrassment. Whether his sudden self-consciousness came from the temporary loss of control or from the fact that his inward fear told him he couldn't sustain the show of strength for any prolonged period of time, wasn't clear. He tried to stare down Bandy, only to quickly avert his eyes and look back down at his desk. Both of the deputy commissioner's shoulders slumped forward and the twitching began again in his wrist.

Captain Bandy cleared his throat. He appeared calm, as if Kasparak's neurotic behavior was nothing new to him. "We don't know that yet, sir," he said. "But I have men working on it."

"My guess," Bolan said, "is that before the day is out you're going to find two dead guards some place in their underwear."

Kasparak turned to stare at Bolan, and his face flashed red again. But this time it was clearly out of rage. "And how would you know that?" he snapped.

"Deductive reasoning," Bolan said. "With a little bit of common sense thrown in." The soldier didn't like Kasparak, and it wasn't just his faint-heartedness. The man exuded all of the shortcomings of an incompetent bureaucrat who slid though years of government employment with his focus on his personal career rather than his actual job. He cost the taxpayers far more than he ever contributed.

Bandy cleared his throat. "That's very likely," he said.

His spirit broken yet again, Kasparak folded his hands on the desk once more and then stared at them. Finally he looked up at Johnny Seven. "You," he said, "I know. We've dealt in the past." His eyes shifted back to Bolan. "But you would be…?" He was trying hard to sound confident again. Bolan would have bet his life that he had a political connection somewhere who had landed him this job.

"Matt Cooper," Bolan replied. "Department of Justice."

A look of surprise fell over Kasparak's face. He swiveled to look at Luiza Polyakova. "It was my understanding it's about drugs."

"It's a matter that concerns the DOJ," Bolan said, not explaining further.

A new respect—bordering on awe—came over Kasparak's face as he turned back to look at Bolan. The soldier watched the deputy commissioner's eyes and saw the window to a politically driven soul. Behind the expression of astonishment, Kasparak's brain was carefully evaluating this new turn of events. The man was trying to determine how he might best use this development to further his own standing.

Bolan was about to leave Rikers Island, and when he did, Luiza Polyakova was going with him. He had anticipated balking on Kasparak's part when he informed the man of that fact in the next few minutes. But now he saw a way to make the transition smoothly, cut through any argument and red tape, and save time. "The DOJ would appreciate your full cooperation," he said.

Kasparak's head rose a full three inches in the air and he literally beamed. "Of course!" he said enthusiastically. "However I can be of service. I'm more than willing to help in any way I can."

"Good," the Executioner stated. "What we need is simple. I want to take Ms. Polyakova with me."

"That's no problem," Kasparak said. "Federal officers do sometimes request a leave for certain prisoners to help on cases. Simply complete the paperwork and—"

"No," Bolan said, stopping him. "No paperwork. With all due respect, Deputy Commissioner, this place is like a sieve. If six prisoners can get out of their cells, get guard uniforms and attack another prisoner, you've got a serious information leak. If there's a paper trail, word that Luiza is helping the Justice Department would be on the streets before we were. It'll leak out eventually anyway, but I want to delay it as long as I can."

Kasparak withdrew back into the frightened-bureaucrat persona again. "But Agent Cooper, we have policies."

"My boss said to tell you that he'd be grateful for this favor on your part," Bolan said. "Very grateful. Do you get my drift?"

Kasparak brightened again but his face still held an element of fear. Like most political animals, he felt more comfortable accepting favors than risking anything by doing them. Finally he said, "I suppose it will be all right. But there are state and federal investigators on their way here right now. I can't let you go until they've interviewed you."

Bolan glanced at his watch. Already it was late afternoon, and getting tied up with prisoner officials for the rest of the day wasn't on his schedule. "It's late," he said. "And they'll have plenty to investigate today without us. Why don't you tell them we'll all be back here bright and early in the morning. Does 8:00 a.m. sound okay?"

Kasparak was still hesitant. "I suppose—"

"Good," Bolan said and stood. "It's all settled, then. But Luiza needs a place to change clothes. She can't be running around in orange coveralls."

Kasparak lifted the phone on his desk. "I'll have one of the guards bring up her—"

"No," Bolan said. "Leave the clothes she wore here where they are. Some prisoner is likely to see what's going on and as far as you and Rikers are concerned, she's still here, remember?"

Kasparak gulped visibly, a lump in his throat swelling and then disappearing like a boa constrictor swallowing a small pig. "Oh. Yes. Certainly." He replaced the receiver.

"I have clothes for her right here." Bolan lifted the large briefcase.

Kasparak pointed to a side door of the office. "Washroom," he said.

Polyakova had remained seated on the couch. As the soldier turned toward her, she looked up at him timidly. "Do I have anything to say about this?" she asked.

"Sure," Bolan said. "Go with me or stay here and look through the yellow pages for a lawyer." He paused. "Or, more likely, a funeral director."

Polyakova took the briefcase and disappeared into the washroom.

Johnny Seven had remained quiet during most of the conversation. But now he said, "What are we going to do?"

The soldier didn't want to discuss business in front of a self-serving politician like Kasparak. "We'll talk later," he said. He turned back to the desk and smiled. "No need to bother the deputy commissioner any more than we already have."

Kasparak didn't seem to take the remark as an insult. In fact, he seemed relieved to remain ignorant of more than he already knew. He stood to get some big favor from the DOJ, and that was enough to satisfy him. He looked far more relaxed than he had when the conversation first began.

A few minutes later, Luiza Polyakova reentered the office wearing an expertly tailored navy blue woman's suit and high heels. She had redone her makeup yet again, and the overall effect was near staggering. Bolan led her and Johnny Seven out the door.

The soldier hurried them down the hall to a row of elevators, then changed his mind when he saw the light indicating that one of the cars was on its way up. It might very well be the investigators Kasparak had mentioned, and he didn't want to bump into them on his way out. Taking the Russian by the arm, he hurried her toward the stairs, then ushered her and Seven onto the landing. The door closed behind them just as the bell sounded down the hall, indicating that the elevator had arrived.

Bolan glanced back through the mesh-glass window in the door long enough to see two men step off the elevator and start down the hall toward Kasparak's office. They might as well have had New York State Police stenciled across the backs of their pinstriped suits.

Bolan stayed outside the locker room with Polyakova while Seven picked up both of their weapons from the lock-boxes at the front of the prison building. While they waited, he reflected on all that had happened so far, where they stood and what they knew. Perhaps more importantly, he realized, the attempt on Polyakova's life meant the enemy already knew the situation.

A plan of action was beginning to form in Bolan's mind, but he would wait until they were away from Rikers to talk about it. He led the way across the parking lot to the Toyota Highlander he had rented upon arriving in New York and took the wheel while Johnny Seven opened the passenger's door for the woman. None of them had spoken since they'd left the deputy commissioner's office, and the silence seemed to be uncomfortable for the DEA man. As Polyakova slid into her seat, Seven looked across at Bolan and said, "I'll say one thing for you."

"What's that?" Bolan asked as he stuck the key in the ignition and started the engine.

"You guess women's clothes sizes well." He glanced at Polyakova and grinned.

Bolan smiled. The navy blue suit did fit Polyakova perfectly, but it wasn't because Bolan guessed sizes well. There was another reason.

As they pulled out of the parking lot and started across the bridge linking New York's most famous jail to the rest of the city, the soldier said, "We need a place to go sit and talk things out. I'll find a motel."

Polyakova looked across at him for a moment, and even though her eyes were still filled with fear a tiny smile played around her lips. "We could go to my place instead," she said, reaching out and fingering the cuff of the blue suit coat. "You know the way."

In the rearview mirror, Bolan could see a baffled look on Johnny Seven's face. The conversation had taken a turn he couldn't possibly have understood.

Polyakova leaned back in the seat and sighed quietly. "I don't know how you really are at guessing women's sizes," she said, her smile still in place. "But you have excellent taste in clothing." She paused and stroked the arm of the jacket again. "I almost wore this today anyway."

BOLAN DID KNOW THE WAY to Luiza Polyakova's apartment, and he guided the Highlander back toward it as a light rain began to fall over the Big Apple. He had stopped there as soon as he'd rented the vehicle, wanting to check out both the small but elegant loft and the art gallery below it before he met Polyakova for the first time. He had seen nothing that led him to believe the Russian woman was anything but what she claimed she was—a successful art importer and gallery owner. There were no traces of drugs or drug activity of any kind. The apartment was small and comfortably furnished but not luxuriously so. The furniture and other items he'd seen could have easily been afforded on the money he suspected she made in the art business.

Knowing he would be taking her away from Rikers, he had pulled the navy blue suit from the first hanger he came to in her closet and added a pair of dark blue shoes he suspected she wore with it.

Bolan had no intention of setting up a base of operations at Polyakova's apartment. Whoever wanted the woman dead wasn't going to give up now, and as soon as word leaked out of Rikers that she was gone, the gallery-apartment would be the first place the next assassins checked. They would stop only long enough for her to pack additional clothes and for him to talk things over with Seven.

Bolan hadn't decided whether he wanted the DEA man along on the rest of the mission. And he wanted to make that decision before Johnny Seven knew his plans. If he wasn't going to be along for the long haul, there was no sense in his knowing what was about to go down.

The sun had fallen, casting the city into darkness. The rain grew stronger as they entered Greenwich Village. Home to artists, poets, writers and musicians, it also claimed its share of freaks, weirdos, drug peddlers and criminals of all varieties. Bolan drove the Highlander slowly through the crowded traffic as the sights and sounds of the eccentric residents drifted through the windows. Many of the pedestrians had taken refuge from what was beginning to be a downpour, but many more ignored the rain, some seeming even to glory in it.

They passed a long line of street venders who had closed the side panels over the stalls to protect bagels, hot dogs, sandwiches and a thousand other items from the rain. Luiza Polyakova's art gallery was in the middle of the block, squeezed between a Jewish delicatessen and a silk-screen T-shirt shop. Bolan drove past the darkened front window, turned at the corner, then cut into the alley running behind the three businesses.

Having been there before, the soldier already knew the gallery shared a common parking lot with the deli and silk screener. Through the falling rain, he now saw several other vehicles on the wet asphalt, and half-hid the Highlander between an old Volkswagen and a newer Plymouth sedan. Even if word had already hit the streets that the woman was out, Bolan saw no way the rented Highlander would be recognized by anyone looking for her. But there was no sense in taking chances. In any case, he didn't plan to be at the gallery long.

Bolan, Polyakova and Seven hurried through the rain to the shelter of a green awning over the back door. The Russian pulled out a ring of keys. Bolan heard the buzz of a burglar alarm kicking in as soon as the door opened, and saw the digital pad mounted on the wall as they entered. Polyakova tapped a code into the control pad and the buzzing stopped. The rooms inside the building were dark, and her hand moved toward the light switch. Bolan reached out, taking her hand gently and stopping her. "Leave them off," he said. "No need to announce to the world that you've come home."

The woman nodded her understanding. In the dim light her eyes flickered up at the soldier and Bolan felt the electricity pass between them. He let go of her hand just as gently as he'd taken it and she turned away, embarrassed.

But Bolan had also seen a flicker of fear return to her face during the second their eyes met, and he knew that she was well aware that the threats to her life were far from over. There would be more, and they would be potentially even more dangerous than what had happened on Rikers. The men who came next wouldn't be hampered by, or have to work within, the limitations imposed by prison security.

Polyakova led them into the darkness. Bolan followed, trailed by Johnny Seven. The soldier felt his way with one hand on the wall, while his mind was on the killers he knew they would face in the next few days. One of the many Russian groups known now as the Russian *mafiya* had forced Luiza Polyakova to help them. But she wasn't one of them, and they couldn't afford to let her cut a deal with the attorney general's office to turn state's evidence.

There was only one way to ensure that didn't happen. Just like the old saying about dead men, dead women told no tales.

They passed through a small office at the rear of the building and entered the gallery. Bolan remembered it from earlier in the day. The rest of the ground floor was one large room with dozens of rows filled with oil paintings and watercolors displayed on easels. More paintings had been mounted on the walls, and scattered about the room were sculptures—some free-standing, others on hardwood stands. The entire front of the building was glass, and unlike many of the shops throughout the city, the gallery hadn't resorted to barring itself in at night.

The rain continued to pound the building as Polyakova led Bolan and Seven up a staircase in the semidarkness. When they reached the second floor, she inserted another key into a door. A moment later, they were standing inside the woman's apartment. It was even darker than the gallery and hallway.

Bolan reached out, taking the Russian's hand as she automatically reached again for the switch.

"Oh," she said in embarrassment. "I'm sorry. I forgot."

"Do you have an interior room?" the soldier asked. "One with no window onto the street or alley?"

In the dim light her eyebrows dropped slightly in concentration. "No. Well…the bathroom, but—"

"The bathroom is fine," Bolan said. "Show us where it is. Then I want you to pack enough clothes for a few days. Keep it simple. We need to get out of here as soon as we can and regroup someplace else." He stuck his hand inside his coat and came out with a small flashlight. "Here," he said. "Take this. And remember about the lights."

Polyakova nodded, switched on the powerful beam and then led them down the hall. The building was old, and the bathroom much larger than would have been found in a more modern structure. A tall grandfather clock in the hallway ticked loudly as they passed. Bolan waved Seven through the opening, then turned back to the Russian woman. "Don't take long," he said. "Whoever wants you dead has good contacts at Rikers. For all we know the news that you're out may already have been leaked." He thought of the concern the woman had shown for her appearance earlier and realized packing could turn into a whole night's event if he didn't cut off the problem. "And keep it light. One suitcase."

She looked up into his eyes as if he'd asked her to do the impossible. "One suitcase?" she said. "I can't even—"

"One suitcase, Luiza. Now hurry."

Bolan closed the door behind him and switched on the light. He turned to see a large claw-foot bathtub against one wall.

The sudden brightness caused both men to squint as their pupils adjusted. The only seat was the toilet and Seven had taken it. Bolan moved to the side of the big bathtub and leaned back, facing him. The apartment fell silent, the clicks of the grandfather clock in the hallway the only sounds.

The Executioner had read through Johnny Seven's DEA personnel file on the plane to New York, and found that he had a somewhat unusual background for a federal law-enforcement officer. He had grown up in the slums of Buffalo, where his father had earned a decent living as a freelance magazine writer but dropped the family's existence to welfare-level by being an unlucky gambler. The boy who would someday be known as Johnny Seven had stayed away from the cards and dice, and finished high school. He then spent four years at NYU majoring in journalism. He'd worked as a reporter for several small newspapers in the Buffalo area, then given up the pen for the gun when his application to the Drug Enforcement Administration had been accepted.

That had been nearly two decades ago. The name "Johnny Seven" hadn't come from any gambling-father connection. John Jameson had acquired that appellation from his gun of choice for undercover drug deals and as a backup weapon. In addition to his DEA-issue SIG-Sauer P-220, Seven toted a four-inch Taurus revolver. The .357 Magnum wheelgun had been the first to break the six-shooter mold and had a seventh hole in the cylinder.

In addition to the grandfather clock on the other side of the door, Bolan could now hear the sounds of drawers opening and closing. He studied the DEA agent for a moment.

He still hadn't decided whether or not he wanted Seven along with him on this mission. Someone covering his back was always a good thing—as long as it was the right someone. The wrong man became deadweight at best, and a nightmare in the worst-case scenario. What had caught Bolan's attention in the personnel file, and made him question the wisdom of letting Seven join the party, were the reports of insubordination sprinkled throughout the file.

That could mean that Seven was a troublemaker. If that was the case, Bolan had no use for him. On the other hand, it might just as readily mean that Johnny Seven was an independent thinker who had conflicted with some of the by-the-book bureaucrats in supervisory positions within the DEA.

Seven's file also contained several complaints about the use of excessive force, but while several hearings had taken place, no disciplinary actions had been executed against the DEA agent. Again, that could mean one of two things—he was either one of the sadistic cops who enjoyed hurting others or he was a man who intended to get the job done even if he had to break a few rules. Bolan wouldn't tolerate a sadist. But he knew that he'd have more excessive-force complaints than any cop who'd ever lived if he answered to an established law-enforcement agency.

Johnny Seven had been staring at the floor but now he glanced up and saw Bolan looking at him. Bolan stared deep into the eyes, trying to get a read on the man's brain and even his soul. His instincts told him that Johnny Seven would be a good man to have along. So he decided to lay things on the line and let the man decide for himself whether or not he still wanted in on this case.

"You've got a decision to make," Bolan said. "Decide now whether you want to stay or walk on this thing."

Seven bristled visibly, his face and the top of his bald head turning red as blood flowed to the skin. "Why would I walk?" he asked. "It's my case, and I didn't invite you in on it in the first place. Or are you trying to tell me you're taking this case over completely?" He took several short, angry breaths. "I don't doubt that you can." He glanced at the pocket where the Executioner carried his cell phone. "You've got the stroke to do it, but I don't have to like it."

Bolan stared back at him. "No," he said. "You don't have to like it. But if you stay, you have to do what I tell you, when I tell you. With no questions." He paused a moment. "I've looked through your file. You seem to have had some problems with that in the past."

Rather than anger the DEA man further, the words brought an outright laugh to Seven's face. His chest shook slightly as he said, "Yeah, I've had some trouble taking orders in the past. From idiots. If you get a chance to check that file closer, you'll see that all of those problems came from two supervisors. Both were guys who climbed the back staircase to rank with little or no actual street experience." The chuckling stopped and his face grew serious. "Check and see how I did when Cookerly was my SAC. Or Addington or Applegate. Those were supervisors who'd seen the elephant. I respected those guys. I'd have followed them into hell, and on several occasions, I did." The DEA man sat up a little straighter and continued to meet Bolan's stare. "You strike me as a guy I could follow into hell, Cooper. Don't take that as ass-kissing—I don't do that for you or anybody else. It's just a simple fact."

"There's more than that you need to consider," Bolan said. "I doubt that I work like anyone else you've ever teamed with."

"In what way?" Seven asked.

"I don't just bend the rules, sometimes I break them. Other times I *shatter* them completely."

The two men continued to lock eyes. Finally Johnny Seven said, "I don't really know you yet, Cooper, but I saw what you did back there on Rikers. You were unarmed, going up against two men with guns. I respect that. And that means I respect you. I'll take your orders, and if I end up breaking a few rules or even laws to get the job done, it won't be the first time." Slowly he nodded his head and the scowl on his face began to fade. "Count me in."

While Seven had made a big mistake in how he'd tried to handle Polyakova during interrogation, Bolan's overall impression of the man was good. Again his instincts told him he had made the right decision by giving Seven a chance to be included.

Before he could say more, there was a soft knock on the door. Bolan opened it to find Polyakova standing there with a suitcase the size of Yankee Stadium on the floor next to her. "I'm ready," she said. She looked like a frightened sparrow as her eyes fell to her feet.

The rain continued to beat down on the roof overhead as Bolan reached out and took both of her hands in his. "Look at me," he said.

The beautiful Russian woman looked up.

"We're going to get you out of this mess," the soldier said. "Trust me."

The emerald eyes betrayed a mixture of emotion—fear, confusion and righteous anger among them.

"I do trust you," she answered.

Bolan gently dropped her hands and picked up the suitcase. The apartment was silent except for the tick of the grandfather clock as he led the way down the stairs.

They were halfway down the steps to the art gallery when the front window exploded.

FIRST THROUGH THE WINDOW came a thunderstorm of broken glass, the shards sparkling like diamonds in the streetlights outside the gallery. It was followed by the rain from a real thunderstorm as heavy sheets of water soaked everything within six feet of the front wall.

Then came three men with guns.

The burglar alarm had gone off the second the window broke, activating both the sound and motion sensors Bolan had seen throughout the gallery. But the shrieking, nerve-grinding screech that now raged throughout the room seemed to have no effect on the first man who leaped through the opening. Wearing a dark bomber jacket, he hit the ground on his shoulder and rolled to his feet like a gymnast. In the half-dark room, ten feet from the stairs, Bolan could see the barrel of a large handgun extending from his fist.

The Executioner had instinctively lifted Polyakova's huge suitcase in his hands when he'd heard the sound, and now he hurled it down the steps at the intruder. The hard leather case, which he guessed weighed at least fifty pounds, hit the man in the chest, knocking him two steps back. The gun in his hand went off, the round sailing away to rip through several canvas oil paintings before drilling into the wall. The man caught his balance, and began to turn the gun back toward the stairs.

The Executioner had drawn the .44 Magnum Desert Eagle from the holster on his hip. Bolan fired twice, the muzzle-flash lighting up the darkened gallery like bolts of lightning from the storm. Bolan couldn't tell where he'd hit the man—the points of impact were lost in the darkness beyond the flashes—but he heard the long-barreled handgun fall to the floor as the man in the bomber jacket took a few more paces backward before collapsing.

Two more men vaulted through the broken plate-glass window. As the burglar alarm continued to scream in their ears, the Executioner turned quickly to Seven and Polyakova behind him. "Get her back upstairs!" he shouted over the noise of the alarm.

By the time he had turned back around, more gunshots had added to the pandemonium. Bolan felt a round zip past his eyes as his head turned. Raising the big hand cannon, he squeezed the trigger and another Magnum hollowpoint round roared from the Eagle and dropped a tall, shadowy figure in a dark trench coat. A gasp of final breath escaped the man's lips, somehow finding its way through the noise to the Executioner's ears.

Bolan swung the big automatic to the side and popped another round into a shorter, wider shape. Again he couldn't tell where he'd hit the man, but it hadn't been a kill shot. The thicker shadow dropped to one knee and tried to bring the pistol in his hand back up.

The Executioner lowered the Desert Eagle, then raised it slightly until he felt the barrel come on the mark. It was no different than pointing a finger, and his next two rounds drove the man from his knees to the floor.

Outside the shattered window, thunder boomed like the angry shouts of a hundred giants. Lightning flashed just as a new face peered around the corner of the broken window. Bolan swung the Eagle that way, but before he could pull the trigger the target had jerked back onto the sidewalk. A second later, running footsteps splashing water could barely be heard around the alarm, wind, rain and the thunder.

Bolan moved carefully down the stairs, the Desert Eagle again aimed at the men on the floor. It had been too dark to see where his rounds had hit, and "dead bodies" had been known to come back to life to kill men who thought they'd survived. When he reached the floor he slowed even further, sliding carefully across the tile and stopping briefly next to each body on the floor. The hand cannon stayed up and ready as he jammed a finger into the throats of the men. He detected no pulses.

As he hurried to the window, sporadic gusts of wind threw rain into Bolan's face. The Desert Eagle held tightly against his ribs and aimed outward, he looked up and down the block—deserted except for a mangy hundred-breed mongrel who sat passively across the street as if the gunfight had been staged for his personal entertainment. Satisfied that no second wave of gunmen was about to strike, the Executioner stepped out through the broken glass.

Barely visible through the downpour, he saw a running figure two blocks down dart around a corner.

Something caused him to suddenly twirl back around. He stepped back through the window into the half-lit gallery, the burglar alarm still blaring in his ears. He wasn't sure how, but he knew there was at least one more of the enemy, alive and well, within the room.

More rain drove through the window, soaking the Executioner's back as he retraced his steps back into the gallery. Behind him, in the distance, the wail of police sirens added to the pandemonium already filling his ears.

Bolan moved cautiously behind a row of paintings, looking between the canvas toward the staircase he had just descended. It wasn't Seven's or Polyakova's presence he'd felt just now. Seven had taken the Russian woman back up the stairs as he'd ordered, and he'd have seen them if they'd come back down. He crept up and down the row, moving back and forth until he had reached a vantage point from which he could view the entire room. No one.

That left only one place where the presence he had felt could be hiding. Dropping lower behind the canvases, the Executioner began making his way toward the small office.

As he neared the staircase, a swarthy figure suddenly appeared at the top of the steps. The Desert Eagle rose. But a second later, Bolan made out the broad figure of Johnny Seven. The DEA man held his SIG-Sauer in his right hand, the 7-round Taurus in his left. He was about to start back down the stairs.

The Executioner raised his empty hand and shook it violently over his head to catch Seven's eye in the dim light. Johnny Seven saw him and froze in place. The Executioner's index finger moved down to his lips for silence, then pointed toward the rear office.

Seven understood, and nodded. He trained both his autopistol and revolver toward the rear of the building.

Bolan motioned for him to stay where he was, then crept on, making his way through the forest of canvas and easels. In his mind he heard breathing, but he knew that was the only place it could be—in his mind. The gallery was still a cacophony of diverse racket that would have covered such sounds even if they'd been right next to him.

The Executioner stopped at the last row of paintings before the office. By his count, he had fired six rounds from the big .44 Magnum. He had two left. Not wanting to be disarmed—even for the second or so it would take to drop the nearly spent magazine and replace it with a fresh box—he curled his left hand under his jacket and pulled the Beretta 93-R from under his arm. He flipped the selector switch of the sound-suppressed machine pistol to burst mode, then moved on.

A muzzle-flash partially blinded the Executioner as he stepped around the last row of paintings. A split second later, an explosion sounded over the screech of the alarm, the pounding rain and the ever nearing sirens. He reacted rather than acted, firing with both right and left hands simultaneously, and sending a deafening .44 Magnum hollowpoint round as well as a sound-suppressed trio of 9 mm slugs back at the flash.

An obscure specter that had stepped into the doorway leading to the office was driven back against the wall next to the door. Still half-blinded by the sudden light, the Executioner watched it slump to a sitting position on the floor before rolling over onto its side.

Bolan crouched low as he hurried on through the doorway, squinting both ways, hoping his suddenly contracted pupils would pick up any more gunmen who might be hiding in the office. But he was alone.

With another dead body.

As his eyes began to readjust to the darkness, the Executioner saw that the door to the rear parking lot was slightly ajar. Part of the wooden frame had been ripped from the wall, and what must have happened suddenly became clear. The gunman had kicked in the door after the alarm went off. The roar coming from the speakers around the gallery had masked the noise.

Bolan hurried back to the main room and found Johnny Seven at the bottom of the steps. The DEA man could see through the doorway to the office and knew what had happened. Seven knelt next to the dead man who had worn the bomber jacket and began going through his pockets.

"Don't waste your time," Bolan said. "They won't have ID on them." He hurried back to the steps and yelled up to the second floor. "Luiza! Come down! We've got to go!" When he got no response, he took the stairs in three long leaps and found the Russian woman in her living room. She was sitting with her back against the wall, her hands clasped in front of her, shaking violently.

Bolan knelt next to her and took her in his arms. For a moment, he held her. Then, as she began to calm, he leaned back to arm's reach and said, "Come on. It's over. But we've got to go."

Polyakova felt like a limp rag as she let Bolan help her to her feet. Barely audible under her breath, he heard her say, "It will never be over. But what cannot be overcome or escaped must be endured."

The words sounded strangely formal under the circumstances, as if she might be quoting the line from a book or a play. Under other conditions Bolan would have been tempted to inquire further, but the sirens were growing louder now as the NYPD raced closer, and the burglar alarm continued to squeal.

Bolan helped the Russian woman down the stairs, thinking of how she had punched the first female convict who had tried to kill her on Rikers Island. The incident stood out in bold relief against seeing her just shaking in terror. But Bolan was reminded that she was like most people when it came to courage. Sometimes it was just there. Sometimes it just wasn't. And often it came only when a person's back was against the wall and there was no one else to help.

"Let's go," the Executioner said as he passed Johnny Seven, still on the floor.

"The cops will be here in a minute and—"

"That's why we've got to go. Grab the suitcase." Bolan had no more intention of answering questions the rest of the night than he had of keeping the appointment with Deputy Commissioner Kasparak and the Rikers investigators in a few hours.

The Desert Eagle in one hand, Luiza Polyakova in the other, Bolan hurried to the back door and swung it open. He peered outside. When he was satisfied that the area around the gallery was clear, he hauled the woman across the lot to the Highlander. He had her in the passenger's seat and was halfway behind the wheel by the time Seven opened the door and jumped in the back.

Bolan hit the window wipers as he pulled out of the alley onto the street.

"So," Seven said as they passed the front of the gallery, "I take it we don't intend to stick around and explain to the locals what happened."

"You've got it," Bolan replied.

"Well, it's not as if you didn't warn me," the DEA man stated from the back seat.

"You can still take off if you want," the soldier said.

Behind Bolan, Seven snorted loudly. "You kidding?" he said. "I'm having the time of my life. There's just one thing I'd like to ask of you, though."

"What's that?" Bolan asked.

"Next time, let *me* kill one of the scumbags, okay?"

"You'll just have to be faster," Bolan answered.

A block from the gallery, the Highlander met two black-and-white squad cars going the other way.

3

The Red Brick Hotel was actually one of New York City's famous brownstones. The layer of bricklike shingling covering the front of the building around the entryway was apparently enough to warrant the name.

It sat a few blocks from Polyakova's gallery. Bolan remembered the hotel from years before as a modestly priced place several steps below the Hilton but an equal number above a Bowery flophouse. What he remembered best—and what was most important now—was the fact that the Red Brick had enclosed parking.

At least one of the attackers—maybe more—had been at the gallery and escaped. That meant the Highlander had to be considered exposed, and if they planned to stay somewhere for any length of time, Bolan wanted to get it off the streets and out of sight.

Bolan sent Seven up the concrete steps and into the lobby to secure a room. He and Luiza Polyakova stayed in the vehicle, double-parked along the street. Bolan kept one eye forward along the street, the other on the rearview mirror, as they waited.

The rain hadn't let up and it pounded the roof and windshield of the light SUV. The wind was unusually strong for the city, and now and then a gust rocked the Highlander. What little hair Johnny Seven had on the sides of his head was soaking wet and blown over his ears when he returned a few minutes later holding a key. The DEA man got in. Bolan twisted the steering wheel and guided them down a narrow drive between the hotel and a small grocery store to the rear of the building, then up a ramp.

They found an empty space on the second floor of the parking garage. The Executioner killed the engine, grabbed Polyakova's suitcase and got out.

Five minutes later they all stood inside the room on the third floor. Sparsely furnished, it consisted of a double bed, a desk, small table and mismatched chairs. All of the furnishings looked as if they might have been picked up at a garage sale. Bolan set the suitcase down on the floor next to the wall and pulled the chair out from the desk. When he turned around, Seven was coming out of the bathroom with a towel and began drying the straggly hair at the sides of his head as he took a seat on the edge of the bed next to the Russian woman.

"Okay. Luiza, I need you to go over it all again. And this time, don't leave anything out. No matter how small or how unimportant some detail might seem, I need to know." He paused a moment and looked into her emerald eyes. "After all that's happened in the past few hours, I think you can figure out where you stand. You're smart enough to know that unless we help you, you're going to die. And the only way we can help you is by finding whoever wants you dead."

Bolan sat waiting, expecting another flood of tears that would rival the storm raging outside, but the impending shower didn't happen. Instead, Polyakova's deep green eyes took on a weary, resigned look.

"Where do you want me to start?" she asked.

"At the beginning. Tell me how you met the men who forced you to help them."

Polyakova sighed. "It seems so long ago," she said, and for a moment her voice sounded like a little girl's. "I had opened my gallery here in New York only two years ago. I had been making a modest living, and I was happy. I am not a person who demands wealth. If it comes, fine, but it has little to do with happiness."

Bolan and Johnny Seven sat quietly, listening.

"Then a childhood friend of mine—an art dealer in Moscow—

called me," Polyakova went on. "He offered me an extraordinary price on several dozen paintings that he couldn't sell in Russia because of the lagging economy. I went home to Moscow to arrange for shipment and to visit my family." She stopped speaking for a moment and shivered. Whether it was from the rain or the memory, Bolan couldn't be sure. "I was leaving the art dealer's office when I was approached on the street by a man. It was Rabashka."

Polyakova paused, took a deep breath, then continued. "Rabashka explained what he wanted me to do. He had paintings of his own that he wanted to ship with mine. I knew they must be stolen and I suspected they wanted to smuggle drugs of some kind, as well. The words 'stolen' and 'drugs' were never used by him, you understand. He claimed it would simply allow him to avoid unnecessary and tedious paperwork and excessive import fees. He always used the word 'he' rather than 'us,' but even from the beginning I knew he could be only a messenger. Nestor Rabashka was terrifying." She shuddered again, and this time Bolan knew it wasn't from the rain. "But he wasn't the sort of man to manage such an intricate operation. I knew what he wanted to do had to be illegal and I told him I wouldn't do it."

Bolan waited. More was coming. And while he didn't know exactly what it would be, he'd have bet his life he could have laid out the general scenario. When the woman had refused, they would have done something to frighten and intimidate her.

"Two days passed and nothing happened. I forgot about the repulsive man." She closed her eyes for a moment, then went on. "Then, the day before I was to fly back to New York, we were awakened to find my parents' cocker spaniel dead on the kitchen table. His throat had been cut and his...private parts were in his..." The recollection was too terrible for her to go on. She leaned forward, covering her face with both hands.

Johnny Seven, who hadn't shown any compassion toward the woman when they were in the interrogation room, now reached to his side and took her hand. He looked up at Bolan and shook his head grimly, his face telling the soldier that if these men were within his reach right now they'd already be dead.

"You can skip the rest of the details," Bolan told her. "We get the picture."

Polyakova pulled her hands away from her face, but still no tears formed in her eyes. She had cried her tear ducts dry, and now her beautiful face just looked tired. "No, there is more that you must know," she said. "My sister and brother-in-law lived in the same building. They had a cat. He was treated similarly. His head was cut off and he was left under the covers in their bed while they were at work."

Seven's jaw tightened even further. The angry red returned to his face and the top of his head, his breathing deepened and he looked as if he was either going to find the men responsible for such atrocities within the next thirty seconds or have a stoke, one or the other. He did neither, however, and the Russian continued.

"The message was clear enough," she said in a weak voice. "I received a phone call that evening. It was a strange voice I had never heard before, and have never heard since. It said, 'Families are as easy to kill as family pets.'" She stopped again, took a tissue from her purse and blew her nose. "I had already paid my friend the art dealer and we had agreed that he would ship the paintings the following week. But now I called him and said there was a change of plans. I instructed him to turn my paintings over to Rabashka, who would make all of the arrangements. Then I flew back to New York. A week later, when I went to the airport to take possession of the shipment, Rabashka was there. And he has accompanied every shipment since."

Bolan nodded silently to himself. It wasn't a bad scheme. Polyakova had no criminal record and ran a well-respected business. While anyone was subject to search by customs, officials would have no reason to flag her for any special attention. As he understood it, the bust at the airport the day before had been nothing but pure dumb luck. Something about rats eating into the paintings and spilling the heroin onto the floor. Then an anthrax scare before they found out what the white powder actually was. "How many shipments have they brought in since then?" Bolan asked.

The woman laughed again, even more sarcastically than before. "Twenty? Forty? I've lost count. I tried not to think about it in between. I can check my records if it is important."

"All from Russia to New York?" Bolan asked.

She shook her head. "No. Some have come from other cities. London. Paris. Prague. But Rabashka has always been with them, no matter where they originated."

Bolan nodded. It sounded as if whoever was behind all this was based in Moscow but had markets in America and all over Europe. "When the shipments came here from cities other than Moscow," he said, "were there always stolen paintings involved in addition to the heroin?"

Polyakova looked up at the ceiling, frowning. "I...think so," she said. "But it is not something I could swear to."

"Think hard," Bolan coaxed her. "It's important. I suspect the main moneymaker on this deal is the heroin and the stolen art is just a profitable sideline. But it would be a whole different market, and it might give us a lead we wouldn't get otherwise."

The beautiful Russian woman closed her eyes and frowned again. "Yes," she finally said. "Yes, in addition to the bags of white powder—which he always put in a large gym bag—I distinctly remember Ontomanov taking paintings away with him from my gallery. At least most of the time. I am certain of it."

"Ontomanov?" Bolan prompted.

"Yes. I believe his first name is Agafonka. He is the man who always came by the gallery to take away the drugs."

"And these are the only two men you had contact with?"

She nodded.

Johnny Seven still held her hand in a brotherly fashion. "What were you paid to do all this?" he asked now.

Polyakova turned to him, shaking her head passionately. Although she held his hand, the Russian woman hadn't completely forgiven Seven for the initial interrogation on Rikers. "I was paid nothing, Mr. Jameson," she said through clenched teeth.

"My reward for helping them was that my family and I continued living." Now she pulled her hand back away and placed it in her lap.

"How did you contact them when you needed to?" Bolan asked.

Polyakova turned back to him. "I didn't," she said. "They contacted me. And Rabashka must have been in touch with Ontomanov because whenever I returned from the airport he would be waiting at the gallery."

The Executioner didn't doubt her, but he had been around criminal enterprises that exploited honest people before, and he knew they would have given Polyakova a number to call in case of emergencies. "They didn't want you contacting them?" Bolan asked.

"No. Not unless it was an extreme emergency. They gave me a number but I have never used it." She crossed her legs and Bolan was again reminded what a desirable woman she really was. "No emergencies came up. Until today. And I wanted no more contact with either man than I had to have."

"You have the number with you?" Bolan asked.

Polyakova nodded at her purse, then turned back. "I am sorry, Mr. Cooper," she said. "You really are trying to help me, and you have risked your life to do so." She looked hesitantly at Johnny Seven next to her, then took his hand again. "As have you, Mr. Jameson. And I am sorry I can't remember more details about the shipments."

Bolan nodded. "That's okay. The important shipment is the next one," he said.

Polyakova and Seven both looked at Bolan as if he'd lost his mind. Both of them knew that whoever was behind Rabashka wasn't going to trust Polyakova now that she'd been busted. The fact was, they were trying to kill her, and a person usually didn't try to kill the one he planned to continue doing business with.

Rather than explain, Bolan stood up and walked to the phone. He took a seat on the edge of the bed, his back to the beautiful Russian woman. Pulling out a calling card, he tapped a number into the instrument. As he waited, he glanced at his watch. It was long past the time the Justice Department building shut down for the night, but Brognola was often there burning the midnight oil. A moment later, however, he got a recording. "You have reached the office of Hal—"

Bolan pushed the button down to disconnect the line, then hung up and entered another number. If Brognola wasn't wearing his Justice Department hat, the Executioner knew there was a good chance his Stony Man Farm helmet was atop his head. Again, he waited for the line to connect, but this time he knew it would take longer. First the call had to be bounced to confuse any possible intercepts. He listened to the strange series of beeps and clicks as it did.

Finally the call connected at the top-secret Stony Man Farm counterterrorism installation. The voice that answered said simply, "Hello." It was Barbara Price, the Farm's mission controller.

"Hello yourself," Bolan said.

"Well, well, well," the honey blonde said.

Bolan pictured the woman on the other end of the call in his mind. He and Price had a very special relationship, and it was the closest thing to romance a man with Bolan's fast and furious lifestyle would ever be permitted. "Hal around?"

"I'll put you through."

A moment later, Hal Brognola used Bolan's mission code name to greet him. "How are you, Striker?"

"I'm still alive. But I need some help."

"Ask," Brognola said around the ever present stump of an unlit but well-chewed cigar in the corner of his mouth, "and ye shall receive."

"Item One—we had a little incident at Rikers earlier in the day."

"So I heard," Brognola said. "If I got the right score, the game ended with good guys 2, convicts 0. I'm not counting the women you had to fight."

"They weren't hurt," Bolan said. "But a few more points got scored at Polyakova's art gallery about an hour ago. Four more, to be exact."

"I figured that had to be you," Brognola replied. "Need me to fade the heat with the cops on both counts?"

"Right. I'm scheduled to report back to Rikers and talk to the investigators in the morning. I won't be there. And the cops were arriving at the gallery when we left. They'll eventually put two and two together." He paused to draw a breath, then said, "I don't have any idea where we'll end up before all this is over, Hal. Almost certainly Russia. Maybe some other places. I don't need any over-enthusiastic cops who don't know what's going on getting warrants out for me because I didn't let them interview me."

"Not a problem, Striker," the head Fed answered. "Now, you said, 'Item One,' inferring more than one item, but you lost me. Was all that Item One or were they Items One and Two and now we're ready for three?"

"We're ready for Two. Three and Four will be coming up. First I'm taking DEA Agent John Jameson along to cover my back. Can you get him temporarily on loan to Justice?"

"That's no sweat. The new DEA director is an old friend. Tell Jameson he's covered. Next item?"

"Hang on a second." Bolan turned away from the receiver and looked at Polyakova. "Find me that emergency number Rabashka gave you," he stated. Returning to the phone, he continued, "Got a number I'd like Aaron to try to run down," Bolan said, referring to Aaron "the Bear" Kurtzman, Stony Man's computer genius. "My guess is it won't lead anywhere useful but it's worth a try. And here's a name for you while she's finding the number—Ontomanov. Agafonka Ontomanov."

On the other end of the line Bolan could hear Brognola start to write. "You want to spell that, Striker?" he asked.

The soldier complied. By the time he'd finished, Polyakova was handing him an address book. She had opened it to the letter *E* and was pointing to an entry that said simply, "Emergency." Bolan read the number over the phone and listened as the Stony Man Farm director of Special Ops Group wrote it down along with the name. "I'll see what the Bear can find for you, big guy," he said. "Anything else?"

"Not at the moment. Tell Aaron to move as quickly as he can. I need the info ASAP."

"Consider it done. You'd better get busy, Striker. That's why we pay you the big bucks."

Bolan couldn't help but grin as he hung up. He had never been paid big bucks. The fact was, he had never been paid at all. He was a loner, a crusader for justice who had embarked upon his own personal war, for his own personal reasons, long ago. He answered to no one, although he had an arm's-length relationship with both Stony Man Farm and the U.S. Department of Justice. Sometimes they financed his missions; other times he robbed from the criminally rich and used that money to save the innocent poor they mistreated. But either way, he had been on his own, calling his own shots, since the beginning. And he would still be on his own when the bitter end inevitably came.

Bolan turned back around on the bed so he could see both Polyakova and Seven. "You're temporarily assigned to a Department of Justice task force," he said.

"And the rest of that task force is where?" Seven asked, but his face reflected that he already knew the answer.

"You're looking at it," Bolan said. He stood and moved back to the chair. Pulling it closer to the bed, he leaned forward and took Polyakova's hands again. The emerald eyes seemed to widen as they met his. "I have a plan," the soldier said.

The beautiful Russian woman sat quietly, waiting.

"It has to involve you. And I won't lie to you. There's more than a little danger and risk involved."

Her eyebrows rose slightly. "You are telling me there was no risk and danger today?"

"No," he answered. "There was plenty of risk and danger today. I'm telling you there'll be more."

"Today was more dangerous than any day I have ever known before," the woman said. She stopped and a serious look brought the eyebrows back down. "But I don't think it was such an extraordinary day for you. I think you must've had many days like this."

For a brief second, Bolan felt the same fatigue he saw on Luiza Polyakova's face. It fell over him like a heavy wave of warm sea water. "More of them than I can remember," he replied. "But what my life is like is not the topic of discussion here. I want to make sure that you know from the beginning what you're getting into. And if you don't want to do it, I'm not going to make you." He stopped to let the gravity of her situation sink in before she made her decision. "Yes, today was risky, but if you say yes to my offer, tomorrow is likely to get worse."

Polyakova squeezed his hands. "It seems to me that every day from now on will be worse if I don't help you," she said. "My alternative is what? Return to jail?"

"Not necessarily," Bolan answered. "I could probably arrange it so that you stayed at home if you promised to be available as a witness."

The woman laughed softly—a nervous laugh of resignation. "Ah, yes, I could stay at home. That home with the broken windows downstairs that let in the rain and men with guns. How long do you think I would be home before I was killed?"

"Not long."

"And how long do you think I would last if I went back to jail?"

"Not even as long as at home. Whoever the puppet master is who's pulling the strings of men like Rabashka and Ontomanov has long arms. And they'll reach out to someone else at Rikers."

She nodded. In contrast to the way she had behaved during the attempts on her life, she was staying calm, weighing her options rationally without panicking or showing any emotion whatsoever. "I could return to Moscow," she said.

"Yes, you could," Bolan agreed.

The Russian laughed skittishly again. "But I think that would be like going straight inside—how do you say it?—going straight inside the place where the lion lives."

Bolan smiled. "Right into the lion's den," he said.

"His den, his living room, his bedroom, whatever." Polyakova might not be able to word the old aphorism correctly, but she had no problem with the basic concept. "What it means is that Moscow is where the man lives who wants me dead most of all."

"That would be my guess."

"Then I will stay with you," she said firmly. "At least when they try to shoot me, I will be with a man who can shoot back."

Next to her, Johnny Seven cleared his throat. After practically causing the beautiful Russian woman to have a nervous breakdown earlier in the day, he had spent the entire time they had been in the hotel room trying to make peace with her. He wasn't sure it had worked.

Polyakova turned to look at Seven, and finally a smile that wasn't spawned by fear or restlessness broke across her face. In the emerald eyes the Executioner now saw forgiveness for the man next to her—a man she now realized had just been doing his job to the best of his ability. But in the same eyes he also saw hope, hope for her own future.

The Russian woman took Johnny Seven's hand again. "All right," she said. "I will be with *two* men who can shoot back."

Seven laughed with his own mixture of emotions—gratitude and embarrassment.

Polyakova turned back to the Executioner. "So," she said, "tell me what you want me to do first."

Bolan did. But by the time he had finished, Luiza Polyakova was no longer smiling.

THE BAD GUYS KNEW the rules of the game just as well as the good guys.

Seated in the chair next to the desk at the Red Brick Hotel, Bolan lifted a slice of pizza to his mouth. Whoever was behind the stolen art and heroin shipments that Rabashka had escorted to Polyakova's art gallery obviously knew Polyakova had taken a fall. He knew the law would be pressuring her to help them, and he was doing his best to see that she died before that could happen.

The Executioner took a bite, thinking while he chewed. All he had to do was somehow convince that man—whoever he was—that he not only shouldn't kill the beautiful Russian woman but that she had somehow convinced two federal agents to defect and enter the drug trade with her. In other words, all he had to do was convince the man to ignore all conventional wisdom and throw common sense completely out the window concerning him and Johnny Seven.

No problem. Piece of cake.

Across the room, still sitting on the bed, Luiza Polyakova played with her pizza more than ate it. Knowing they would have to wait on the return call from Stony Man Farm, and since none of them had eaten since morning, Bolan had sent Seven out to get food. The man had come back with more pizza than the Executioner had thought twice as many people could eat. But Seven sat at the desk now, finishing the last of it.

Bolan had just taken a drink from a can of cola when the phone rang. He stood and walked over to the bed, lifted the receiver, then sat back down in the same spot where he'd been when he'd made the original call an hour earlier. "Hello," he said.

"And how are you?" The voice was that of Aaron "the Bear" Kurtzman. The Executioner had expected it to be the computer wizard who called back.

"I'm fine," Bolan said. "What've you got?"

"Good news and bad news. Which first?"

"I don't care."

"Bad news, then. The phone number, as I'm sure we both expected it would, traces to a cell phone. I could run the details down to you about exactly how that means it could be anywhere, with anyone, but you already know that, too."

"It was a long shot but worth a try, Bear," Bolan said. "Okay, I'm ready for the good news."

"It wasn't hard to find out who Agafonka Ontomanov is," Kurtzman came back. "Young. Twenty-seven. Came over from St. Petersburg when he was fifteen with his parents and he's been involved in the art business one way or another ever since. No arrests unless you want to count a few speeding tickets and one reckless driving. He races cars as a hobby, and I guess he does the same on the highway."

"If he's never been arrested, how'd you come up with all this so fast?" the Executioner asked.

"Elementary, my dear Striker," Kurtzman answered. "He's been in the legitimate art business—buying, selling and he's even been an auctioneer at times—all these years but he's also been suspected of dealing in stolen works of art and running drugs. I hacked into the customs and DEA database and cross-referenced his name. He's mentioned in several intel reports as a suspect, and the narcs even have an intelligence file on him." He paused. "Aren't you working with a DEA dude? He didn't know anything about Ontomanov's file?"

"No," the soldier replied. "But if he hadn't worked any cases the man was suspected in, he'd have no reason to. Anything else about the guy?"

"Just about what you'd expect," the computer man said. "He's a high roller. Likes to gamble but doesn't have a problem with it. Toots a little coke now and then, but he seems to be handling that, too—so far. I already mentioned the fast cars, and he likes fast women, too."

"No connection you can find between him and the phone number I gave you?" Bolan asked.

"Nope. No links that I found. Which doesn't mean it *isn't* his phone. May very well be."

"Okay, Bear. Tell everybody hello for me."

"I will. Come tell us yourself sometime. It's been a while."

"No rest for the wicked," the Executioner said.

"Not when you're after them, there isn't." Kurtzman hung up.

Bolan dropped the receiver back into the cradle. Polyakova had moved closer to him on the bed while he talked to Kurtzman and now, as he turned toward her, his knee slid up against hers. A jolt of electricity seemed to pass through the soldier, and in the green eyes that now turned his way he could see she'd felt it, too. Casually moving his leg back away, he ignored the sensation and said, "Okay, how good of an actress are you?"

The woman shrugged. "I don't know. I suspect it depends on the part."

"The first role is pretty easy," Bolan said. "All you've got to do is play yourself. Call the emergency number and see who answers. Did Rabashka tell you it would be Ontomanov?"

"No."

"But he didn't say it *wouldn't* be, either?"

"No."

"Then maybe it will, maybe it won't," Bolan said. He continued to stare into the Russian woman's eyes. In them he saw the trust she had placed in him. "Act frightened."

"That shouldn't be hard."

"Tell them you were arrested and that Rabashka was killed."

For a moment, she looked puzzled. "But...surely they must already know—"

"They do but you're playing dumb. Tell whoever it is that people are trying to kill you and you need help."

A look of understanding came over Polyakova's face. "They will offer to come get me."

"I'd stake my life on it," Bolan agreed.

"You are staking *both* of our lives on it." She glanced up at Seven, who had finished the pizza and was dropping the empty box into the trash next to the desk. "All three of our lives."

"Yes, I am. There's no other way."

Slowly she nodded. She looked at the phone. "Now?"

"Now," Bolan said.

The two changed places and the Russian tapped the numbers into the phone. Bolan moved closer, pressing his face close to hers so he could hear what was said on the other end of the line. Again he felt the electricity brought on by the nearness of the woman. Polyakova turned her head to the side and let out a nervous cough.

A moment later a voice said, "Hello."

"Who am I speaking to?" Polyakova said in a half-panicked voice. "Is this Agafonka Ontomanov?"

"Ah, Luiza," the voice said pleasantly. "I have been waiting for your call."

"I was arrested!" she blurted out. "Rabashka was shot down and killed in front of me!"

Bolan grabbed a notepad and pencil from the stand by the phone. "Ontomanov?" he wrote on the paper, then held it in front of her.

The Russian woman nodded.

"Yes, I know all that," Ontomanov said quietly. "Where are you now?"

The woman ignored the question. "People are trying to kill me!" she more or less screamed into the instrument.

Bolan suppressed a smile. She was doing a good job so far. Playing her part just dumb enough that there was a chance Ontomanov would buy it.

"Where are you now, Luiza?" the Russian on the other end of the line asked again. "I will come and get you."

Bolan leaned back to catch the woman's eye and shook his head. He didn't want her playing things that dumb or Ontomanov would smell a rat.

Polyakova caught on immediately. "I won't tell you!" she said, her tone coming out both angry and terrified at the same time. "For all I know it is you who have sent the people to kill me!"

Ontomanov laughed softly and confidently on the other end of the line. "Luiza," he said. "That is ridiculous. Who knows if anyone is trying to kill you? Maybe it is your imagination, eh? But it's not me. We are partners. Tell me where you are and I'll come get you and protect you."

Bolan had held on to the notepad and pencil, and now he wrote "Tell him you'll meet him somewhere" as fast as he could.

"I will meet you somewhere," she said.

"Where?" Ontomanov asked.

By then, Bolan had written, "Romeo's Submarine." Romeo's was a large, well-lit, all-night sandwich shop a half mile from the Red Brick Hotel. Below the name of the restaurant, the Executioner had scribbled, "Do you know it? If so, give directions."

Polyakova nodded. "Do you know where Romeo's Submarine is?" she asked Ontomanov.

Bolan had pressed his head against Polyakova's. "Of course," he heard the young Russian say. "When can you be there?"

Bolan held up one finger.

"I will be there in an hour," she said.

"Come alone," Ontomanov stated.

"Of course I will come alone!" the woman practically screamed into the telephone. "Everyone else in the city is trying to kill me!"

Both the Executioner and Polyakova heard clicks in their ears as Ontomanov hung up his end.

Bolan moved back away from the woman on the bed next to him. In one hour, they would meet the only contact Polyakova still had who could lead them to the Russian in charge. Ontomanov would be expecting her to be alone. And he would be expecting to take her away from the public eye and either kill her himself or have someone else do it for him.

Again the Executioner knew his job was simple. All he had to do was keep that from happening, and at the same time not have to kill Ontomanov in the process. If the young Russian died, they ran straight into a brick wall as far as further ins to the organization went.

Bolan stood and flipped the tab on another soda. He walked back to the desk and sat in the chair.

Yes, it was simple. At least on paper.

Putting it into practice was going to be the tricky part.

ROMEO'S SUBMARINE WAS playing the name for all it was worth. The sign over the front door featured a long, skinny submarine sandwich. But reality stopped there, and smokestacks made of pepperoni, as well as a bread-stick periscope, extended upward from the top bun. Little cartoon men—dressed in seventeenth-century British sailor suits—were busy atop the bread passing stacks of pickles, mushrooms, olives and heads of lettuce down through port holes to their counterparts in the middle of the sandwich. Below, the sailors who weren't reaching up to accept the cargo were busy swabbing the lower deck with mayonnaise, mustard and ketchup.

Seated in the Highlander across the street, Bolan watched

Polyakova walk beneath the sign and enter the sandwich shop. Johnny Seven was already seated inside, alone, at a table near the rear. He had gone in five minutes earlier, and it appeared the pizza hadn't been enough to satiate his appetite. What looked like a corned beef on rye was quickly disappearing from the basket a waitress had brought to his table along with a bag of chips.

Romeo's was still crowded as the clock made its way toward midnight. Bright from the overhead lights, it had all the ambience of an all-night diner. The clientele was a mixture of partyers getting ready to call it an early evening, night-shift workers on their way to the job and street people taking advantage of the shelter as long as they could. But the important thing was that it was crowded.

Bolan had picked Romeo's for Polyakova to meet Ontomanov because he knew it would be busy—even late at night. And he doubted the Russian would resort to violence in front of so many eyes.

Unless he had to.

Bolan glanced at his watch, then stepped out of the vehicle. He had on blue jeans, running shoes and a navy blue T-shirt. Hanging open, the long tail outside his jeans, the soldier wore a faded denim shirt as a make-shift jacket. Beneath the shirt, in a Cordura nylon and Concealex shoulder rig, the Beretta 9-R rode under his left arm. Counterbalancing the sound-suppressed 9 mm machine pistol under the other arm was a magazine pouch bearing two extra 15-round mags and an inverted Concealex knife sheath. Extending from the sheath was the black Micarta grip of a Tactical Operational Products Loner. The wide four-and-a-half-inch blade was blackened, and in addition to a wickedly curved primary cutting edge, four inches of back edge had been honed to razor sharpness. The back of the tip, however, was blunt. This allowed the strength needed for prying and also drastically widened any cut made by the back edge when the thicker steel hit flesh at the end of a stroke. Designed with the police undercover officer in mind, it had proved to be both a widely accepted fighting blade and utility knife.

As Bolan pocketed the Highlander's keys and crossed the street, he felt the Desert Eagle digging lightly into his right hip. He had chosen to carry the big .44 Magnum in a simple leather Yaqui slide drop-in holster for concealment. In the warm humid weather following the spring rain, he was pushing things to wear anything but a light concealment garment like the shirt, and the Yaqui slide was as low-profile as they came.

The Executioner waited in the middle of the street as a slow-moving taxi puttered past in front of him, then he stepped up on the curb in front of Romeo's. Scattered around his belt in nylon pouches and shoved into his back pockets he had four extra magazines for the Desert Eagle. He was a man who believed in being prepared for any situation that might arise. But this night, he was praying that neither of the guns nor the knife would be necessary.

As he neared the front door of the sub shop, he thought of the fourth weapon he had added to his arsenal at the last minute. It rode in a breakaway Kydex holster just behind the Desert Eagle, and might well mean the difference between a live Russian who could further the mission and a dead one whose demise resulted in a sudden dead end.

Bolan opened the glass door and entered Romeo's, well aware of the fact that his was a precarious situation. He needed Agafonka Ontomanov alive if his plan had any chance of succeeding. Ontomanov and Rabashka had been Polyakova's only contacts within the organization. And with Rabashka dead, the man Polyakova was about to meet was his last hope.

The Executioner took in a breath of stale tobacco smoke as he entered the submarine shop, hearing the chatter of at least two dozen conversations coming from the tables and booths around the room. He walked directly to the counter, ordered coffee and waited while an acne-faced girl in her late teens turned to the counter behind her. He knew from past experience what kind of men he was dealing with. Loosely termed the Russian *mafiya* by the press, the general population had picked up on the term and now used it to designate any of the many large, well-organized ongoing criminal enterprises based out of

Moscow, St. Petersburg and a dozen other formerly Communist cities in Eastern Europe. Their influence spread across the globe, however, and in less than a decade they had made themselves into a power with which to be reckoned within the realms of organized crime in America. New York was one of their strongholds.

The girl set a steaming paper cup of black coffee down on the counter. Bolan dropped two dollars next to it, picked it up and turned back toward the crowd. Next to the table where Polyakova sat, two young couples who had been talking about a movie were just getting up to leave. Bolan walked slowly that way as a boy in a white apron began wiping down the linoleum top with a damp rag. A second later, Bolan pulled a racing form from his back pocket and took a seat in one of the steel-and-plastic chairs, facing the door. He ignored Polyakova and, and as she had been instructed to do, she ignored him.

Bolan's face fell to the racing form as he sipped his coffee, but his eyes kept watch on the front door. In his peripheral vision, he could see Seven several tables away. The DEA agent had finished his sandwich and was reading the comics section of a newspaper. The conversations around the room continued as the patrons of Romeo's Submarine discussed such diverse topics as abortion, the Yankees, the war on terror and the evening rain.

Bolan kept his ears open, catching bits and pieces of each conversation he could hear. Somewhere among the tables, he suspected members of Ontomanov's organization might already be in place. There were several tables of men only. Some were talking. Others weren't. But of those who were, he detected no foreign accents.

Which, of course, meant little. Like the criminal elements of the Italian, Irish, Jewish and other immigrant communities, the Russian mobsters were equal-opportunity employers. They often contracted out to local thugs to do their dirty work for them.

Customers—several men who could have been gunmen—came and went as Bolan, Polyakova and Seven waited. Close to twenty minutes later, as the bottom of the paper coffee cup was starting to appear and he was thinking about going back for a refill, Bolan saw the glass door swing open.

Agafonka Ontomanov walked in.

4

Ontomanov wore a black suit with a white shirt. His straw-blond hair was long, expensively permed, and a tiny gold cross hung from his left ear. He stopped just inside the door—much like a patrol cop answering a disturbance call at a bar—and looked around. His eyes fell on Luiza Polyakova, and he walked directly to her table.

Bolan lifted the empty coffee cup, pretended to take a sip and set it back down.

Agafonka Ontomanov pulled out the chair across from Polyakova and sat down. His voice was low, whispering, as he said, "You must come with me." His English was good—as it had been on the phone, but like many people when speaking a second language, Ontomanov's speech was more formal than that of native-born Americans. And he might have been in the country for twelve years, but he hadn't lost the accent he must have had when he arrived with his parents at fifteen.

"No," Polyakova said, as she'd been ordered to. "How do I know I can trust you? How do I know it is not you who is trying to—" She stopped suddenly and her eyes shot around the room to see if anyone was listening. Then, in an even lower voice, she said, "How do I know it is not you who I must fear?"

Ontomanov let out a sigh. He closed his eyes, rubbed both temples with his fingers, and said, "Luiza, be reasonable. We have done good business with you. Why would we want to ruin that?

"Because you are afraid I might talk to get out of trouble. You are afraid I will be a witness against you in order to gain leniency for myself."

Bolan lifted the racing form and frowned at it. But inside, he was grinning. Polyakova was a natural actress. Her lines were being delivered even better now than when they had rehearsed them on the way to Romeo's.

Ontomanov waved a hand in front of his face, dismissing the idea as ridiculous. "There would be no reason for you to do that," he said, leaning even closer. "These charges are nothing. They will never be proven. Already I have hired one of the city's top attorneys for you. By the time it goes to court you will have your own personal dream team." He beamed a lady-killer smile that Bolan suspected got him what he wanted most of the time.

But this night, it didn't. Not with Luiza Polyakova. "I don't believe you," she said. "If these charges were really so easy to beat, why did you not bond me out? Why did I have to do so myself?"

Ontomanov shrugged his shoulders, reached inside the jacket of his suit and pulled out a gold case covered in intricate engraving. "I sent a man with money," he said as he opened the case and took out a long, slender cigarette. "He was to go to your arraignment and provide your bond, but by the time he arrived, you were already gone." From another pocket he produced a gold lighter. The engraving matched that on the cigarette case. "What I do not understand is when you were arraigned. Or even *if* you were arraigned." Flame danced from the lighter to the end of the cigarette. He drew in a long breath, and as the smoke came back out said, "If you were not, that can only mean one thing. And it is not good for either me or you."

A waitress came by with a coffeepot and filled the Executioner's cup without being asked. The conversation at the table next to him stopped until she had left again.

"Where is it you want me to go?" the woman asked.

"I will take you to a house," Ontomanov said. "A house where you will be safe."

"Who is trying to kill me, if not you?"

For that, Ontomanov obviously had no good answer. He was being forced to rely on the hope that she was so upset she would trust him as a familiar face in a sea of desperation. He shifted uncomfortably, then said, "We are not sure, but we are in the process of finding out."

"Who?" Polyakova asked loudly.

Bolan had told her that at some point she should draw attention to their table. This was the way she had chosen to do so. And it couldn't have worked any better.

While all of the heads within hearing distance in the sub shop turned her way, three men seated at a table ten feet away all showed special interest. One, around the same age as Ontomanov himself, even reached reflexively into his coat. Bolan casually scanned the rest of the restaurant. If Ontomanov had other men inside, they hadn't shown themselves.

He glanced across the room toward Johnny Seven. The DEA man met his eyes briefly, then glanced away but nodded his head. He had seen the backup Russians, too.

"Luiza," the Russian gangster said under his breath. "Lower your voice."

"I am sorry," Luiza whispered. "But I'm upset. I can't be sure what to do. How do I know I can trust you?" She was playing perfectly the part of frightened and confused woman, on the edge of giving in. Her next move would be to finally agree to go with the man. They would stand and walk out of the submarine shop. Bolan would follow, and take Ontomanov down before they reached his car. Seven would step just outside the door and wait until the other three Russians came out the door, then get the drop on them and hold them at gunpoint until the Executioner had time to get Polyakova and his new prisoner out of the area. Then they would all meet up back at the Red Brick Hotel, entering through a rear entrance and taking the back stairs to the room.

At least that was the way it was supposed to go.

"I don't know what to do," Polyakova said.

Agafonka Ontomanov was young, immature and impatient. He had heard enough. His face suddenly changed from pleasant and relaxed to one that would have rivaled Charles Manson. "Then I will help you decide," he said. He tucked the cigarette case back into his coat, and when his hand came back out it held a blue-framed STI Ranger with a stainless-steel slide. As quickly as it had appeared, the .45-caliber pistol disappeared under the table. His eyes shot around the room. All three of the men at the backup table had their eyes locked on Ontomanov. But besides Bolan and Polyakova, none of the other customers had noticed.

The woman's face froze in fear. The Executioner continued to study the racing form.

Ontomanov reached out with his free hand and tore several white paper napkins out of the black dispenser on the table. He covered the gun in his lap, then whispered. "You will come with me, Luiza. And you will come quietly. If I must, I will shoot you here."

"But if I go with you…you will kill me."

The smile of a carnivorous beast came over Ontomanov's face. "Then you must chose whether you prefer to die now or later," he said quietly.

Bolan's eyes shot to the back of the room. Seven was looking the other way and showed no sign that he had seen the gun. But the three men at the other table had, and their faces reflected both shock and confusion. The Executioner had to guess that producing the gun was a development even Ontomanov hadn't anticipated. It had all the earmarks of a rash and impatient decision on the young man's part.

"Now, Luiza," Ontomanov whispered through gritted teeth, "we will stand. You will walk to the door with me. And you will smile while we walk. If you do not, I will kill you here." He stopped for a moment and his tongue shot out, nervously licking his lips. "Do you understand?"

Slowly Luiza Polyakova nodded. The fear in her eyes was real now, her acting performance was over. But she didn't look toward the Executioner as he feared she might, and he had to hand it to her. She was keeping it together better than he would ever have guessed as their plan went to hell in a handbag.

The two stood. The napkins didn't completely cover the gun, but Ontomanov used them to camouflage the shape of the weapon until he could get it back out of sight under the lapel of his jacket. They started toward the door.

Farther back among the tables, the other three men also stood.

Bolan leaned forward and reached under the tail of the denim shirt, behind where the Desert Eagle rode on his hip. In one fluid motion he propelled himself to his feet and stepped around the table directly in front of Polyakova. The collapsible ASP baton flew out of its breakaway Kydex holster and into his hand.

The Executioner flicked the sectional rod with his wrist and suddenly, instead of a short six-inch stick, he was holding twenty-one inches of steel club in his fist. With his other hand, he brushed Polyakova out of the way.

The Ranger was coming out from under Ontomanov's jacket as Bolan drew the ASP back over his right shoulder. As the gun came up, he brought the steel baton across his body, striking the Russian squarely on the wrist. A sickening sound, like the snap of a pencil breaking, filled the air. The .45-caliber pistol fell to the floor and Ontomanov screamed.

Bolan brought the ASP back across his body in a backhand strike, coming down hard on Ontomanov's collarbone. Another crack of bone issued forth and the Russian fell to the ground.

By now the three men at the other table were charging the Executioner's position, their hands all under their shirts or in their coats. The man in the lead was less than five feet away, and a small .380 Talon semiautomatic was already in his hand.

Bolan turned and took a long, sliding step straight toward the man. The ASP came around in a horizontal arc and struck the oncoming gunman squarely across the forehead. The resulting pop sounded like a watermelon falling on concrete. Screams and a few groans now issued forth from the mouths of the customers who had seen what was happening.

The man directly behind the leader tripped over the falling man, flying forward and dropping the revolver in his hand as he crashed into the Executioner's chest. Bolan turned to the side and caught the falling man across the back of the neck with the pommel end of the ASP, helping him onto the floor.

The third backup gunner skidded to a halt, a good fifteen feet away. He gripped a Taurus PT 911 pistol in both hands, and was bringing it up as the Executioner brought his arm back over his shoulder once more.

A split second before Russian could find his target, Bolan threw the ASP with the force of a major-league pitcher unleashing his best fastball. Flying past the heads of several shrieking and ducking patrons, the baton flipped end-over-end across the room, the tip striking the gunman squarely between the eyes. Two things followed. The baton collapsed in on itself, returning to its carry size, and the gunman fell dead on the floor.

Bolan drew the Desert Eagle and swung it across the room, scanning to see if Ontomanov had any more men in the room who he might have missed. If he did, they weren't about to act like it right now, and he hurried back to where the drug dealer lay on the floor.

Johnny Seven, SIG-Sauer in one hand, 7-shot wheelgun in the other, arrived at his side as the Executioner hauled the injured Russian to his feet. The crowd inside the submarine shop was still screaming, and Bolan feared some well-meaning citizen might mistake them for the bad guys and intercede, getting himself hurt in the process. He nodded toward the room. "Show them your badge, Johnny," he said, then whispered, "Buy me enough time to get these two out of here. We'll meet back at the room as planned."

Seven knew what he meant. His badge case came out of his pocket and flashed long enough to be seen but not identified. "Take it easy, folks," the DEA man said. "Everything's under control. Stay cool. We've been after these men for a long time. Everything's going to be fine. Just bear with us—"

He was still saying a lot without actually saying anything as Bolan carried a moaning Agafonka Ontomanov out the door.

A still frightened but grateful Luiza Polyakova followed.

"I'VE GOT TO GET HIM some medical attention," were Matt Cooper's first words when Seven walked back into the room at the Red Brick Hotel. "He's hurt worse than I thought."

Seven took in the scene quickly. Polyakova sat in the chair Bolan had occupied earlier in the evening. Bolan stood next to the bed where Ontomanov lay, unconscious. "What happened?" he asked, closing the door behind him.

"His wrist and collarbone are both broken," said the big man next to the bed. "He's in so much pain he can't keep his mind straight long enough to answer questions, let alone do the rest of what I need him to do."

Seven squinted at the bed where the Russian seemed to be sleeping peacefully. "He doesn't look like he's in that much pain to me," he said.

"That's because he was making so much noise I had to administer some anesthetic," said the DOJ man.

Seven looked closer and saw the new lump on the man's jaw. It hadn't been there when Cooper carried the man out of Romeo's. Already it was beginning to discolor.

He glanced down at Bolan's right hand. The knuckles were red.

Seven laughed under his breath and shook his head. "Yeah, you do break a rule here and there, don't you?" he said, not expecting any answer. He wondered briefly if he would ever be able to collect the pension that awaited him in a few more months. More than likely he'd be fired before he could retire. And if he kept hanging around with the DOJ agent, there was a good chance he'd even end up in prison himself.

Seven forced the thoughts from his head. He had never been what in cop parlance was known as a "homesteader"—an officer who always went by the book, kissed ass and was afraid of his own shadow. He was what was known as an "explorer." A risk taker. Someone who wasn't afraid to take a chance with his life, and wasn't above bending or even breaking a few laws himself in order to take down the bad guys.

"You know a doctor?" Bolan asked as Seven took his still damp sport coat off and let it fall to the floor next to the wall. He took a seat on the edge of the bed. The DEA man knew what kind of doctor his partner meant. In every city in every town in all the world, there was at least one physician who still practiced medicine after his license had been revoked. Some had drinking problems. Others succumbed to one or more of the various drugs over which they had practically free rein. Once in a while, a doctor got caught up in some illegal business deal that involved his practice and the medical board took his or her ticket away. But for whatever the reason, they had to make a living and very few of them chose to sweep buildings or dig ditches. It was to unlicensed doctors such as this that criminals took their injuries. Physicians practicing illegally didn't report gunshot wounds and other cases of violence to the police.

"Guy right here in the village," Seven said, looking up at Bolan. "I busted him a few years ago. Had a Talwin problem and was handing out scrips right and left to support it."

"He owe you a favor?"

Seven shrugged. "We didn't push it hard. He lost his license but didn't do any time. I'm sure he could use the money."

The big man next to the bed lifted the phone. "Call him," he said.

Seven rose and took the receiver. A few minutes later, he had former general practitioner Francis Clarence on the line, and a few minutes after that Clarence was on his way to the hotel. While he was talking on the phone, Seven felt a hand on his belt. Before he could turn, Bolan had pulled his handcuffs from their case and was wrapping one bracelet around Ontomanov's uninjured left wrist. The big man secured the other end of the cuffs to the bedpost. The Russian slept through it all.

Hanging up, Seven sat back down on the corner of the bed. Bolan moved over to Polyakova and took her hands again, talking to her in a low voice, telling her what a good job she'd done at Romeo's, basically calming down the terrified woman. Seven just shook his head in silent awe. He had worked with a lot of good cops in his day, liked to think he was a pretty good law-enforcement officer himself, but he'd never seen anybody who could operate like Matt Cooper. He could be Mother Teresa one second and turn into a timber wolf on methamphetamine the next. He was whatever he needed to be at the moment, and he played every part perfectly. And he was a good man—Seven could tell that. He had no doubt that Cooper was on the right side. What he did doubt, however, was that he was a Justice Department agent. Sure, Jameson had talked to the President of the United States earlier, and he knew Cooper had backing. But the Justice Department? He didn't think so. The President didn't give his personal phone numbers out to field agents.

Bolan and Polyakova were still talking quietly when a soft tapping sounded on the door. Bolan looked up and nodded at him. Seven's hand dropped automatically to the holstered SIG-Sauer as he walked to the door and looked through the peephole.

A moment later, Francis Clarence came shuffling through the door carrying a suitcase.

Clarence had aged badly during the three years since Seven had seen him. What had been distinguished patches of white at the temples had spread until the entire head of hair had become an unhealthy yellow-gray. The flesh around Clarence's jaws sagged like a basset hound, and his coloring was that of a man with liver cancer. He moved like a stoned zombie, and Seven had no doubt that he was. Stoned, anyway. As to the zombie part, the doctor appeared more to have died and *not* returned to life than to have turned into a zombie.

Bolan turned away from Polyakova toward the man on the bed. Seven walked Clarence over to where Ontomanov still slept. There were no introductions.

"What did you give him to make him sleep?" Clarence asked.

"He got knocked out," Bolan said. "Blow to the head."

This didn't seem to surprise the doctor or have any effect whatsoever. He shoved Ontomanov's legs slightly to the side, set the suitcase down on the bedspread and opened it. Pulling out a hypodermic syringe and a small vial, he drew a colorless liquid into the needle.

Seven watched, figuring Clarence wanted to make sure his patient didn't awaken while he worked on him. But as soon as the hypo was full, the doctor quickly rolled up his sleeve and plunged it into his own arm. A look of dreamy satisfaction came over him as he shot the drug into his vein. When he had finished, he tossed the uncovered needle back into the suitcase and said, "There. All ready to begin. Where's he hurt?"

Seven shook his head, turned away and simply walked to the table by the window.

"How long is this going to take?" Bolan asked as Seven dropped into one of the chairs.

"Broken wrist?" Clarence said, his voice slightly more sluggish than it had been a few seconds before. "Long enough to set. Then I have to make a cast." He pointed to the suitcase with a wobbly finger. "Set. Brace. I brought one with me." He closed his eyes for a moment as if in some other world, then opened them again. "But to answer your question, I should have him on his feet and moving in an hour or so. And you'll have five hundred dollars less in your pocket."

Seven watched as Bolan reached inside his pants and came out with a roll of bills the size of a softball. Peeling several off the top, he stepped forward and shoved them into the front breast pocket of Francis Clarence's threadbare sport coat. "Here's a thousand," the big man said. "Make it thirty minutes."

JUST BEFORE LEAVING, the raggedly dressed doctor rolled up his sleeve again. Using another vial and needle from the suitcase, he fired himself up once more.

Bolan had watched the unlicensed physician as he worked on Ontomanov, making sure the man wasn't too messed up to perform his duty. But Francis Clarence had proven to be one of those addicts who was still competent under the influence, and considering the fact that he might well go into withdrawal without the Talwin, they were probably better off having him work stoned than straight .

The Executioner gave Clarence another two hundred dollars for some pain pills that the doctor assured him would balance Ontomanov somewhere between torture and incoherence. The

Russian had begun to come around again by the time the neck collar had been fitted, and now Bolan forced two of the pills down his throat before walking the doctor to the door and bidding him farewell.

The Russian was fully awake by the time Bolan closed the door and returned to the bed.

The pain pills had kicked in almost immediately, and Ontomanov looked at his wrist handcuffed to the bed. "You will pay with your life for this impertinence," he growled.

The Executioner didn't answer. He simply stopped next to the bed and reached down, grabbing the still drying plaster cast, and shook it back and forth.

Ontomanov screamed at the top of his lungs.

The doctor had removed both Ontomanov's jacket and shirt earlier, and they lay on the bedspread next to him. Bolan grabbed the shirt, wadding it into a ball and stuffing part of it into the Russian's mouth to silence him. With the jacket he tied the man's uninjured arm to the opposite bedpost. Moving the hurt limb brought another scream, but it was lost behind the makeshift gag. Ontomanov's chest heaved up and down as he sucked air in through his nose. Gradually, as the pain in his wrist subsided, he calmed down.

"Now," the Executioner said, "are we straight about who's in charge here?"

Slowly the Russian nodded.

"If I take the shirt out of your mouth, are you going to scream again?"

The question got him a shake of the head.

Bolan reached out and yanked the shirt away. Ontomanov coughed and shot daggers at the Executioner from his eyes. In a quiet voice, he said, "You are violating my civil rights."

"Yes," Bolan replied, "I most certainly am. And I plan to go right on violating them as long as I have to."

"I will sue you," Ontomanov stated. "I am a naturalized American citizen."

"Congratulations," the soldier said. "But I understand the test isn't really all that hard."

"I will sue you and retire a rich man," the Russian growled.

"Ontomanov," Bolan said wearily, "I suspect you're already rich by most standards. You've gotten that way by selling illegal drugs that poison Americans—your *fellow* Americans, according to you. You also deal in stolen works of art, and who knows what else." He paused a moment, then said, "But I'm about to give you a chance to redeem yourself."

"Where am I?" Ontomanov demanded. "Who are you?"

"You're in a hotel room. And I'm the guy you're about to help."

"I will never help you!" the Russian yelled. "Go ahead! Take me to jail!"

"It doesn't seem to be sinking in, Ontomanov," the Executioner said. "I'm not a cop. And you aren't going to jail." He caught a quick glimpse of Johnny Seven in his peripheral vision as he glanced toward the window. The DEA man didn't look all that surprised. Seven was smart. Bolan had already broken far more rules than any legitimate federal officer could get away with, which the DEA agent had to know meant only one thing.

He had paired up with a man to whom the rules simply didn't apply. All that counted was the end result. The innocent had to quit suffering, and the guilty had to paid for the suffering they had already inflicted.

"What do you mean I will not go to jail?" Ontomanov said, his face beginning to twist into a mask of semiunderstanding.

Bolan looked back down at him. "What I mean is just what I said. You aren't going to jail. You may go into the East River before this is all over, but I promise you won't do a day in jail."

"Bah! You are bluffing!" Ontomanov cried out with a sudden resurgence of confidence. "Take me to prison! I will never help you with anything!"

Bolan jammed the shirt back in the man's mouth. This time, when he grabbed the cast, he shook it harder. Ontomanov writhed back and forth, up and down, flopping like a fish on the bed. His eyes widened in pain, and a strange sputtering came from his mouth around the shirt.

The Executioner dropped the arm and allowed him to quiet again. Then, removing the shirt, he said, "Shall we start over?"

Ontomanov's eyes were orbs of horror now as it finally sank in that it was no game. He wasn't in the hands of the police. He was in the hands of a man who, in order to see justice done, could be ruthless. After several moments of silence, he gasped out, "What is it you want me to do?"

"That's more like it," the Executioner said. "First I want you to tell me who you work for."

"I work for myself. I am an art—"

Bolan stuck the shirt back in and shook the cast.

By the time he removed Ontomanov's gag, tears had begun rolling down the Russian's cheek. Bolan ignored them. "Same question, second chance," he said. "Waste my time again and I'll go to work on your collarbone. Who do you work for? Who's behind the shipments you've been picking up at Luiza's shop?"

"I knew only Rabashka," Ontomanov said. "The man who was killed. He is the only man I knew."

The Executioner reached out slowly, lifting the shirt off the bed and into the air.

"Wait!" Ontomanov half screamed. "It is true! Rabashka was the only man I have met!" When the Executioner stopped with the shirt in midair, he lowered his voice. "But I have spoken to another man on the phone. This man is above Rabashka. He is…was…Rabashka's contact."

Bolan didn't stick the shirt back in Ontomanov's mouth, but he didn't set it back down on the bed, either. "Go on," he said.

"This man has direct contact with Moscow," Ontomanov stated.

"Who is he?"

"I don't know. I call him Gregor."

The shirt moved closer to his mouth and he shouted. "Please! I'm telling you the truth. I don't know his last name! Or if that is even his real first name!"

"Is he here in the U.S. or in Moscow?"

"Here. I think. I can't be sure."

Bolan inched the shirt closer to Ontomanov's face just to keep his attention. "Who *do* you know in this drug-and-art smuggling organization?"

"No one above me," said Ontomanov, looking nervously at the shirt. "Only the men who work directly for me. Some of them you saw tonight at Romeo's." His eyes widened as his mind seemed to race back to the submarine shop. "Are they all dead?"

"I don't know," Bolan said. "And I don't really care. But that's the last question you ask me. You want a chance of saving your skin, you answer questions rather than ask them. You understand?"

Slowly Ontomanov nodded his head.

Bolan sat silently for a moment, wondering how much of what the Russian was saying was true and how much was the desperate attempt of a man in pain trying to save his own life. Could he really not know any more than he professed to? Maybe not. Polyakova had known very little, and most successful drug-smuggling syndicates were tight-lipped—even within their own organization. But if Ontomanov had never met anyone above him in the criminal organization, how did he get recruited in the first place?

The Executioner asked the question, afraid he already knew the answer. He was right.

"Rabashka," Ontomanov said. Rabashka had recruited him.

"But you talked with this mystery man, Gregor?" Bolan asked.

"Yes."

"Then you can call him for me."

Ontomanov shook his head. "No. I don't have a phone number for him. He always called me."

"Where?"

"At my apartment."

The Executioner turned to face the wall, suppressing a sigh. It was apparent nothing was going to come easily on this mission. On the other hand, it rarely did. This meant he would have to alter the plan he had already constructed in his mind on how to approach the next step of the mission.

"So there's no way for you to contact him?" Bolan asked, hoping against hope that Ontomanov had some other means. Mail drop. E-mail. Anything.

"No. As I said, he contacts me."

Bolan looked past the tears into the man's eyes. His next question was vital, and he wanted to make sure Ontomanov didn't lie. "When was the last time you spoke with Gregor?"

"Yesterday," Ontomanov said. "Before the plane arrived."

Bolan stared hard into the dull gray eyes of the man on the bed. "If that's the case, how did you know Luiza had been busted?"

Ontomanov caught the hard stare and grew nervous. "It was all over the news. Everybody in New York knows about it!" he said anxiously.

Bolan nodded his understanding. It was the explanation he had expected, and unless he read the man wrong, it was the truth. That was why Ontomanov hadn't been surprised when the woman called him. But it meant one other thing, too.

"Johnny," the Executioner said over his shoulder. "Uncuff him." As the DEA man moved around to the side of the bed, Bolan glanced down at the black sport coat he'd used to tie the cast on Ontomanov's arm to the bed. He had knotted it tightly, and it might take hours to work out those knots.

Reaching under his arm, the Executioner drew the Loner knife with his left hand. Ontomanov's eyelids shot up in surprise as he heard the clicking sound as the steel came out of the sheath. The black blade appeared just inches above his face. But before he could speak, Bolan slashed down across his body, severing the jacket with one clean slice. He grabbed Ontomanov's good arm and yanked the man to his feet.

"Where are we going?" the Russian asked. He was confused. Only a second before he had thought his throat was about to be cut and now he was being pushed toward the door.

"To your apartment."

"My apartment? Why?"

Bolan still had the knife in his left hand and now he grabbed Ontomanov with his right, spinning the man back around to face him. Gently he placed the wickedly curved blade against the man's throat and said, "Because you're expecting a phone call."

THE RINGING WAS LOUD in the silent office, shaking Zdorovye from a half sleep behind his desk. He jerked his crossed feet off the desktop and found that his left leg had gone to sleep. For a moment, the leg was numb. Then, as blood shot back through the starved limb, needles of pain pricked his skin like a thousand tiny knives. He began to rub it as he tried to wake up.

Rather than go home at the end of the day, Zdorovye had waited at the office, anxious to learn that the problem in New York had been resolved. He felt certain Gregor would tell him that the woman was dead. But now some harbinger of doom filled his soul, and he grabbed the receiver and lifted it to his ear with a mixture of hope and trepidation. "Yes?" he mumbled, still rubbing his leg. Through the window, he could see a gray dawn beginning to light the Moscow skyline.

"We've still got problems," said the voice from America.

"What do you mean?" Zdorovye asked, suddenly wide awake.

"The hit at Rikers didn't go down. Couple of Feds were there and stopped it."

Zdorovye's tongue felt as if he'd slept with steel wool in his mouth. His sinuses were clogged, and that didn't add to his mood. "Well, try again. You should have plenty of people available there."

"No such luck. The Feds took the woman with them."

"You couldn't stop it?"

"What could I do? I sent men to her gallery."

Although he was awake now, Zdorovye realized his brain still wasn't running in high gear. He was about to ask if they had killed the woman there, then realized that if they had, Gregor would have told him so immediately.

"What happened?" Zdorovye demanded. The needles had left his leg and it was feeling better, but nausea was beginning to sour his stomach.

"The Feds were there with her. They killed all but one of our men."

Zdorovye leaned forward across the desk, still absentmindedly rubbing his leg with one hand. It was all starting to sound like one of the Americans' action-adventure movies. "Who are these two federal men?" he demanded. "Rambo and Arnold Schwarzenegger?"

"Going by what happened at Rikers, and what the guy who got away at the gallery said, one of them seems to be both. Big guy. Tough looking—looks like he's been there, seen it all and brought back the T-shirt. The other Fed—he's DEA—is good but not in the same league."

"Do you know who the big man is?"

"Justice Department is what he claims. Name's Matt Cooper."

"You say that as if you don't believe it."

"I don't," said the voice on the other end. "Several things don't add up. Why would the Justice Department be taking this away from customs and DEA? And this guy never hangs around for follow-up investigations. He took off before the other Feds and state agents could talk to him about the Rikers deal. And he and John Jameson—he's the DEA agent—left the art gallery before the cops got there." There was a pause. "You have any ideas?"

"How should I know?" Zdorovye said with more venom in his voice than he intended.

"Just being polite," said the voice on the other end. "Sometimes two heads are better than one."

Zdorovye shook his head silently, looking blankly at the sword hanging in front of him. The man he called Gregor was right. And it wasn't his fault everything was suddenly going to hell. "Call Ontomanov," he said. "Tell him to get some of his men together and hunt down the woman."

"There's no need for Ontomanov to find her," Gregor said. "She's already found him."

For a moment Zdorovye was speechless. "What do you mean?"

"I mean she called him and he arranged to meet her at a sandwich shop. He didn't know the Feds had her—thought she'd bonded out on her own."

"You didn't tell him the federal officers had taken her?"

"I hadn't talked to him yet," said the other man. "I tried to call him all afternoon. See if *you* can reach that whoremonger when he's shacked up with some of his girls. He won't answer the phone."

Zdorovye shook his head again in disgust. It was a true comedy of errors, bad luck and bad timing on everyone's part. It reminded him of a series of old American slapstick movies. "Well," he said into the receiver, "where is Ontomanov now? Does he have the woman?"

"No. The two Feds got him."

Zdorovye suppressed a curse. "What do you mean? They killed him, too?"

"Maybe," Gregor replied. "But I don't think so." He then told him about the meeting.

"Were you at the sandwich shop?" Zdorovye asked.

"Of course not. I'm getting all this from the one man who survived that incident. This Cooper bashed everybody's head in with one of those collapsible batons." There was a pause, then the voice said, "Look, Anton, do you want me to take care of this problem personally?"

Zdorovye didn't hesitate in saying, "No. We can't take the chance of exposing you. I need you right where you are." But he also couldn't resist taking at least some of his frustration out on the other man. "Besides, it sounds to me like this Cooper would just kill you, too."

The voice on the other end of the line went quiet now. Zdorovye could hear the man's irritated breathing. But the truth was the truth. Gregor was a skilled mole but not an assassin. When the Soviet Union had fallen, he had stayed in place but shifted his focus to private enterprise, namely Zdorovye's drug-smuggling ring.

Zdorovye sighed to himself. He had insulted the man and he didn't need problems with the him right now. So, to soften his earlier comment, he repeated, "You are simply too valuable to risk, my friend."

There was another silence on the other end, and Zdorovye could imagine the man in America weighing the sincerity of the statement. Finally the voice said, "We can send more locals after them, but I've got a bad feeling we're just going to lose more men."

"Do you have a better idea?" Zdorovye asked.

"No. Not yet."

"I do," the Russian said. "Movlid."

"Movlid Akhmatov?" Gregor asked incredulously. "He's a madman, Anton. I would have assumed someone had killed him by now."

"Many have tried," Zdorovye replied. "But no, Movlid is alive and well." He stopped a moment to rephrase what he has just said. "Well, he is alive at least. Whether or not Movlid has ever been well is debatable."

"You won't get that debate from me," said the other man. "He's the original loose cannon, Anton. Like I said, I can't believe he's not dead or in some asylum by now. He's actually still working?"

"He has left Moscow and gone home to live. But, yes, he is still available. I have used him a few times. Expensive, but the best."

"He's the best, all right. Or the worst, I suppose. Depends on your point of view."

"Keep your phone with you," Zdorovye said. "I will contact you and let you know when Movlid is coming."

"You're going to call him now?"

"There is no way to call him. I must go see him in person."

"I should have figured as much. He's probably living in the woods some place with a pack of timber wolves and they're all screwing the sheep before they kill and eat them. Where is he?"

"Just keep your phone handy," Zdorovye said. "Goodbye." He hung up, then lifted the phone again and called for a cab. Walking swiftly to the closet of his office, he located the small overnight bag he kept packed for emergencies. Quickly he checked it to make sure his clothing, toiletries and other items were all there.

Finally Zdorovye walked back to the desk, opened the bottom drawer and pulled out a hard plastic case. Flipping the latches, he opened the lid to reveal a Heckler & Koch Mark 23. The .45-caliber ACP double-action pistol was a civilian version of the U.S. Military's official Special Operations pistol, and was used by the elite forces of the Army, Navy, Air Force and Marines. It could hold eleven rounds with one in the chamber.

Zdorovye double-checked to make sure it held all eleven now, then dropped the gun and slipped three extra magazines into the side pocket of his bag. He started to turn back, then stopped. Reaching back into the case, he pulled out the remaining two magazines.

He was going to visit Movlid Akhmatov. Gregor had exaggerated about the wolves—but not by as much as he probably thought. Considering who Akhmatov was, where he lived and the decadent lifestyle he pursued, it was always best to be prepared. For anything. He glanced up at the sword hanging on the wall, and for a moment considered taking it. It was a sword of honor— of romance and adventure, and should he be forced to kill Akhmatov, it would be fitting to do so with such a weapon. Immediately he discarded the idea. Honor, romance and adventure were one thing. Pragmatism was another. And he knew that if Akhmatov ever decided to kill him rather than work for him, he wouldn't last two seconds within sword range. He might not at gun range, either. But at least the odds were better.

Dropping the extra two .45-caliber magazines into his bag, Zdorovye lifted it and walked out of his office to meet the cab.

MADDUX MANOR, directly across from Central Park in Manhattan, was a luxury building complete with security and a doorman. Bolan guided the Highlander slowly past the front doors in a quick reconnaissance before turning into an all-night parking lot two blocks down. As the attendant—an old man who had retired NYPD written all over his wrinkled face—limped over to the vehicles, the soldier turned in his seat to face Ontomanov, who was riding shotgun. "If this guy, or the doorman at the building, or anybody else for that matter asks, you were in a car wreck and we're bringing you home from the emergency room. He—" Bolan thumbed over his shoulder toward Johnny Seven, in the back seat directly behind him "—and I are your friends."

Glancing at Polyakova, he added, "Considering her accent, we can make her your sister. Got it?"

Ontomanov didn't respond.

Bolan reached out toward the cast. "I asked if you understood."

The Russian pulled the cast back toward his body protectively. "I understand," he said.

The attendant, however, couldn't have cared less. He reached the window and Bolan rolled it down. The man didn't even bother glancing inside, and Ontomanov's cast and neck collar didn't become an issue. Bolan handed the old man a fifty-dollar bill. "Keep a close eye on it," he said.

The old man turned silently back to his tiny shack as they all got out.

The doorman stood just inside the glass doors to the Maddux building. Before he would open them, Ontomanov would have to show ID at the security window.

"My goodness, Mr. O!" blurted out the young woman seated behind the glass window. She wore a blue security guard uniform, and what she lacked in physical beauty she made up for in enthusiasm. Leaning closer to the crescent-shaped hole at the bottom of the glass, she went on. "What happened to you?" Her face showed true concern.

Next to him, Bolan saw Ontomanov force a smile. "It is what I believe we call here a fender bender," he said in his Russian accent. He reached back awkwardly with his injured arm, banging the cast against his leg and grimacing as he groped for the billfold in his back pocket.

"Looks like more than a fender bender," said the girl. "More like a major collision."

Ontomanov nodded his head as he continued to try to find his pocket. "Major collision, yes," he repeated. "I will make the correction in my mind and add the term to my English vocabulary."

The young security woman seemed to notice for the first time his struggle to locate his billfold. "What are you doing, Mr. O?" she said. "You stop that, now—you're hurt!" She waved them toward the front door. "You have your friends take you in and put you to bed! I know your number and I'll enter it in the log." With a smile that spread from ear to ear, she lifted a pen and tapped it on a large book, open in front of her.

Ontomanov nodded, relieved. Bolan and Seven flanked him on the way to the door. Polyakova followed. Bolan saw the door-man's eyes move involuntarily to the Russian woman's chest as he swung back the door.

Ontomanov's condominium was on the seventeenth floor. They found an elevator marked L-20 and took it. A moment later, they stepped off and followed Ontomanov down the hall.

Bolan left Seven and Polyakova to watch the Russian as he quickly scouted the apartment for any surprises. The living room was a sterile black-and-chrome horror of high-tech furniture with a fake fireplace set into one wall. Another wall had been made of synthetic stone, and water trickled down the would-be rocks to fall into a pool of goldfish at the bottom. Cherubs in flight, holding miniature bows and arrows, were mounted along the waterfall's path. A coffee table between the counterfeit fire-place and couch held three large books. The Executioner would have bet his life none had ever been opened.

The kitchen was spotless—apparently never used. But the bedroom took the prize as the most crass room in the house. On-tomanov had reverted all the way back to 1965 with no apolo-gies. Against one wall was a round bed covered by a leopard bedspread. In the hutch at the head of the bed was a control sys-tem that undoubtedly made the bed revolve. Strobe lights were mounted on the wall, and when he looked up Bolan saw what he'd known he'd see on the ceiling—the mirror that was in-evitable considering the rest of the garish decor.

Bolan was no interior decorator and had little interest in such things, but this was obviously the lair of a would-be ladies' man, and he couldn't help but wonder if old copies of *Playboy* and *Penthouse* hadn't been smuggled into the Soviet Union and found their way into the hands of an adolescent Agafonka Ontomanov.

In a drawer by the bed the Executioner found a Walther PPK.

In the closet a sawed-off double-barreled shotgun rested against the wall. In the bathroom, he uncovered a 9 mm Smith & Wesson 459 semiautomatic pistol in the cabinet under the sink. The Executioner unloaded all three firearms, returned them to their points of origin and dropped the ammunition into his pocket. A quick search of the rest of the apartment disclosed no other weapons or contraband of any kind.

Returning to the living room, Bolan waved Polyakova, Johnny Seven and Ontomanov toward the chairs and couch.

"What do we do now?" the Russian asked.

"First I tell you what you're going to say when the call comes." Bolan pointed toward the phone on an end table. "Then we wait."

5

Before the fall of the Soviet Union, few people outside of Eastern Europe could have found Chechnya on the map. Fewer still had known that this small Trans-Caucasian country had been the birthplace of Russia's three most powerful crime families.

While they had begun in Chechnya, and still maintained their home bases in that war-torn former Soviet territory, each of the groups had secondary offices in some of Moscow's finest hotels. The Central syndicate smuggled drugs, ran prostitution and extorted protection money from markets, retail stores, restaurants and other business. Ten percent of the gross was customary, and everyone from the largest corporation to the newspaper boy on the street paid up or lived to regret it.

The Ostantinsky cartel—named after the Ostantinsky Hotel out of which it operated—shipped stolen merchandise of all kinds between Moscow and Chechnya and throughout the rest of Europe and America. Whether someone wanted a microwave oven hijacked from a truckload in France or an untaxed television from Japan, the Ostantinsky organization could get it.

The Automobile group was the smallest in size and power but every bit as ruthless as the other two families. As the name suggested, their specialty was stolen vehicles—most of which were brought in from Europe. They also owned and operated Russia's largest chain of gasoline stations.

Movlid Akhmatov had been the illegitimate product of a romance between the daughter of an Ostantinsky don and a Central soldier. He had been raised by both criminal families, where larceny and murder were taught alongside potty training and table manners. But he had taken to crime, vice and perversions of all kinds far beyond what even the normal Russian mobster could imagine.

Movlid Akhmatov had grown up to be the worst in the land of the bad. And no man who knew him could say he felt no fear when the Chechen crossed his path.

Zdorovye's helicopter flew over the last in a series of peaks within the northern Caucasus mountains and began its descent into the valley below. The house, built on the side of one of the foothills, was old, dating well back into the 1800s. It hadn't been restored, nor even kept up in any way. It lay in shambles; the fence broken and wood scattered across the ground, the roof and walls one step from crumbling down. Anyone who didn't know better would assume it had been deserted years ago, and that its only possible inhabitants would be wild animals.

And they wouldn't have been far from wrong.

The chopper touched down and Zdorovye turned to the pilot. "Wait!" he shouted above the sound of the rotor blades above his head. Digging into the overnight bag between the seats, he jammed the Heckler & Koch pistol into his belt beneath his jacket. Then he filled his pockets with the extra magazines.

Zdorovye stepped down from the helicopter and bent low, making his way out from under the whirling blades. As he walked toward the house, he felt the air behind him gradually grow less turbulent. But the gentle breeze blowing in from the direction of the house seemed to bring with it a scent of debauchery. Unconsciously the Russian patted the gun in his waistband for reassurance.

He saw no signs of life around the house. As he made his way toward the crumbling stone path leading up the side of the foothill, he wondered how much of his perception of Movlid Akhmatov was real, and how much imagined. The man was a killer—there was no doubt about that, not in the mind of anyone who knew him—but was he really the mad dog, ready at any given second to bite through the leash that restrained him and attack whoever was closest?

Zdorovye didn't know, but if he had to place a bet, he'd bet yes. He knew that most reputations—both good and bad—were inflated. When men became legends, regardless of the reason, the stories of their accomplishments were almost always exaggerated into the realm of pure fiction. But with Akhmatov, Zdorovye wasn't so sure.

He had still seen no signs of life as he reached the steps. But Zdorovye felt eyes upon him. Watching. Waiting.

The Russian's mind flew back to Afghanistan. So long ago, it seemed now. He had first met Movlid Akhmatov when he'd been stationed there with the tank crew. Akhmatov and several other drunken Spetsnaz troopers had come into a bar the Russians had set up. It hadn't taken too many shots of vodka before a fight had broken out, and the Spetsnaz crew had cleared out the room. But that hadn't been enough for Akhmatov. The fight seemed only to have whetted his appetite for blood, and as soon as the last regular soldier was down he had turned on his own men. Akhmatov had been the last man standing. The crazed Chechen had even beaten two of his own Spetsnaz brothers to death.

Zdorovye had been lucky. He had been knocked to the floor early during the encounter, and feigned unconsciousness beneath a table during the remainder of the battle.

There couldn't have been more than twenty steps leading up to the ramshackle house, but it seemed to take hours as the man from Moscow lifted one foot after the other. Brawling, he remembered, had been the least of Akhmatov's crimes in Afghanistan. Not long after the fight in the bar, the Chechen had been found guilty of rape and murder in a court-martial. By then, he was already famous for such acts, but up until that time his only victims had been Afghan women. When he performed the same atrocities upon a Russian colonel's secretary, his acts could no longer be swept under the rug. He had been sent to Siberia, where he could kill fellow prisoners and no one would bat an eye.

In a tree farther up the mountain, a bird suddenly took flight and Zdorovye's hand shot toward the gun in his belt. He wiped his palm on the leg of his pants, knowing the watching eyes had seen. He had betrayed his fear—never a good thing to do when a vicious animal was watching.

Akhmatov had spent less than six months in the Siberian gulag. The KGB, having heard of him, decided on an experiment. They wouldn't have to train him to kill as they trained other men. To Movlid Akhmatov, killing came as naturally as breathing. With Akhmatov they would attempt to tone down rather than train. Much like a lion tamer trying to gentle a lion, they would see if they could somehow direct his ferociousness in the directions they wished it to go.

Zdorovye reached the top of the stone staircase and started up the crumbling wooden steps to the front porch. For the most part, the thousands of hours and rubles spent on Akhmatov had been successful. By the time Zdorovye left the Soviet army for the KGB, Akhmatov had already been an active field operative for nearly two years. His specialties, which came as no surprise to Zdorovye, were assassination and immoderate interrogation— a KGB euphemism for torture. He was rumored to take special delight in such interrogations, and when Zdorovye once stumbled upon one of the Chechen's efficiency reports, the supervisor had noted that the man was "exceptionally creative."

Such simple words, Zdorovye had thought. But so telling.

The Russian knocked on the door. He waited, knowing that Akhmatov knew he was there. The man had been watching him and still was. He would answer the door when he decided to do so.

More politically powerful than even the Soviet army, and with far less qualms about civilian death, the KGB had had no trouble covering up Akhmatov's frequent indiscretions with civilian women. After all, what was a dead woman here and there compared to the good of the Soviet Union? Viewed through the broad lens, what difference did the occasional dissected mother or strangled sister or wife really make? Toward the end, there had even been rumors of cannibalism on Akhmatov's part. But Zdorovye found that hard to believe, even from a man like the

Chechen. At some point, legend really did take over and surpass even the most vicious of killers.

Inside the house, footsteps padded softly toward the door. Zdorovye felt his stomach muscles tighten. After the fall of the Soviet Union, Akhmatov had returned to his native Chechnya and worked for his families—first in the Ostantinsky, and then the Central crime syndicates. But that hadn't lasted. With his peculiar tastes and lusts, Akhmatov had found an everyday life of crime far too mundane. Soon, he was on his own and hiring out his gun—and knife, and garrote and bare hands—to the highest bidder. Zdorovye had never heard the Central or Ostantinsky side of the story, but he couldn't help suspecting that both Families were more than happy to see him go.

Finally he heard a sound on the other side of the door. Zdorovye waited, wishing one of his last thoughts before the door opened hadn't been about the cannibalism rumors, false as they must be.

A stench the likes of which Zdorovye had never experienced before blew out the door as it opened. It was a sweet, sickly odor that seemed to carry its own tangible aura of evil. The man from Moscow stood waiting, having to will his hand to stay away from the hidden pistol. The gun would do him no good, he knew suddenly. If the Chechen decided to kill him, he would never see it coming.

The door swung back slowly. "Come in, Anton," said an unseen voice that Zdorovye would have sworn had fire and brimstone attached to it.

The stench from within the house was almost unbearable, but Zdorovye didn't intend to offend the Chechen. He stepped inside. Trying to will his mind away from the smell, he forced a smile. "It is good to see you again, Movlid," he said.

Akhmatov had his own smile, and he used it often. It had very little, if any, humor in it. Though he had never actually witnessed any of the Chechen's immoderate interrogations or his depredations with women, Zdorovye could imagine the man using a smile exactly like this one when he performed such acts.

The house was dark. From somewhere in the corner, Zdorovye heard a painful mewing sound. At first, he thought it must be a cat that was sick or injured. But as the whimpering continued, he realized the sounds were human—female.

Akhmatov saw him looking that way. The Chechen jerked his head in that direction, as well. The humorless smile became a scowl that would have stopped Satan in his tracks. Though he didn't say a word, the whimpering in the corner suddenly cut off.

Akhmatov turned back and the leer returned to his face. "Come in," he said to Zdorovye. "Sit down. I will bring us vodka and tea."

The very thought of any substance in the house entering his bloodstream horrified Zdorovye. He raised his wrist toward his face and looked at his watch. "I wish I could, Movlid," he said, "but I am running late." The nauseous odor that had first hit him when the door opened continued to fill his sinuses, and Zdorovye became convinced that such a smell must itself be toxic. "There are two men who must die in America," he told Akhmatov. "And a woman."

As soon as he had said "woman," the Chechen's eyes lit up. "Tell me more," he said.

Zdorovye did, running down the entire situation. "She must die before she can testify. And you won't be able to get to her without going through them."

"But you said she knows very little."

"She knows enough that, together with other things the Americans may learn, we could have problems." He stopped, drew a deep breath and regretted it immediately as the reek in the room threatened to gag him. Before he could stop himself, he had blurted out, "Movlid, what is that smell?"

The lecherous smile stayed in place on the Chechen's face. "Cooking," he said. He turned briefly toward the corner where the whimpering had been. "Go check on it," he ordered, and immediately the sounds of someone crawling, or perhaps sliding, across the floor could be heard.

Akhmatov turned back to Zdorovye. "Dinner," he said. "We are having something very special tonight. You are invited."

Zdorovye's wristwatch shot to his eyes again. "I'm sorry, Movlid, but like I said, time is a problem." He tried to take the next breath in through his mouth, shallowly. "You will have to go to America," he said. "All expenses, of course, will be covered. And I will pay you one hundred thousand American dollars apiece. That is a total of three hundred thousand."

Akhmatov chuckled, the sound seeming to rumble from the depths of hell deep within his chest. "I can add," he said. "But you are wrong. You will pay me two hundred thousand dollars apiece. For a total of four hundred thousand."

For a moment, Zdorovye was quiet, wondering how the Chechen could claim the ability to add in one breath and then contradict the statement with a faulty sum the next. Then he understood.

And that understanding must have shown on his face. For with another rumbling laugh, Movlid Akhmatov said, "Yes, old friend. The woman is free."

LUIZA POLYAKOVA HAD TAKEN a nail file from her purse and busied herself working on her nails as they waited. The sudden ring of the telephone startled the Russian woman, causing the file to tumble from her hand onto the black leather sofa. She jumped up, then leaned down to retrieve the file, and as she did, her skirt rode up high along the back of her thighs.

Bolan turned away, moving toward the phone on the table. The woman was beautiful—there was no denying that fact—but this was no time to allow himself to be distracted. He watched silently as Johnny Seven grabbed Ontomanov's arm and ushered him to the extension phone in the bedroom. The Russian had been tight-lipped since realizing his only chance of survival was to cooperate, refusing to talk unless asked a direct question and answering with nothing more than a nod or shake of the head whenever possible. That was fine with Bolan—as long as the nods and shakes came at the right times.

Bolan leaned down with his hand over the receiver and waited. A few seconds later, the soldier heard the DEA man say

"Okay…now" from the bedroom. He lifted the phone and placed his free hand over the mouthpiece before holding it against his ear.

How they played it from this point depended upon whether or not this mystery man Gregor knew that Ontomanov was in the hands of U.S. agents. If he didn't, Ontomanov had been instructed to try to set up an emergency meeting with him. Bolan and Seven would be surprise guests. But if Gregor already knew the Executioner had Ontomanov, Bolan would come on the line and take over negotiations.

From the bedroom came Ontomanov's voice. "Hello?"

"Hello," said the voice on the other end. "Are you alone?" The accent was Russian but the words were clear and precise. It was the voice of a Russian who had spoken English for many years and knew it well.

"No," Ontomanov said. "I am with two American policemen."

Bolan nodded silently. Good. Ontomanov had done what he'd been instructed to do. The man on the other end wouldn't have asked the question if he didn't already know they had Ontomanov in custody. So there was no sense in trying to lie. Not when they were about to attempt to gain the mystery man's trust.

"What do they want?" asked the voice.

Bolan could see Polyakova sitting nervously on the couch, holding her breath. He dropped his hand away from the mouthpiece and said, "Let's cut out the middleman. I'm Cooper. What do I call you?"

On the other end of the line all he heard was breathing. Finally the voice said, "You may call me Gregor. But I suspect our mutual friend there has already told you that."

"We can cut out the formalities and the B.S., too." the Executioner answered. "There are two ways to work this. Luiza can go back to jail, I can cut Ontomanov's throat and then come after you." He waited a second to let it sink in, then said, "You like that plan, Gregor?"

A soft, gravelly chuckle came from the other end of the line. "You Americans always sound like your Hollywood movies. You have no idea who I am, where I am or how to find me. Torture Ontomanov all you want. He doesn't know, either."

"Maybe we can find you, maybe we can't," Bolan said. "But it's something you'll have to think about from now on, because I promise I'll spend the rest of my life looking for you. So, sleep well, if you decide that's the way you want to go."

Gregor's low, rattling chuckle came over the line once more, but it sounded a little more hesitant, as if he actually was considering the fact that looking over his shoulder the rest of his life might take the fun out of things.

"There's another option," Bolan stated. "With it, you get a full night's rest every night. And we all get rich."

"I am already rich," Gregor replied. "But I will keep the sleeping part in mind. Go on."

Bolan didn't expect the man to go for what he was about to propose—at least not at first. To do so, Gregor would have to be a fool, and fools didn't succeed in the drug-smuggling business as he had. No, the Russian would insist on proof that what the Executioner was about to propose was sincere. "You have a nice little setup going," Bolan said. "All my partner and I want is a part of it."

What had been a coarse chuckle on the other end now blossomed into a full-blown belly laugh. "Ah," the man said, and now even the trace of Russian accent was gone. "You want to be in business with us?" The laughing continued. "You must take me for a complete moron, Agent Cooper."

"No," Bolan stated. "But I take you to be greedy enough to chance it." He waited a second before continuing on. "Think about it. You'd have a Justice Department agent and a DEA agent on the payroll. Between the two of us, we could get any information you'd ever need. If the heat's on in New York, you can switch deliveries to Miami. If something's coming down in Miami, you change to Chicago or Los Angeles, and so on." He stopped for a moment, then added, "If you'd had us on the payroll yesterday when the rat chewed through your painting, we could have even found a way to cover that up."

Silence fell over the phone line again.

Bolan waited. The man was thinking about it. Weighing the risks, the pros and cons.

"This could be a setup," Gregor said. "In fact, I'd lay nine-to-one odds that it is."

"If short odds paid off, everybody at the racetrack would go home a winner."

Once more a slow and steady breathing was all that came over the line. Then Gregor said, "I am aware of the way you police officers work. When you are using an informant, he must prove his reliability before you trust him. So, I will work it that way myself. Before I begin to trust you, we must find some way for you to prove you are reliable."

"I've already thought that one out," Bolan said. "And it's simple. We do a drug deal with you. You have your people bring in another load, and my partner and I take possession of it. Then we turn it over to your buyers here in the States. You following me?"

"Go on."

"By having us take possession, and then distribute it to your dealers, we get our hands dirty. We break the law. You can stay out of the whole thing and just watch so it's no risk to you." He waited a second, then added. "If you're right, and it is a setup, all you've lost are a few men who work for you."

The breathing on the other end of the line went on again for several seconds. Then Gregor said, "There's one major hole in your plan."

"Where?" Bolan asked. But he knew what was coming, and already had an answer for it, as well.

"Now that she's been busted, customs is going to go through everything headed for Luiza Polyakova's art gallery with a fine-tooth comb."

"That's easy, too. Once the evidence of the bust gets lost and the case has to be dropped, every cop who was involved is going to be mad as hell. They'll want Luiza worse than turkey on Thanksgiving. So they'll hang back and follow orders when we tell them there's still a top secret investigation going on, and they need to steer clear of her so she doesn't get suspicious."

"No, they'll want to be part of the investigation," Gregor said.

"Of course they will," the soldier replied. "But they'll understand when they aren't. If we have to let somebody in on things for whatever reason, we'll send them on rabbit chases that will still keep them a long way from the action."

Yet another long pause, and Bolan knew the man was thinking it over. But he suspected Gregor was about to take the bait. It was a good plan—just complex enough to catch the interest and sound feasible. And Gregor could see that if he and Seven really could be trusted, they'd all have one sweet deal lined up for a long time to come. There was still some risk on Gregor's part, but drug dealers were used to calculated risk, and Bolan was betting that the man's greed would win out in the end and he'd chance it.

"We're all getting older," Bolan finally said. "What's your answer?"

"You have a partner, and so do I," Gregor said. "Give me fifteen minutes. I need to make another phone call." He hung up.

The grin on Bolan's face was still there as he placed the receiver back in the cradle. He walked over to the couch and sat next to Polyakova. A moment later, Seven pushed Ontomanov back in and they found seats.

Almost exactly fifteen minutes had gone by when the phone rang again. Bolan grabbed it.

"It's a go," Gregor said. "But we're going to keep this first deal small. The men I don't mind risking. Money, that's another thing. I'm willing to risk five kilos that this isn't some cheap Fed trick. You will take possession of the heroin, then you will turn it over to our buyers and take their money. Then you will give the money back to us. Do you understand?"

"I should," Bolan answered. "It was my idea."

"I'll call you back again with the details as soon as it's arranged," Gregor said. "Now, let me talk to Luiza."

The soldier has suspected that was coming, and he didn't like it. The woman had been exposed to more violence and terror in the past twenty-four hours than most people experienced in a lifetime. She was still shaky, and a slip on her part now could blow the whole deal. "She's not available at the moment," Bolan said.

He looked across the room to where the woman was nervously working her fingers with the nail file. Gregor, too, knew she would be frightened, and he wanted to exploit that fright with more threats against her family. He knew that if the Executioner's proposal really was some elaborate trap, she was likely to come clean in order to protect them.

"Then I will talk to her when she is available," Gregor stated. "Until then, tell her to remember the pets." He hung up.

Bolan dropped the receiver back into the cradle and turned toward the couch.

Polyakova had heard only half of the conversation, but that was enough. "He wanted to talk to me?" she asked, her hands trembling in her lap.

The soldier looked her square in the eyes. He had to tell her something, and that something had to sound realistic. "He said he hoped you were worth it."

A puzzled look came over the beautiful Russian woman's face. "What does that mean?" she asked.

"He was insinuating that there was something more than business between you and me," Bolan said.

Polyakova sat up straighter and nervously tugged at the hem on her dress. She looked at the wall when she said, "Is there?"

The Executioner didn't answer.

THE EXCHANGE WAS at El Cuchillo Rojo, which meant "the Red Knife." For anyone who didn't speak Spanish, the flashing neon sign above the door interpreted the words with pictures. The sign showed a hand wielding a red-handled *navaja*—sometimes referred to as a Spanish gypsy knife—cutting into a thick beefsteak.

Following the Spanish tradition of late dining, El Cuchillo didn't even open until 8:00 p.m. Customers still filled the front dining room when Bolan stepped through the door at almost 4:00 a.m. He had decided to pick up the heroin alone, checking Ontomanov and Polyakova into another hotel nearby and leaving them under the supervision of Seven. Gregor still suspected the whole act could be a police trap, but Bolan knew the Russian might well be setting his own snare, and if Ontomanov, Polyakova, Bolan and Seven were all in the same room, taking them out in one fatal sweep wouldn't be that hard. He could surround the place with men who came in with machine guns, or simply set off a bomb and kill everyone inside.

As he closed the door behind him, Bolan thought of the three people back in the hotel room. He would have preferred leaving the Russians in the custody of some of the Stony Man Farm experts, but there was no time for that. Besides, Seven was proving to be a level-headed man who kept his cool when the gunfire started.

The thick and not unpleasant odors of fish, saffron, wine and the smoke of expensive cigars filled the Executioner's nostrils as he walked through the main dining room. Gregor had called Bolan's cell phone only a few minutes before and instructed him to proceed directly to the back room of the restaurant. Bolan made his way through the tables past a large bar against the right-hand wall. A bartender poured Spanish brandy into a pair of snifters as the soldier walked past. The man didn't look up, nor did any of El Cuchillo's other patrons.

Still, Bolan made sure his hands were never far away from his unbuttoned sport coat as he walked. Both the Beretta and Desert Eagle were only a split second away.

Many of the men and women in the main dining room were drunk. The others were busy getting that way as the Executioner threaded his way between the tables. Stepping through the open door, he found himself in a narrow hallway. He half expected someone to meet him and guide him the rest of the way to where the deal was about to go down. When they didn't, he started down the hall on his own, passing a darkened banquet room, then one in which several men and women wearing aprons were eating. Like the people in the front room, they paid him no mind.

Two men sat at a table in the last room at the end of the hall. Both were in their early thirties and looked fit—but in different ways. The one seated closest to the door wore a skintight gray T-shirt that threatened to rip out across his broad shoulders and

back. His head was shaved but he sported a bushy brown han-
dlebar mustache and matching goatee. Both were carefully
trimmed, as if the time he saved on the top of his head went into
grooming the hair below.

Even seated, the Executioner could tell the other man was
taller—over six feet, he guessed. His reddish-brown hair was cut
into a close brush cut, but he, too, wore a goatee. His T-shirt was
black and, while his arms were not as large as his friend's, the
sinewy cuts of biceps and forearms extended from the sleeves.

Both men's legs were hidden behind the white tablecloth that
hung over the edges to the floor. A dozen other tables just like
it, empty, were spaced around the room. More importantly than
the men's legs, however, were their hands, which were also out
of sight beneath the tabletop. The Executioner had no doubt that
both men held guns—aimed his way.

On the table between the two men was a black briefcase.

The Executioner walked halfway into the room and stopped.
"I'm looking for Leon and Rotislav."

The bulky man smiled. "You have found them," he said. "I
am Leon." He nodded toward the other man, indicating that by
process of elimination he had to be Rotislav. "What can we do
for you?" Leon's accent was so strong it sounded as if this might
be his first trip outside the Russian walls.

The Executioner took a step forward and glanced down at the
briefcase. "I think you know," he said.

"No. Tell us." This from the Rotislav, whose Russian inflec-
tion was as thick as his partner's.

"You talked to Gregor?" Bolan asked. It was then that the soft
humming he had heard upon entering the room finally sank in.
He glanced up to see a small red light half-hidden between stacks
of clean dinner and salad plates on the table in the far corner. A
video camera.

Leon and Rotislav were recording the meeting. Gregor not
only wanted proof that the Executioner and Seven were crooked,
but also he wanted leverage that he could apply against them later
should he ever need it. As his eyes moved back toward the table

where the two men sat, Bolan noticed a slight rustling beneath the tablecloth hiding the video camera. A quick scan of the other tables in the room showed no more movement. But it didn't have to in order to tell him what was going on.

There were other armed Russians beneath the tables.

The Executioner suppressed a smile. He had expected no less, and if they wanted to videotape him he would play along. He looked back to Leon. "Gregor said you had five keys of smack for us. And that you'd tell us where to take it." There. He had said it. He had incriminated himself on tape for all the world to see. That should satisfy the man.

And it did seem to be exactly what the two men at the table had been waiting for. The bulky man stood, flipped the catches on the briefcase and opened the lid. Bolan noted that he turned slightly to ensure a better camera angle. From inside the brief-case, he lifted a large plastic freezer bag high into the air. It was filled with an off-white powder.

"Do you want to test it?" Leon asked.

The Executioner lowered his eyes, shook his head and laughed softly. Then, looking back up, he said, "What would be the point? It's your stuff, going to your people. I'm just the middle man on this deal." He glanced back at the camera again, for the first time letting the two Russians know he was aware of it. "But yeah, sure, if it'll make you happy. Just for the record, Department of Justice Special Agent Matt Cooper, who is now engaged in the illegal trafficking of dangerous controlled substances, is about to field-test this heroin to make sure he doesn't get ripped off." He looked back to the two men at the table and said, "That okay, boys?"

Leon scowled back at him. Rotislav growled something under his breath. Neither of them liked the fact that he had spotted the camera.

Actually Bolan had anticipated the field test and Johnny Seven had provided an unmarked undercover DEA test kit. The Executioner pulled the small plastic vial of colorless liquid from his pocket and unscrewed the lid as he walked on up to the table. Drawing the Loner knife from under his coat, he slid the razor-sharp primary edge of the blade along the top of the plastic, then shook a tiny amount of powder into the vial. Twisting the cap back into place, he shook the solution until it began turning blue.

Bolan looked first at Leon, then Rotislav, letting a cruel smile creep across his face. He stepped around the table and walked toward the video camera in the corner. When he was directly in front of the lens, he stopped, leaned down slightly and said, "The test proves positive for heroin. Now, if this tape is being viewed by law-enforcement officials, rest assured that by now I'm sitting on a beach somewhere sipping rum and cola. Hope the rest of you are happy with your salaries, benefits and retirement packages. I *wasn't.*"

Straightening back up, the Executioner turned around. "Anything else you guys think you might need on tape?" he asked innocently.

The two men's faces turned red from both embarrassment and anger. Bolan returned to where they sat, keeping one eye on them and the other on the tables around the room where the other Russians were hidden. "Where do I take this?" he asked Leon.

The bulky Russian reached into the back pocket of his faded Levi's and pulled out a folded sheet of paper. "Your instructions are all there," he said.

Bolan dropped the paper along with the used test vial into the briefcase with the heroin and shut the lid. He started to leave, then stopped and turned back toward the room. With the briefcase in his left hand, he drew the Beretta 93-R with his right as he walked swiftly to the table where he'd seen movement earlier. When he reached the tablecloth, he lashed out with a vicious kick that sent his foot flying through the linen and under the table.

The toe of Bolan's shoe met something solid, and he heard a loud grunt of pain. Turning to face the camera one last time, he said, "Don't ever think I'm stupid, Gregor."

Then, without another word, the Executioner walked out of the room.

6

Duane Park was like dozens of other street intersections around New York—a tiny triangle of grass with a few benches calling itself a park.

Bolan parked the Highlander two blocks from Hudson on Duane Street and got out. He walked along the deserted sidewalk past the nineteenth-century buildings that made up that part of the Tribeca area of lower Manhattan. Ahead he could see a red-brick building with a variety of rounded arches, a mansard roof and what looked like Roman details. Farther down on Duane was another structure with a cast-iron front.

Bolan stepped off the sidewalk and listened to the rubber heels of his black-leather-and-nylon assault boots pound softly against the street. He crossed to the park, his eyes flickering right and left, his senses on alert. After leaving El Cuchillo Rojo he had returned to the hotel room where Ontomanov, Polyakova and Seven waited, informing the DEA man of what had transpired.

Now Bolan wore black jeans, a black T-shirt and a black Australian outback coat. The long dusterlike garment wasn't necessary to hide the Desert Eagle, Beretta, Loner knife or the extra magazines for his pistols, but it came in handy when trying to conceal a weapon the size of the 9 mm Calico machine pistol that hung under his right arm. With the 50-round drum snapped in place on top of the gun, and an extra 100-round drum mag hanging from the other side of the shoulder sling, the system created considerable bulk.

Bolan stepped onto the grass and walked to the center of the park. He knew that if Gregor had decided to kill him rather than continue the test, now would be the time. There was always the possibility that the Russian would change his mind and decide the rewards from being in business with two federal agents weren't worth the risk. There was also the possibility that the reason for this isolated meeting place was that Gregor's men could grab Bolan and force him to reveal where Polyakova was.

Taking a seat on the bench in the center of the park, Bolan lifted his wrist and stared at the luminous hands of his watch. He knew he had been followed when he left El Cuchillo Rojo, had seen the car behind him as soon as he'd pulled the Highlander onto the street. But a series of turns down alleys and back streets had lost his pursuit, and by the time he returned to meet with the others at the hotel he was satisfied that he was alone.

The headlights of the car cruising slowly down Hudson toward the park caught his attention. The lead vehicle—a Ford LTD—was followed by two more cars. Bolan watched them slow and park along the street.

The Executioner tightened his grip on the briefcase, letting his other hand move closer to the Calico. The moment of truth was at hand, and he would soon know if his plan was working or not. The traditional method of climbing the ladder to the top of the Russian drug-smuggling operation had failed—his informants didn't even know the people above them. But as soon as he had gained Gregor's confidence, the Executioner would change tactics and run the mission more like a war than a police investigation. Playing cop hadn't worked. So he would revert back to what he really was. A soldier.

There were two things that still worried him, however, two things that he had to find a way around. First he had to complete this drug deal, and possibly others, without letting the white poison actually get into the hands of men who would put it on the streets. Pulling that off without blowing his cover wouldn't be easy. At the same time, he had to maintain his guise as a Justice Department agent gone bad until he could end the threat to Polyakova's family. If he was unsuccessful at that, she could kiss them all goodbye.

But first things first, Bolan told himself as the car doors began to open. He had five kilos of heroin in his briefcase that he was supposed to turn over to these men. He couldn't do that—five keys might not be much compared to some drug deals, but it was enough to ruin many lives. So, how was he going to maintain his cover without giving these men the dope? He didn't know. As happened so often to the warrior, the time for battle had arrived before he could fully prepare. But, as soldiers did in such situations, the Executioner would go with what he had, stay alert, think on his feet and take advantage of any opportunity that might present itself.

Three men got out of the Ford LTD. They were joined by seven others from the other two cars. An even ten dark figures made their way across the street and into the park.

Bolan stood in front of the park bench as the ten men fanned out. He was directly under an overhead light, and clearly visible. But so were they. The streetlights behind them made the men look like walking police silhouette targets, and he could almost see the X-rings in the centers of their chests. His jaw locked hard as the old familiar battle adrenaline began to creep through his veins, sharpening his senses. It was the "fight or flight" response to threat and danger.

But flight had never been an option with the Executioner.

The men walked forward and formed a semicircle around him. Bolan noted that several had their hands in the pockets of overcoats. A vastly overweight man stepped forward. Thick wet lips glistened in the park lights. Above the lips was a stringy mustache that would have looked more at home on an adolescent than on the middle-aged face who spoke to Bolan now.

"I believe you have something for us." Another thick Russian accent.

"And I believe you have some money for me?" the Executioner replied.

"The heroin first."

Bolan gave him a smile. "I'd have thought you'd want me to say that. For the camera, I mean. Which one of you has it, by the way? I want to make sure you get my good side."

The thick-lipped Russian didn't return the grin. "Yes," he said. "You are a very funny man. I understand you like making the movies. And kicking people under tables."

The Executioner shrugged. "It was a stupid place for them to hide."

"Give us the briefcase."

"Give me the money."

For a moment there was a long silence. Then the Russian finally reached into his overcoat.

Bolan reached under his own coat. His fingers wrapped tightly around the grip of the Calico.

Several of the men saw the movement. "There are ten of us, American," the fat man with the stringy mustache said. "You think you can shoot us all?"

The Executioner stared back at him. "I doubt it," he said. "But I think we both know who's going to be first. Don't we?"

The dark form didn't answer. He pulled out a large brown envelope and stepped forward, extending it toward the Executioner. "Count it if you like," he said.

Bolan shook his head. "No need." He traded it for the briefcase.

The fat Russian turned to go, then, as if as an afterthought occurred, turned back. "Oh, yes," he said. "One other thing. The man you kicked under the table. He was my brother and you broke his kneecap."

"Send me the hospital bill."

The portly Russian threw back his head and laughed. "That is not so bad," he said. "You are a very funny man. And I forgive you for his knee." Then the smile faded from his face. "It is my other brother for whom I cannot forgive you. You killed him at the art gallery." A second later there was a pistol in his hand.

The Executioner swung the Calico out to the end of the sling and flipped the selector switch down to full-auto. Pulling back the trigger, he sent four lightning-fast rounds into the rotund belly in front of him. The Calico was a big machine pistol, and the 9 mm rounds had light recoil. It wasn't much different than shooting .22s.

The Russian dropped the Makarov from his fist and opened his mouth. Blood spewed between his fat lips. It was followed by a loud belch, and then the man regurgitated as he fell to his knees, then forward onto his face.

Bolan swung the machine pistol to the left. He could see a man trying to bring a gun up into play, having just drawn it out of the side pocket of his coat. Another three rounds exploded from the Calico. It was too dark to see where they hit, but the man ended up on his back.

Return fire now whizzed past the Executioner, at least one round catching the tail of his long coat and whipping it back around his legs. He dived to the side, away from the bench and out of the light, rolling across the grass as more explosions sounded in the still night. The bullets sliced into the carefully tended lawn to the side of his head as he moved, tossing blades of grass into his face. He came to a halt on his belly and raised the Calico with both hands.

A pair of quick bursts ripped from the Calico toward a well-illuminated target—a gunman wearing a light tan trench coat that reflected both the park lights and the moon. Bolan saw all six holes appear in the chest area, and for a second they looked like additional buttons on the coat. Then the blood—black rather than red in the darkness—shot forth, ruining the illusion. The man in the trench coat went down.

But another gunner just to his side, a short, squat man with what looked like a .45-caliber Strayer-Voigt pistol, swung his weapon the Executioner's way. Bolan shifted his point of aim and pulled the trigger again. Another staccato of fire caught the man on the left side of his chest. The force twirled him halfway around. Bolan's next series of rounds stitched up and down his back. A dark baseball cap fell from his head as he toppled away.

Bolan rolled again, coming to a halt behind another bench.

The slatted wood offered little concealment and no cover—all it could do was further distort his outline in the darkness. But it was the best he had. Bringing the Calico up into play again, he reached out with his left hand and grasped the fore grip just in front of the downward ejection port. Hot brass sailed past his wrist as a full-auto stream of 9 mm hollowpoint slugs blasted from the barrel. Two, maybe three rounds—it was impossible to be certain in the dim light—struck a man wearing a linen bomber jacket in the left thigh. A bloodcurdling howl escaped his lips as he fell to one knee. Bolan didn't even have to change his point of aim as the man lowered his more vital areas into the steady stream of fire. A dozen 9 mm rounds stitched through the gunner's intestines, lungs, heart and other organs. He, too, fell to the grass.

Return fire splintered the bench, throwing sharp slivers of wood into the side of Bolan's neck. He rolled again, this time maneuvering toward a concrete birdbath ten feet away. The concrete was the first cover of any kind he'd had since the gunfight began. But over half his body was still exposed to the enemy.

The Executioner was about to bring the Calico back up into play when he heard an emphatic voice scream, "Stop! Wait! We weren't sent here to kill you!"

Bolan had already taken up the short slack in the trigger. His finger jerked to a halt, less than a pound of pressure away from unleashing yet another burst of fire.

"Ivan started this!" the same voice squealed. "It is his fault, not ours! You killed his brother!"

Silence fell over the small park again as the roar of the gunfire died down. The rank smell of cordite filled the air as the five men still standing froze in place. They gave every indication of wanting to end the battle, and an idea began to form in the Executioner's mind.

"You!" Bolan shouted. "Talking man! Lower your gun and step forward!"

Slowly, hesitantly—no doubt wondering if the Executioner just wanted a better angle of fire—the man obeyed. He cleared his throat nervously. "There is no need for us to fight," he said.

"Ivan was acting on his own. We were sent here to retrieve the briefcase. Nothing more." He was silhouetted against a streetlight behind him on Duane Street, and Bolan saw him look down and to his left.

The briefcase lay on its side, still grasped in the dead hand of the fat man who had been named Ivan.

Bolan waited, thinking, his instincts telling him the man spoke the truth. The Russians had been in the process of leaving when Ivan turned back and drew the pistol. It was as if he had fought the urge to revenge his brother earlier, beaten it, then finally given in to it at the last second. The bottom line was that one man had started the gunfight for personal reasons and the others had gotten caught up in it.

Suddenly the Executioner saw a way out of one of his dilemmas.

Bolan glanced toward the briefcase, then slowly stood, keeping the Calico trained at the center of the five men still scattered around the small park. As he walked forward, one of them moved slightly. Bolan swung the Calico his way and the man froze again.

Stepping up to the briefcase, the Executioner leaned down and lifted it with his left hand. He moved two steps back toward the bench he had originally sat on, and dropped the briefcase onto the seat. A light wind was blowing through the park, hitting the Executioner in the face as he aimed the 9 mm machine pistol back at the man who had spoken. "You," he said, then swung his head around in an arc to indicate the other men. "And the rest of you. Come in here. Closer. Now."

The Russians moved reluctantly forward. The man who had been speaking was of medium height and weight. He wore a loose-fitting sport coat and pleated slacks. "Don't try to trick us," he said, his voice trembling slightly. "You are good. Very good, in fact. But don't forget there are still five of us."

The Executioner swung the Calico over the ground, around the dead bodies. "And don't you forget what happened to these five," he said. His eyes moved along the line. The Russians had all dropped their weapons to arm's length.

The man in the pleated slacks nodded. "We don't wish to kill you," he said. "Or to die ourselves. Just give us the briefcase as Gregor ordered. We will explain to him that this was Ivan's fault, not yours."

Bolan chuckled softly, just loud enough to be sure they heard him. "You could do that," he said. "But that's not enough. Gregor made a mistake by letting Ivan out without his leash. And when you make mistakes, you have to pay for them." The Calico stayed in place as his left hand reached down, flipped the catches on the briefcase, then opened the lid to reveal the five plastic bags of heroin. Reaching under his jacket, he snapped the Loner knife out of its Concealex sheath and held the blade up in front of him. Then Bolan turned slightly and sliced downward into the case.

Five times the knife rose and fell, and when he had finished the quintet of kilos lay open. Lifting them one by one, Bolan shook them in the air and let the wind take the powder away into the night behind him.

One of the men gasped. "Gregor won't like this," he said.

"You can tell Gregor I don't like people trying to kill me," the Executioner said. "And you can tell Gregor if he wants me dead, he'd better send better men than you." He suppressed a smile. The opportunity he had hoped for had come. He had kept the heroin off the streets and still looked like a criminal. But he would have to play it smart from then on. He wasn't likely to be so lucky again.

Turning back to the man who had spoken, Bolan said, "Did you get it all on tape?"

"What do you mean?" the man asked innocently.

"Don't play stupid," Bolan said. "Like at the restaurant. Gregor wants footage of me breaking the law to prove I'm on his side. Who's the cameraman?"

A red-haired, ruddy-complexioned Russian was standing almost directly under one of the park lights. Now he slowly pulled his coat. A small video camera was slung over his shoulder. "I got nothing once the shooting started," he said.

"That's a shame," Bolan said. "But I think we can fix it." He looked up and down the line of men. Every one of them was involved in the heroin trade. Each played a part in bringing in the poison that went into the veins of Americans, not only creating addicts but also resulting in crimes against innocent citizens so the junkies could score money for more. Each of these men was directly responsible for ruining the lives of children, for the mugging of elderly citizens, for the murders of decent people trying to get a few dollars from an ATM and every other abominable act brought forth by the addiction to their white powder.

And each deserved the death penalty as far as the Executioner was concerned.

Bolan kept the Calico aimed along the line of men as he walked back and forth, looking them each in the eye. Few could meet his gaze, and most looked down or away. But the man standing next to the speaker stared back at the Executioner with a dead, hate-filled glare. Evil emanated from every pore of his body, and the knuckles of his gun hand were clamped white around the grip of a mammoth Wildey automatic pistol. Bolan couldn't be sure of the caliber in the darkness, but the Wildey could be as powerful as a .475 Magnum.

The Executioner stopped three feet in front of the man. Then he turned toward the red-haired man with the camera. "Focus over here," he said. "On us."

A puzzled look came over the cameraman's face, but he swung the lens that way and lifted the camera to look through the viewfinder.

Bolan looked straight into the lens. "You want proof I'm on the other side of the law, Gregor? You want me to do something no cop would do if he planned on busting you?" He paused a second, took a breath, then went on. "You want something you can threaten me with if I ever try to arrest you? Well, get ready."

The Executioner dropped the Calico to the end of the sling. Still looking at the camera, he said, "I'm going to count to three. Then I'm going to shoot this slimy piece of crap standing in front of me giving me the evil eye. You ready?"

Bolan continued to stare into the camera but watched the man in front of him in his peripheral vision. "One," he said into the lens. He waited a second, then said, "Two." As he had suspected would happen, the man with the Wildey moved as soon as the word was out of his mouth.

The big automatic pistol began to rise from the end of his arm.

The Executioner grabbed the grip of the Calico and squeezed the trigger, sending a steady stream of rounds peppering from the barrel. Brass ejected down, hitting the tops of his boots and glistening gold in the white park lights.

The man with the Wildey jerked like a marionette on the end of the strings of a demented puppet master. The big gun flipped up into the air, then fell to the grass. The man fell on top of it.

Looking back into the lens, he said, "I hope you got that, cameraman. Of course if you didn't, I suppose we can always do it again." He glanced down the line at the remaining men.

"I got it," said the Russian with the camera.

The Executioner waved his hand toward the parked cars across the street, and without another word the Russians took off. He kept the Calico trained on their backs until all three vehicles had driven away.

DAWN HAD BROKEN over New York by the time Mack Bolan arrived back at the hotel where Polyakova, Ontomanov and Seven waited. The soldier had planned to use it as his new base of operations, but after what had transpired at the park, he knew another phone call from Gregor would be forthcoming. And the only place the Russian could contact him was at Ontomanov's apartment. So, in spite of the danger to Polyakova, it was back to Ontomanov's.

Bolan left the other three in the hallway outside the apartment and went in first. There was every chance that after the surviving Russians told Gregor their story, the mobster and his boss in Moscow would decide just to kill all of them and be done with it. That, the Executioner thought, would be the wisest thing for them to do. The drug smugglers appeared to have multiple outlets for their illegal fare in America and Europe, and Polyakova's little corner of the trade couldn't have cut into their overall profits that much. There was only one thing he could hope for, one human emotion that might still make Gregor and his contact in Moscow willing to take a chance. Greed.

As soon as he'd checked all of the potential hiding places within the apartment, Bolan returned to the hall and ushered the others inside. He bolted the door behind them and they took seats around Ontomanov's garishly decorated living room. Polyakova sat alone on a couch, her nail file in hand once more. The Executioner had noticed that she used the manicure tool to keep her hands busy when she was nervous.

Johnny Seven, who had been assigned the task of being Ontomanov's permanent baby-sitter, kept an eye on him as the Russian fidgeted in a reclining chair.

They had been there less than half an hour when the phone rang. Bolan picked it up but didn't speak. Finally Gregor said, "Cooper?"

"It's me."

The familiar gravelly chuckle came over the line. "You keep costing me men," the Russian said. "Every time I turn around, you kill a few more."

"It's hard to find good help these days," Bolan replied. "But I wasn't the one who started the shooting."

"So they told me. Ivan was touchy where family was concerned."

"He won't be anymore."

"No, I guess not. But like I said, I'm beginning to run short of soldiers."

Bolan glanced across the room at Seven. The DEA man was still seated on the couch, keeping his eye on Ontomanov. For his part, the Russian continued to move about nervously in his chair, crossing and uncrossing his legs every few seconds. Turning his attention back to the phone, the Executioner said, "Look at it this way, Gregor. The two men you've just acquired are worth a lot more than all of the ones you've lost."

The chuckle came again. "You have a point."

"I think it's time we quit playing games," the Executioner said. "I've proven myself. And my partner's with me. It's time we started making some money."

"I agree," Gregor answered. "But keep in mind, I've got tape of you taking the heroin, then turning it over to the other men. Illegal distribution of dangerous controlled substances, I believe it's called in the U.S. A Schedule I drug if I'm not mistaken."

"So you've read your law books," Bolan said. "Good for you."

Gregor ignored him. "In case you try to trade sides again, this tape will be tucked away in a very safe place. Don't think you can write the drug deal off as part of some elaborate undercover act, either. I've also got footage of you killing one of my men."

"Self-defense," Bolan stated. "He drew first."

"Self-defense?" Gregor asked. His chuckle turned into a raspy laugh. "Your ego overcame your ass on that one, Cooper. It comes off on tape like one of your Old West quick-draw shoot-outs. It ought to take a jury ten, maybe fifteen seconds to find you guilty and recommend a lethal injection."

"Can the threats, Gregor," said the Executioner. "No one plans to switch sides again. My partner and I have a plan. We all work together for a few years, get rich, then Johnny and I retire from the DEA and Justice Department and just fade off into the sunset."

"I've got a similar plan myself," Gregor replied.

"I'm sure you do, so let's get on with our plans. It's time you and I met each other."

The chuckling came again. "That's not the way we play the game around here. No one knows anything or anybody they don't have to know. That's how we keep from getting caught."

Bolan's laugh was sarcastic. "It doesn't seem to have worked all that well for you, Gregor." He turned and glanced across the room as Ontomanov stood, crossed the room and took a seat again, this time in one of the leather chairs. Seven's eyes followed him the entire way. The woman was still nervously working on her nails. "I'm standing here looking at a woman of yours who got busted yesterday. And another guy who'd be in jail if I was actually the devoted law-enforcement officer I'm supposed to be."

"Cannon fodder," Gregor said. "Both of them. I said the way we play it is how we—meaning men like you, me and your partner—stay out of jail. Not them."

Bolan waited silently. He knew there would be more. Finally it came.

"I have one last test for you."

"I'm finished jumping through hoops for you."

"This will be a last test of loyalty. But it will pay you well, too."

"What more do you need?" Bolan demanded. "I moved your drugs and I killed a man on tape for you. You think cops do that as a matter of course?"

"No," Gregor replied. "Normal police don't. But the very talents you exhibited at the park prove you're anything but normal. You could be with the CIA, Defense Department, Homeland Security, any number of little groups who don't play by the same rules the police do." He chuckled again, the sound like ball bearings rolling on a driveway. "I'm afraid you're going to have to prove yourself to me over a longer period of time. And I've got another test before I meet you."

"Let's hear it," Bolan said, making his voice sound weary.

"I want you to kill a man for me. A man you don't know, in a city you won't know about until the last minute. The job will pay a half million."

It was an unexpected development, but the Executioner had learned to expect the unexpected. As always he would play it by ear as he went.

"A half million sounds fine," Bolan said. "For me. But remember I have a partner."

"I haven't forgotten," Gregor responded. "So far, he's been a *silent* partner. I haven't seen jack out of him." He drew in a short breath. "The job pays five hundred large. You can cut it up between the two of you however you see fit."

"Let us talk it over for a minute," the Executioner said. He covered the mouthpiece with his hand. It would do this man good to think Seven had to be consulted first, and it would give Bolan a chance to think things over, as well. A strange feeling was beginning to come over him concerning Gregor. The more he listened to the man speak, the more he noted that the man's vocabulary was filled with Americanisms. Expressions like "I haven't seen jack" and "five hundred large" and the pun about Seven being a "silent partner." That depth of understanding of the language, and the use of such slang, meant he'd been in the U.S. a long time, and that he'd spent a good portion of that time around the American criminal element.

Out of the corner of his eye, Bolan saw Ontomanov stand again. "I must go to the rest room," he told Seven.

"Sit back down," the DEA man said.

Bolan half watched the two men as he continued to ponder Gregor. Who was he? If he had to guess, the Executioner would have said there was a better than even chance the man had once been a KGB officer assigned to the U.S. in some fashion. Since the fall of the Soviet Union, Bolan had come across several such men who, like their brethren in Moscow, had switched their focus from espionage to racketeering when the statue of Lenin came down. The change hadn't been difficult. The main difference was that they made more money now.

Capitalism paid better than communism.

"I *must* go the bathroom!" Ontomanov was practically dancing, standing first on one foot and then the other like a first-grader who needed to empty his bladder. Bolan looked at Seven and nodded. Then, his hand still covering the phone, he whispered. "Just keep an eye on him."

Ontomanov took off for the bedroom with Johnny Seven. The DEA man stopped at the doorway and watched the man continue from there. Bolan heard the sound of the bathroom door closing and returned to his thoughts.

There was another thing about Gregor's voice that bothered him. He'd heard it before. He couldn't say where, when or who, but it was familiar—filed somewhere in the back of his brain, trying desperately to surface to his conscious mind.

The soldier pushed the thoughts from his mind. They would either become clear or they wouldn't, but it was impossible to force them. In the meantime, he'd make one final stab at taking the easy route to the head man in Moscow. Uncovering the phone, he said, "The plan sounds fine to my partner. But he agrees with me. Before we go we want to get together with you and discuss the whole thing face to face. Maybe *you* play the game another way. We don't."

"You will, though," Gregor said. "At least if you want to play in the game at all. And keep in mind that the half million is only the beginning."

It was what the soldier had expected, so he wasn't disappointed. He still didn't know who Gregor was, but he knew the man had a direct line to Moscow. Bolan would have to take the long way to the man at the top, but he would get there with or without Gregor's assistance. And he wouldn't forget the man he was talking to now. He'd come back down the drug ladder and take him out before this mission was over.

"It's a deal," the Executioner stated.

"Almost," Gregor said. "There's one more thing. You used the woman to get into the game. Fine. I understand. But she's no use to you anymore, and she's a liability. We want her."

"You can't have her," Bolan said without pause.

Gregor didn't answer for a moment. Obviously he hadn't been expecting any argument over the issue. "Why not?" he finally asked.

"Because I've grown to like her," Bolan said simply.

"Tsk, tsk, tsk," Gregor replied. "Tits like that have been the downfall of many a good man."

Bolan let a trace of false anger creep into his voice to reinforce the cover. "You let me worry about that," he said. "She's not on the bargaining table. Put it out of your mind."

"I'll let it pass for now. But just in case this actually is some elaborate CIA or other-agency trap, let me remind you that men are ready right now to go after her family in Moscow. And I want your word that if she becomes a problem you'll take care of her yourself."

"I haven't hesitated to kill anyone who needed it yet, have I?" Bolan asked.

"No, but it's different with women. Men get crazy. Even men like you."

"The subject is no longer open for discussion," the Executioner said. "Who do we kill and where do we go?"

"I'll get back to you with the details. Stay there so I can call you."

From the bathroom off the bedroom came the sound of a toilet flushing. "I'll stay here," Bolan said into the phone. "But if you send any more of your goons to kill me, you'd better send somebody a lot more professional than the bozos I've met so far."

The bathroom door opened as the raspy voice came back over the line. "That's exactly what I'm trying to stop."

Bolan glanced across the room to see Seven suddenly take a short step to the side with his left foot, brush the tail of his sport coat back around his side and pull his SIG-Sauer from the holster. Dropping the phone, Bolan shot to his feet and drew the Desert Eagle as the DEA man fired three shots at an unseen target in the bedroom.

A second later, Johnny Seven fired again as Ontomanov stumbled through the doorway, into the living room. Blood poured from his chest. The 9 mm Smith & Wesson 459 pistol Bolan had unloaded earlier fell to the carpet a second before Ontomanov did.

Seven grabbed the pistol off the ground, then knelt next to the Russian. He pressed a finger into the man's throat, then looked up at the Executioner and shook his head.

Bolan hurried back to the phone, hoping to ask Gregor what the last comment had meant. When he pressed the phone to his ear, the line was dead. He looked up at the DEA agent, who still held the SIG-Sauer gripped in his fist. The man's eyes were slightly dilated. He needed something to do to keep busy while the sudden adrenaline dump worked through his system. "We're going somewhere," Bolan said. "I don't know where yet but somewhere. Luiza and I have clothes in the Highlander." He pointed to the bedroom. "Go find some of Ontomanov's shirts. They'll be tight but they'll have to do. He'll have luggage you can use, too."

Johnny Seven looked slightly confused. "But—"

"Go do it, Johnny," the Executioner said.

Without another word the DEA man disappeared into the bedroom.

Bolan looked up at Polyakova. She looked back at him. She had just seen yet another man gunned down, but she didn't look afraid.

Either she was getting used to it or she trusted the Executioner.

NIGHT HAD FALLEN over Moscow by the time Anton Zdorovye returned to his office. The building was dark, the only light in the ancient stone edifice glimmering from the second-story window of his office. He parked along the street in front of the building, let himself in through the front door and walked through the deserted lobby to the elevators. A moment later, the doors rolled back on the second floor.

The former KGB man was tired, not just physically but emotionally, as well. A minute spent with Movlid Akhmatov had to take at least a year off of one's life, and it had taken him far longer than a minute to explain the situation and come to terms with the Chechen. He had never left the front room or ventured more than two steps past the front door, but the experience had still been harrowing. The darkness, and trying not to gag on the noxious cooking odor he dared not think too hard about. Not to mention wondering what kind of…*thing* it had been that Akhmatov kept prisoner in the disintegrating ruin. The ghastly, pathetic whimpering noises had sent shivers all the way up his spine.

Zdorovye opened the door to the outer office. Amalia, and the two armed guards who posed as office help during the day, had gone home. He passed the secretary's computer hutch and went straight to his desk in the rear office, where he opened the bottom drawer. Pulling out a bottle of vodka and a small glass, he set them on the desktop and dropped into his chair, shaking his head in disbelief at the day's work. Dealing with Akhmatov was like dealing with Satan himself.

Slowly the former KGB man filled the glass with vodka. He stared at the opposite wall, his eyes on the sword, his thoughts on the father he had never known. He was drained of strength, as if he'd just finished a marathon or two-hundred-kilometer bicycle race. Perhaps it was the fear that the Chechen induced in him, or the pure and simple evil that seemed to flow from Akhmatov's every pore. Whatever it was, it robbed Zdorovye of all potency as if Akhmatov were some sort of energy vampire.

Zdorovye downed the glass of vodka in one fast gulp, then stood. He walked to the wall and stared at the sword, letting the alcohol hit his empty stomach and bounce back up to his brain. With the warmth in his belly came a calmer outlook on the situation. Things were not so bad. And they were about to be cleared up for good. The woman and the American federal agents would soon be dead, and Akhmatov would return to that stinking, run-down energy-vampire castle in the Caucasus Mountains. Zdorovye nodded silently as he stared at the sword that had killed his father. In his mind he saw the Chechen, clad in a long black cape, climbing the steps to his house as lightning flashed in the dark sky and thunder boomed down on the mountains. Good, Zdorovye thought. Let him go home. Let him torture whatever poor creature he kept captive there, and sleep in a coffin or whatever else he did. Zdorovye hoped never to see the maniac again.

The phone rang and Zdorovye jumped, whirling on his heels. It continued to chime shrilly in the night as he hurried back to his desk and ripped the receiver from the cradle.

"Yes?" he said into the instrument.

"Good afternoon," said the voice from America.

"It is night, Gregor," Zdorovye answered. "And I am tired. What do you have to tell me? Please get to the point."

"The situation has changed since last we spoke," Gregor said. "I think, for the better."

Zdorovye let out a sigh. "The Americans are dead?" he asked. Already he was trying to decide on a way to break the news to Akhmatov. Certainly, he would pay the Chechen for his services even though they hadn't been needed. First because even though he hoped never to have to use the man again, he suspected he would. But second, and far more importantly, he didn't want the crazed mountain animal coming after him. The problem was that Akhmatov would still be angry. He had wanted the woman. Zdorovye didn't care to speculate about in what way.

"No," Gregor answered. "The American agents are alive and well and so is the woman. In fact, the large American has killed several more of my men."

"Gregor," Zdorovye said. "I am tired. Did I hear you correctly? If this is true, how can the situation have taken a turn for the better as you said?"

"It seems the Americans don't want our organization broken. They wish to become part of it."

Zdorovye cursed in Russian. "Gregor, have you taken leave of your senses? It is the oldest ruse in the world for both police and espionage. They are setting us up, old friend."

"No," Gregor said. "I don't think so."

Zdorovye sat back down in his chair. He listened as the man in America went on to tell him about the meetings at the restaurant, the shoot-out in the New York City park and the videotapes in which the American agent not only entered into an illegal drug deal but also killed a man.

"He is on our side," the voice on the other end of the line finished.

Zdorovye reached up, rubbing his weary face in order to clear his head. He wouldn't have to tell Akhmatov that the Russian woman and Americans were dead. But this new development presented another dilemma.

"Have you engaged Movlid yet?"

Zdorovye pursed his lips, leaned forward and poured himself another drink. "Yes. I have just returned," he said.

"No wonder you are worn-out," Gregor responded. He chuckled in the low, rough voice Zdorovye had grown to despise over the years. "Did you return with all of your limbs and body organs still intact or are they in his stew pot?"

Zdorovye chose to ignore the remark. Anticipating the next question, he said, "He is already on his way to the U.S."

"On your plane?" Gregor asked. "You could contact him."

"No," Zdorovye said as he lifted a fresh glass of vodka. "The Chechen makes his own arrangements—you know that. He will tell no one where he goes or how he performs his work. But the job always gets done."

"Surely you must have some way to reach him?" Gregor asked. "This arrangement with the American agents could be quite profitable, I believe."

Zdorovye downed two more ounces of vodka, throwing it back against his throat, feeling it burn in his belly once more. Gregor's words were irritating, and he said, "Did you not hear what I just said? There is no way to contact him. Once he is gone, he is gone. The job cannot be stopped. These Americans and Luiza Polyakova are as good as dead."

Silence fell over the international connection.

The vodka hit Zdorovye again and he relaxed. "But it is too bad, I suppose," he said after a moment. "Perhaps you are right. From what you have told me about these federal agents it could have been profitable."

"Perhaps it still will be," Gregor said. "You haven't seen what this man Cooper is capable of. Don't be so sure it will be him who dies instead of Movlid."

The very thought brought a laugh to Zdorovye. He almost spurted vodka from between his lips. Finally he got the fiery liquid down his throat and said, "Fifty thousand dollars says the Chechen will fly back with Cooper's scalp on his belt."

Gregor laughed. "Considering the Chechen's bizarre appetite, you may well be right. In any case, the bet is on."

"Only one of us will win the bet," Zdorovye said. "But neither of us can lose when you consider the larger picture."

"No," Gregor agreed. "If Cooper kills Akhmatov, then we can look forward to many profitable years in business with the DEA and Justice Department."

"And if the Chechen kills the American and the others," Zdorovye said, "we are no worse off than before. We have accomplished our original objective and the heroin pipeline will remain intact." He took another sip from the glass and found it was empty.

"I am sending Cooper to London," Gregor stated. "For the Briton."

"Good," Zdorovye answered. "It is time that situation was resolved. Is there anything else we should discuss?"

"Not at this time."

"Good. Then goodbye." Zdorovye hung up. He had consumed a third of the bottle of vodka in only a few minutes and, along with the call form Gregor, it had taken the edge off his nerves. Thinking more calmly now, he could see that he really had no downside in the matter at hand. Regardless of who lived or died, he would come out on top.

Zdorovye walked to the wall, the bottle gripped by the neck in his left hand. He took the sword down from its hangers and stared at the dark red bloodstains near the guard. A quiet voice in the back of his brain was now all that bothered him. It was a voice telling him things might not be going quite as smoothly as he suspected. Gregor had quickly accepted the bet from him, and he had never known the mole to wager whimsically. This Cooper had to indeed be a man of impressive talents.

Then again, Zdorovye thought as he replaced the shashqa on the wall, Gregor didn't know Movlid Akhmatov as he did. He hadn't seen the evil in the man's eyes or known how totally ruthless the Chechen could be.

Anton Zdorovye had. And that memory caused him to lift the bottle to his lips and drink again.

7

Movlid Akhmatov shrugged out of his black trench coat, folded it and laid it over the chair next to the seat he was about to occupy in the small bar. He glanced through the glass at the airline ticket counters across the hall. He was playing a hunch, but he had always trusted his instincts in the past, and they had rarely led him astray. This time, those instincts told him the two American agents and the Russian woman would be traveling by air.

A waiter walked over to the table. "What can I get you, sir?" he asked pleasantly.

Akhmatov continued to stare out the window. "Vodka," he said. He didn't realize how he had pronounced the word until he heard the waiter laugh and say, "Wodka? Hey, man, you're the real thing, huh? Russian?"

Akhmatov looked up at the smiling man, and the smile vanished.

"Yes, sir," the waiter said, taking a step back. "Vodka. I'll get it right away." He turned on his heels and was gone.

From the inside breast pocket of his suit coat, the Chechen produced a well-worn paperback book. Friedrich Nietzsche was his favorite writer and philosopher, and *Beyond Good and Evil* was by far, in Akhmatov's opinion, his ultimate work. There was, indeed, a realm beyond the bad and good that manacled the common man. It was a realm where superior beings made their own rules, and even broke those rules when they chose to do so, simply creating new ones when the time was right. Akhmatov opened the book arbitrarily and read a passage, then looked back out the window. For another moment, he watched the people in the airport come and go, buying tickets at the counters or asking questions about incoming and outgoing flights. Reluctantly he returned the book to his pocket. He couldn't afford to be distracted right now. He was looking for two men and a woman. He had descriptions.

The waiter came back carrying a shot glass on a tray. As he set it down he said, "It's on the house, sir," and was immediately gone again.

Akhmatov downed the shot in one gulp without taking his eyes off the counters. He saw three sets of two men and a woman. But none of them even remotely fit the descriptions. The first three were all in their late seventies or early eighties. The second were African-American. The third were two nuns and a priest.

The Chechen had arrived in New York a few hours earlier and taken a cab directly to the house of a former Spetsnaz trooper now working as a bodyguard for a Russian hockey star. The man hadn't seemed happy to find Akhmatov banging on his door, but he had done what the Chechen wanted, turning over a Colt .38 Special and one of the old U.S. Army .45 pistols Akhmatov had always liked. He had told the cabbie to wait, and they had gone from there to Ontomanov's apartment.

The apartment had been empty, but there were signs that people had recently been there. Not the least of those signs was Ontomanov's dead body—still warm—on the living-room carpet just outside the bedroom. Overall, the apartment had been tidy. The exception was one drawer in the bedroom containing T-shirts, and another drawer with socks and underwear. Both were open, and that had caused Akhmatov to wander into the closet where he saw a shirt half falling off a hanger. It led him to believe that someone had hurriedly grabbed other shirts off the bare hangers in front of it. Looking overhead, he saw a lone leather suitcase. The dust around it showed it had been shifted, and the lack of dust next to it suggested another suitcase had recently rested by its side.

All of which, had led the Chechen to the airport.

"Excuse me, sir," the waiter asked nervously. "Could I, er, get you another vodka?"

Akhmatov ignored the man. He got up, put on his coat and walked out of the bar. He moved silently along the wall opposite the ticket counters, still watching the men, women and children who came and went. Police officers, airport security personnel and Homeland Security guards patrolled the area. He hadn't been to America since the terrorist attacks on the World Trade Center and Pentagon, but he had heard they looked like an armed camp.

The Chechen walked toward a newsstand roughly halfway down the long wall. From there, he knew he could peruse the books and have a clear view of the ticket counters. Ahead, he could see the priest and the two nuns looking at a rack of paperback novels just outside the alcove. Their backs were to him but something had struck them funny, and their bodies all jiggled in laughter.

Akhmatov had walked up behind the three, ready to turn into the tiny store, when one of the nuns suddenly spun 180 degrees and stared straight at him in horror. It amused the Chechen, and he smiled. Her hand shot to the crucifix around her neck like a gunfighter slapping his holster. She took a step back, and her back struck the priest.

Movlid Akhmatov laughed softly as he walked past.

The Chechen found a magazine rack that allowed him to face outward, and pretended to scan the titles. Once in a great while, he got the feeling he might be different than other men. That wasn't quite right, he thought as he looked up at the top rack, where he saw periodicals entitled *Penthouse* and *Playboy*. He knew he was different than other men in many ways. He was stronger, tougher, smarter. But sometimes he got a glimpse into his soul that suggested he might be different in ways he didn't understand. He often wondered why other men took killing so seriously, and even seemed emotional over it. To Movlid Akhmatov, that made no sense. And it wasn't that he was without emotion as one of the weak-minded psychiatrists in Moscow had suggested. Alone, with the women he made love to, he was *pure emotion*. He brought out pure, bare, stark emotion in them, as well.

Their screams proved their passion. Their moans proved their love for him.

Akhmatov shrugged his shoulders. He suspected he wasn't only more intelligent but also more sensitive than other men.

The Chechen looked up at a bare-breasted woman on the cover of one of the magazines. The woman had long blond hair and green eyes, and he knew she, too, would love him if he could only spend some time with her. For a moment, he wondered how she would look if he removed those breasts. As good, perhaps better, he suspected than the woman he had left chained at his house a few hours ago. His thoughts shot back to her, and he hoped she wouldn't die before he returned. There was work to do on her yet.

Movlid Akhmatov's head suddenly jerked up over the top of the magazine rack. Across the hall, at one of the ticket desks, he saw a tall, muscular man wearing jeans and a light black jacket walk to the end of the line in front of the American Airlines counter. Standing just to the side of the line was a shorter, balding man. He was broad, and looked very much like a former Olympic weightlifter with whom Akhmatov had once trained. That man had had layers of muscle beneath the excess weight, and this one appeared to, as well.

Standing next to the broad man was one of the most beautiful women the Chechen had even seen. She had long blond hair cascading down her shoulders like a golden waterfall. As he watched, transfixed, she removed her sunglasses and revealed a pair of hauntingly green eyes. Akhmatov glanced back up at the magazine. The two women looked very much alike.

Moving around the side of the magazine stand, the Chechen left the book stall and crossed the tile toward the counter. An elderly woman was in front of the trio. A middle-aged couple had just fallen in behind them. Akhmatov patted the Colt in the outside pocket of his jacket. He could possibly shoot them all now

and still get away. The .38-caliber pistol had a hammer shroud
and could be fired from within the pocket. The roar would dis-
rupt everyone around him for a few moments and there was
every chance in the world he could simply walk out of the airport before anyone even realized what had happened.

Akhmatov moved to the end of the line behind the middle-
aged couple. He felt the excitement rising in his chest, and a familiar heat swept through his groin. He reached into his pocket
and found the grips of the Colt. The big man in black was the
one Zdorovye had said was the more dangerous of the two. He
would shoot him first.

Taking a step to the side, the Chechen lifted his coat slightly
until he knew the barrel of the revolver pointed straight at the center of the man's back. His finger began to tighten on the trigger.
Then the blonde glanced his way and he relaxed his grip. Her eyes
fell on him for only a second before moving on. But it was enough.

Akhmatov knew a woman in love when he saw one, and this
woman he had been sent to kill—Luiza Polyakova—was in love
with him.

He would have to kill her—he had given his word—and he
would kill her, but before she died, she deserved the chance to
show her love for him. Taking her back to the Caucasus would
be a problem, but surely he could find some isolated spot there
in New York where no one could hear her shrieks of ecstasy.

The Chechen pulled his hand out of his pocket. He would wait.

The elderly woman finished at the counter and the man in the
black jacket stepped forward. Akhmatov tapped the middle-aged
man in front of him on the shoulder. When the man turned and
looked into his eyes, he whispered, "May I cut in front of you,
please?"

The man looking up at him seemed to shrink. He swallowed
as if something had caught in his throat. He started to speak but
seemed unable to get the words out. "Please…go ahead."

Akhmatov stepped forward behind the blonde, who had moved
up with the heavy man to join the tall American at the counter.
He turned away from them but leaned back slightly, listening.

"London," he heard the man in the black jacket say. "Three tickets." The counter attendant gave him a flight number, a time and a gate, and Akhmatov heard a rubber stamp come down on the counter. A second later, he saw the three people move away and he turned to the counter.

"London," Akhmatov said. "One. Business class."

As soon as he had his ticket, the Chechen hurried to a row of telephones against the wall. A moment later, he had placed a call to a former Soviet MVD sergeant living in Liverpool. He didn't know exactly what the man now did for a living but he knew it involved some form of illegal gambling. "You must meet me in London," he told Pavel Petrov when the call connected. "I will need guns."

The man on the other end seemed no happier to hear from him than the former Spetsnaz officer had been. "I can't do it, Movlid," he said. "I no longer—"

The Chechen clicked his tongue against the roof of his mouth. "Pavel, Pavel, Pavel," he said in the voice of one scolding a child. "If you won't come to me, then I must come to you."

"Where do I meet you?" asked the former MVD man.

After the conversation ended, Akhmatov started for the gate, then passed a uniformed police officer and remembered he had one last stop to make first. Looking up, he saw two picture signs above the hallway. One featured the silhouette of a woman, the other a man. Following the arrow leading off from the figure wearing pants, he entered the men's room and proceeded directly into one of the stalls.

Five minutes later the .38 and .45 pistols were at the bottom of a toilet tank and Akhmatov had passed through the security checkpoint without incident.

PARTIALLY HIDDEN behind London's Wallace Collection—one of the city's less famous but more excellent art galleries and museums—was Durrants Hotel. An unusually old-fashioned inn for a city that was fast becoming known for rooms that resembled motels in the Midwestern U.S., the Durrants was still a family-run operation. The restaurant was revered for superior food at modest prices, and featured oak-paneled walls. All in all, the hotel had a "mom and pop" atmosphere no longer considered quaint in a modern city.

Best of all, the Durrants was only a few blocks from the Smith-Williams Art Gallery.

One concession to modernism the hotel had made, however, was electronic locks. Bolan inserted the key card into the door and waited for the tiny green light to appear. When it did, he heard a click and pushed the door open. Polyakova started to go in but the Executioner took her arm and shook his head. He nodded Seven through the opening first.

Comprehension of this break in chivalry lit up the woman's eyes as the DEA man slid his hand under his sport coat and entered the room. Bolan followed, his own hand disappearing beneath his jacket. Instead of the familiar grips of the Desert Eagle or Beretta 93-R, he felt the thick handle of a Browning Hi-Power. They had flown commercial from New York to London in case Gregor had men watching them, and carrying weapons aboard the aircraft would have drawn other unwanted attention when they were forced to fill out an endless number of forms. Bolan had chosen to arrive in London unarmed. The 9 mm Hi-Power pistols had been waiting for them at Heathrow when they touched down, deposited in a locker by a British Special Air Services officer who had been trained at Stony Man Farm.

Whether or not it was all an exercise in futility, the Executioner would never know. But he did know that Gregor was still suspicious of him and he still hadn't shaken the feeling he had gotten at the airport that they were being watched. He couldn't prove it, but he didn't have to prove it to know it.

Bolan left the luggage in the hallway with the woman and followed Johnny Seven into the room. The DEA man lifted the tail of his buttoned sport coat and clumsily drew his own Hi-Power as he ducked into the bathroom just inside the door. The Executioner heard the sound of a plastic shower curtain being drawn as he moved to the open closet door opposite the bath. Seeing it empty, he passed the closet and dropped low to check under the bed before moving on to the large picture window at the other end of the room. The curtains were open, and through the glass he saw that the room looked out onto the alley. Several taller buildings stood behind them in the next block. Just outside the window was a small walkway-balcony that apparently ran around the building. Ten feet to his left was a staircase from the second floor to the ground. The Executioner glanced back at the picture window and saw hinges. In case of fire, it could be turned into a door that would lead to the common steps.

Bolan walked back to the door and ushered Polyakova inside as Seven came out of the bathroom. He had seen no advantage in mentioning that he had unloaded all of Ontomanov's guns before the DEA man shot him. Johnny Seven, while proving to be fearless and trustworthy, had so far been a step behind the Executioner every time shots were fired. Finally getting in on the action seemed to have given him confidence, and Bolan didn't intend to take the chance of ruining that self-assurance.

Bolan stepped back into the hallway, grabbed the suitcases and carried them inside, letting the door close behind him. Seven stood next to the bed in the small room, stuffing his pistol back into his pants against a too-tight striped shirt he had taken from Ontomanov's closet. The shirt not only didn't fit, but also it clashed terribly with his worn and frazzled sport coat. Polyakova had actually winced when he had come out of Ontomanov's bedroom wearing the combination back in New York.

The outfit hadn't bothered the DEA agent in the least, but what Bolan had noticed irritated him was the way the tight shirt threatened to pop the buttons over his stomach. Seven still looked like a powerful man but he was nearing retirement age, and like so many men in law enforcement, had developed a weight problem. Bolan had noticed that he kept his jacket buttoned over the shirt, which meant he had to lift it to get to the Browning. Hardly an advantage to start a speedy draw. The man was letting vanity get in the way of performance, and Bolan knew he had to do something about that before it got the DEA agent killed.

Bolan set the suitcases on a pair of metal-and-canvas luggage racks along the wall. Jack Grimaldi, Stony Man's ace pilot, should have arrived in one of the Farm's Learjets by now with both men's regular weapons. They'd be hearing a knock on the door any time now. In the meantime, he'd take care of Seven's clothing problem.

The DEA man dragged the suitcase he had taken from Ontomanov's apartment in from the hall and, with the luggage racks both full, dropped it on the bed. Bolan walked to a door leading to the adjoining room and made sure the bolt lock was in place.

The soldier came back in and saw Polyakova looking at the bed. She glanced up and their eyes met for a moment, then she blushed and turned away. Bolan walked to his suitcase and opened it, pretending not to have seen her embarrassment. He had considered leaving Luiza behind, hidden somewhere where she'd be safe, but he had a plan for London, and that plan needed her art expertise. Unzipping his suitcase, he pulled out a clean T-shirt, socks, a pair of khaki pants and dropped them on the bed. Then he turned to Seven and reached into his pocket for his money clip. He shoved several hundred-dollar bills into the man's hand and said, "While we're waiting, go downstairs and change this for British pounds. And I saw a men's clothing store just down the street."

Seven took the money and nodded. "Thanks." He kept his jacket buttoned as he hurried out the door.

As soon as he was gone, Polyakova said, "Did you do that on purpose?"

Bolan had turned back to his suitcase but now looked up. "What?" he said, then saw the look on her face and suddenly knew what she meant. She was standing five feet away but he could still feel the heat radiating between them. "No," he said softly. "I didn't do that on purpose."

The woman took a step closer to him and her green eyes bore into his. "I wish you had," she whispered, and then she was suddenly in his arms.

Bolan felt the beautiful Russian woman's full red lips press against his as his arms encircled her, and hers wrapped around his waist. She hugged him tightly, pressing her body into his, and pulling against his back as if trying to force the two of them to become one. Bolan was lost in the embrace, stroking the long blond tresses that fell down her back. For a brief moment in time, there were no Russian drug dealers, no murderers, rapists or thieves in all the world.

Then the knock came.

Bolan leaned back, holding Luiza Polyakova at arm's length. Her face was flushed a soft pink. One long strand of golden hair fell over her left eye. She muttered something in Russian—some curse word that wasn't in even the Executioner's extensive Russian vocabulary. Then she laughed softly. "Perhaps later," she said. "When we have time."

Bolan smiled and turned to the door.

In his faded brown leather bomber jacket, Jack Grimaldi looked every bit the air ace that he was. "Howdy, Striker," he said as Bolan opened the door and stepped back.

Grimaldi walked in carrying two musical instrument cases. One was for a guitar, the other big enough to hold a viola. "I've felt like Al Capone ever since I stuffed these full of—" The pilot suddenly saw Polyakova standing there, her face still flushed, and stopped in his tracks. "Whoa, son!" he said, turning back to the Executioner. "Did I come at a bad time?"

"Drop the gear and have a seat," Bolan told him.

The woman stepped over the desk and pulled her ever present nail file from her purse. She sat down and began to work furiously on her fingernails.

Grimaldi followed the first order, setting the cases on the floor next to the bed. But he ignored the Executioner's invitation to sit and turned back toward the door. "No time, big guy," he said. "Five of your friends need me to pick them up in the Belfast and drop them off near Madrid, stat." He glanced back at Polyakova, and even a well-disciplined man like the pilot couldn't keep his eyes off her chest for a flicker of a second. "Besides that, the hormones are bouncing off the walls in here. I'm afraid I'll get hit with a ricochet." He grinned at the Russian woman. "Ma'am," he said, and then with a wink at Bolan he was out the door again.

Polyakova laughed when he had gone. "I think he knew," she said.

Bolan smiled at her. She started toward him again but he shook his head. "You said it yourself," he told her. "Later. When we have time." He tore his eyes away from hers and walked to the black cases on the floor, lifting them both up and setting them on the bed next to the suitcase already there. He forced himself to concentrate on opening the latches. He didn't need to be thinking about the two of them together right now. He needed to keep his mind on keeping her alive.

The guitar case Bolan opened held Seven's Taurus, his SIG-Sauer, ammunition and other accessories. The Executioner closed it and opened the bigger container. Inside was an M-16 A-2 and various other guns, including the Beretta and Desert Eagle. His constant companions had flown over the Atlantic in their holsters, and he took off his jacket and slipped into them now. He checked both magazines and chambers, flipping the safeties back on when he was done. Drawing the Loner knife from its sheath, he tested it against his thumbnail. The edge bit into the nail with no effort.

Bolan dropped the Browning Hi-Power into the case, then dug through the rest of the guns and other equipment, sorting it. He glanced up once at Polyakova. She had taken a seat in a chair at the table by the window and faced away from him, looking through the glass at the buildings across the alley. When he had finished, the soldier closed the case again and latched it.

Bolan heard footsteps in the hallway and walked to the door, his hand on the butt of the shoulder-holstered Beretta. The peep-hole had an extrawide field of vision, and he was able to see for several yards both ways, up and down the hall. He watched another hotel guest wrestle his baggage past their rooms. The burly man set two suitcases down in front of a room across the hall and two doors down, stuck his card in the door, then entered.

As the door was closing, the Executioner saw Johnny Seven come walking down the hall carrying two large sacks. He waited until the man was almost at the door, then opened it for him.

The DEA agent walked in, smiling nervously. He still wore Ontomanov's striped shirt beneath his sport coat as he walked to the bed. Seeing the guitar and viola cases on the bed, he said, "Looks like either your man arrived or you've got talent I didn't know about." He dropped the sacks on top of the suitcase.

"Your stuff is in the guitar case," said the Executioner.

Polyakova had continued to stare out the window, but now she stood and walked across the room. "Come on," she said, smiling at the DEA man. "Let's see what you bought."

Johnny Seven was facing away from him, but Bolan saw the back of the man's neck turn red. "Well…" he said.

"Come on, Johnny," she said. "I'll bet you're handsome." Bolan could tell she had begun to like the DEA agent after all they'd been through together. But she would get her revenge for the way he had treated her initially one way or another, and teasing him now was as good a way as any.

Seven reached self-consciously into one of the sacks and pulled out a folded Harris tweed sport coat. "It was on sale," he said, as if he'd done something wrong.

"Put it on," Polyakova encouraged him. "I want to see."

The DEA man's face was redder than ever as he took off his jacket.

The beautiful Russian woman took the threadbare sport coat and giggled. "I will throw this one away for you, Johnny," she said. "You should have done that yourself a long time ago."

Bolan wouldn't have guessed it was possible, but the DEA man turned yet a deeper shade of crimson as he stuck his arms into the new coat. "Hey, give me a break," he said. He pulled several new shirts, a pair of jeans and a pair of corduroy slacks from the other bag and set them on the bed. Then he rolled up the plastic sacks and started to stick them in his suitcase.

"Wait," the woman said, frowning down at the crumpled plastic in the DEA man's hands. "There's something else in there."

Seven looked hesitantly at the beautiful Russian woman, then said, "Oh, what the hell." He unrolled the sacks, shook them over the bed, and a Harris tweed driving cap fell out. He laughed apprehensively again. "I always kind of liked these things," he said, then quickly added, "And it was on sale, too."

The Russian lifted the cap off the bed and placed it on his head. Her eyebrows lowered as she studied it for a moment, then adjusted it to a slight angle. "You will look dashing, Johnny," she said, then looked down from the cap to the jacket. "What is remarkable, is that they even go well together."

"What is that supposed to—?" the DEA man started to say.

She interrupted him. "Here," she said, reaching down to the bed and lifting a cream-colored turtleneck. "Change your shirt."

Johnny Seven shrugged.

Bolan cleared his throat. "If the fashion show is over now," he said, "we all need to sit down and work out our battle plan." He walked to the table by the window and took a seat. Polyakova joined him in the same chair she had occupied earlier.

Seven took off his new jacket, then looked at Polyakova self-consciously before turning his back to her. Bolan saw him suck in his stomach as he stripped off Ontomanov's tight stripes and pulled the turtleneck over his head before slipping back into his new Harris tweed. Bolan tried not to smile when the DEA man wore the cap to the table.

But, after all, she had told him he looked dashing. And such words from a woman like Luiza Polyakova held their own kind of power.

THE SMITH-WILLIAMS Art Gallery was several times larger than Polyakova's Greenwich Village establishment. In addition to contemporary oil paintings, the building housed rooms devoted to watercolors, sculpture, chalk and charcoal drawings and the work of several well-known photographers. It was located six blocks down George Street on the same side of the street as the Durrants Hotel. Well within walking distance.

Bolan hailed a cab just the same, directing the driver to take them several miles away—almost to Regent's Park—before doubling back and arriving at the site from the other direction. The soldier, seated in the back of the taxi with Polyakova, kept an eye on the side-view mirror during the trip, watching for a tail. He saw none.

Seven stayed in the front seat of the cab as Bolan and Polyakova got out. He would return to the Durrants, then walk back to the art gallery, arriving five to ten minutes after them in order to appear to be alone. Bolan didn't expect anything to go down on this recon mission, but the DEA agent would serve as backup just in case it did.

Bolan took the woman's arm, waiting for one of London's double-decker buses to pass before escorting her across the street. "You know your lines?" he asked quietly as they approached the glass door leading inside.

"I think so," the Russian woman said. She looked up at him and smiled, her green eyes dancing. She had shown more good humor in the past hour than she had the entire time the soldier had known her. Her mood change had begun as soon as he returned the impromptu kiss that had happened shortly after Johnny Seven left on his clothes shopping spree.

The door was pushed outward by a man wearing a bright red doorman's uniform, complete with cap and gold braid running down the shoulders. Bolan followed Polyakova into a foyer where they saw a guest book. Going immediately into the roles they had rehearsed only moments earlier, Polyakova said, "I'll sign us in, sweetheart," and stepped up to the podium where the book lay open. As instructed, the Russian woman wrote, "Mr. and Mrs. Matt Cooper, San Francisco, California, U.S.A.," with the gold pen attached with a chain to the stand. She took Bolan's arm and they stepped into the first room of the gallery.

The room reminded Bolan of Polyakova's own business back in New York. Paintings covered the walls, and more stood on easels in staggered rows throughout the area. The Russian took Bolan's hand and pointed toward a painting to their right. "Look, darling," she said excitedly. "I think that's a Fielding. You know how you love his work. Let's go see." She led him down the row of pictures.

They stopped in front of the painting to which she had pointed. The soldier pretended to study it as he scanned the room with his peripheral vision. A few minutes later he saw Seven, complete in new sport coat and cap, enter the gallery and begin browsing through the easels. There were perhaps two dozen other men and at least that many women viewing the oil works. But none of them matched the description of the man Gregor had sent them to kill.

It was an interesting story Gregor had told Bolan, and in doing so he had probably revealed more about the Russians' overall drug-smuggling operation than he'd realized. The setup in London was similar to the one in New York. A Rabashka-type character—Gregor had revealed no names, of course—accompanied the shipments from Moscow, where they were received at this gallery by the owner, Raymond Smith-Williams. Smith-Williams took possession, and then the "Ontomanov" of England—whoever he might be—arrived to cull out the stolen paintings and heroin. There was a major difference here, however. Unlike Polyakova, Smith-Williams was a willing participant in the smuggling operation. In fact, he had been skimming dope off the shipments for some time now. According to Gregor, the last load of heroin secreted in the picture frames had tested ninety-eight percent pure before leaving Moscow. But after it had passed through Smith-Williams's hands that percentage had dropped to seventy-five.

Which was why Gregor and the man in Moscow had decided it was time for Raymond Smith-Williams to die.

"Do you like it?" Polyakova asked, still looking at the painting. He had told her to say those words.

Now the Executioner answered with the words the art expert had told him to say. "It's not his best," Bolan said. "He seems to have diverted from his usual use of color."

Polyakova squeezed his hand. When he glanced down at the woman, her emerald eyes were dancing once more, and it looked as if she was trying not to laugh. Reaching up, she cupped a soft hand around the back of his neck and stood on her tiptoes as if to kiss him on the cheek. She did kiss him on the cheek, but while she was there she also whispered, "That sounded good. But this role doesn't really fit you." She was grinning impishly again when she lowered herself back down.

The woman led him on through the gallery, making a comment here, a statement there, and Bolan recited a few things she had taught him to say. But overall, he had to agree with her. The role of art critic didn't seem to fit at all. He knew it wouldn't last for long, however, and he continued to look interested as they made their way through the sculpture room across the hall and then to the photography exhibit at the rear of the building. Occasionally he would catch a glimpse of a Harris tweed sport coat and driving cap, and know Seven was pretending to study the paintings just as he was.

The Executioner hadn't yet decided whether this short undercover shift was leading toward an enemy capture or was simply an intelligence-gathering mission. It would depend on several things, not the least of which was how many people were around when they finally found Smith-Williams. In any eventuality, Bolan intended to follow through with Gregor's wish that he terminate the drug-dealing gallery owner. As a knowing participant, the man was just as responsible for the death and horror the white powder brought on as Gregor and the man behind him in Moscow. So he would kill the art dealer as he'd been instructed to do. But not until he had pumped the man for information that would lead him both to Gregor and the big man in Moscow.

They left the photography room and entered an area filled with watercolors. Bolan stared at a still life of a floral arrangement. Polyakova had held his hand the entire time they'd been in the gallery, tugging him gently when she felt it was time that a knowledgeable art expert grew bored and moved on. Now he felt her pull again, and they walked around a corner to another row. Bolan stopped in his tracks as a slender man with his eyes down on a bundle of papers hurried down the aisle, not looking up until he'd already run straight into the Executioner.

"Oh, my!" the man said as he finally looked up. Bolan saw that he wore an ascot and a thin David Niven mustache. "Dear me, my apologies," Raymond Smith-Williams said, brushing some imaginary dust off the yacht club insignia on his navy blue blazer. "Clumsy of me."

Bolan smiled and shook his head. "My fault," he replied.

"No, no," Smith-Williams said. "My mistake. Had my mind on other things, I suppose. Business, you know."

"Ah," Bolan said. "You must be Mr. Smith-Williams."

The Briton beamed. "Yes indeed," he said. "At your service. Yank...pardon me, no offense meant. American, are you?"

Bolan laughed. "'Yank' doesn't offend me," he said. "And yes, I'm afraid I'm about as 'red white and blue baseball and apple pie' as they come." He extended his hand and said, "Matt Cooper."

Smith-Williams shook his hand limply, then dropped it, reaching up to smooth his mustache. "No wonder 'Yank' doesn't offend you, then," he said dryly.

Bolan looked at him curiously.

"Baseball, old man!" Smith-Williams said. "Yanks! Babe Ruth. Perhaps my connection was too vague."

"No," Bolan answered. "I'm just a little slow sometimes." He let go of Polyakova's hand and slipped his arm around her shoulders. "I can be a little rude, too, I guess. Mr. Smith-Williams, meet my wife, Ivanna."

Raymond Smith-Williams looked at Polyakova, and she looked at him. The man was hers for the asking.

"It's a pleasure to meet you, Mr. Smith-Williams," she said, holding out her hand.

The art dealer cleared his throat and took her hand. "Charmed, my dear." He leaned forward to kiss her hand, doing his best to camouflage his gaze at her breasts as a mere hitch in the normal path a pair of eyes would take between the face and hand. It was a gallant, and refined attempt, but it failed miserably. Looking back up, Smith-Williams said, "I do not detect even a hint of Yank in your voice, Mrs. Cooper. Russian?"

"Yes."

"Ah." Smith-Williams smiled. "I have many Russian friends myself, men I have met through business since the borders opened up."

Bolan smiled at him pleasantly.

Smith-Williams stopped, closed his eyes dramatically and held up a hand. "But enough of my foolishness. Are you enjoying your visit to my humble collection?"

"Very much," Bolan said.

"And what, in particular, has caught your interest?" Smith-Williams asked. "Perhaps I could—"

Polyakova stepped in to save him. "We both simply *love* Fielding," she said. "You have a rather unusual piece of his. My husband was particularly impressed with the two Perez-Riverte oils near the front. Matt says he studied under Dali. I don't believe him."

"No," said Smith-Williams sadly. "I'm afraid your husband is correct. If you look closely, you can see the influence." He turned back to Bolan with a new respect in his eyes.

The soldier shrugged modestly.

"Is there anything in particular I could help you with?" Smith-Williams asked them both. Then, before either could answer, his arm shot up to his face and he said, "Oh, dear. Silly of me. I was enjoying this conversation so much I've forgotten I have a customer waiting on me."

"That's quite all right," Bolan said. "We have other business we have to attend to, as well. But we *are* interested in both the Fielding and the Perez-Rivertes. Tell me, do you ever make appointments after regular hours?"

"Rarely," the Briton replied. Then he smiled and looked at Polyakova. "But for the two of you, I must make an exception." He glanced at his wrist again, then added, "Would nine tonight suit you?"

"Fine," Bolan answered.

"Marvelous," Polyakova said, smiling.

"Then we'll see you here, then." With a final smile, Raymond

Smith-Williams spun on his heels and disappeared through the forest of easels.

Polyakova looked up at Bolan. "Ready, darling? We wouldn't want to be late for the ballet."

THEY HAD BEEN BACK at the Durrants less than ten minutes when the window exploded.

Polyakova, sitting in the chair she had laid claim to earlier, screamed at the top of her lungs and dived for the floor. Bolan had been sitting on the bed, studying a London city map. He fell over the beautiful Russian woman, shielding her body with his as he jerked the Desert Eagle from his hip. Seven came sprinting out of the bathroom wearing half a face of shaving cream, a disposable razor in one hand and his SIG-Sauer in the other.

"Down!" the Executioner commanded, and the DEA agent fell forward onto the carpet.

The second shot sailed through the window over their heads, drilling into the mattress and scorching the bedspread and sheets. By the time the third shot sounded, Bolan had identified the weapon as a .308. The rounds sounded more like they had come from an assault rifle than a tightly locked bolt action.

Bolan raised his head right after the fourth shot, pinpointing the source as the roof of one of the buildings on the other side of the alley. Night had fallen over the city hours earlier, but in the lights atop the tall structure behind them he could make out the silhouette of a man. He was standing at the lip of the roof, his weapon resting on the short safety wall running along the side. But now that all three of them were below the windowsill and out of sight, he had stopped firing.

The Executioner looked past the man and saw a huge water tank directly behind him on the roof. At the top of the tank, on the far side, he could just see the top of a steel handrail. It glowed in the lights a good twenty feet higher than the roof itself, and meant a ladder led up the tank on the other side.

Suddenly the sniper rose and sprinted away, serpentining toward the tank. Bolan rose and fired two quick .44 Magnum rounds, but the man zigzagged just as Bolan pulled the trigger both times. Before he could fire again, the sniper had ducked behind the water tank.

The Executioner knew why. Twenty feet higher in the air, the man would have a better angle to shoot down through their window. He grabbed Polyakova and jerked her to her feet. Without a word she followed. "Come on, Johnny!" the Executioner said as he raced by where the DEA man lay on the floor. "He's moving higher!"

Seven leaped to his feet with a speed and grace that contradicted his size and age.

Bolan couldn't be sure exactly how wide the sniper's field of fire would be when he reached the top of the water tank, but the safe thing to do was get Polyakova out of the room altogether. Once in the hall, they would be out of sight completely and have at least two walls between them and the powerful .308 rounds.

The Executioner had already opened the door to the hall when the warning bell went off in his head. But by then it was too late. Suddenly he was staring down the barrel of a Degtyarev PPD-40. The man he had seen earlier enter the room across the hall—the man who had carried the large suitcases—stood just outside his room down the hall. The stock of the submachine gun was pressed into his shoulder.

A half-dozen 7.62 mm rounds erupted from the 71-round drum of the Soviet weapon. The wooden frame around the door splintered, sending sharp scraps of wood through the air as Bolan slammed Polyakova back into the hotel room. She fell back against Seven, who had been sprinting along behind them, and the two came to a standstill just inside the doorway. Bolan heard another explosion from the rear of the room, and another .308 slug zipped through the window to drill through the closet next to where he stood. Wrapping his arms around both Polyakova and Seven, he shoved them both into the bathroom and drew the Desert Eagle.

The 7.62 rounds from the hallway had stopped momentarily, and the Executioner dropped to one knee. Slowly he peered around the corner of the room. He had barely gotten his eye around the corner when another burst of fire drove him back again. He fell to a sitting position against the wall as the rounds cut through the open door, slicing off the top hinge. The door fell forward at an angle, jamming against what was left of the frame.

To his side, the Executioner saw Seven crawl out of the bathroom back toward the middle of the room. Two rounds sailed over his head before he could hide behind the bed. He reached up, grabbing the viola case and pulling it down on top of him, then instinctively rolled into a fetal position against the wall at the head of the bed. He was just in time, as several .308 rounds ripped through the mattress, box springs and pillows at the exact spot where he'd ducked. Feathers filled the air as if a tornado had gone through a chicken farm.

Bolan knew what the DEA man was doing and let him do it. He took a deep breath. He was about to lean back into the hall and fire when another stream of Soviet rounds sent the bottom hinge spinning off into the hallway. The bullet-ridden door fell to the ground, wobbling back and forth from one edge to the other until it finally settled into the carpet.

The Executioner had guessed that the top hinge had been an accident. The bottom one proved it was not. The hit man had trapped them between him and his partner on top of the building to their rear. And now he was making sure they couldn't even close the door between them.

Drawing the Beretta with his other hand, Bolan flipped the selector switch to burst mode. He scooted lower in his sitting position until only his shoulders and head were still against the wall. Then, suddenly, in one fluid movement he rolled off the wall onto the floor and extended his upper body through the doorway, firing with both hands.

A quick burst coughed from the sound-suppressed 93-R as its big brother bellowed out a pair of .44 Magnum slugs. All five rounds flew straight at where the man had been when Bolan first saw him, and where he'd still been a moment before when his attack had destroyed the door.

The problem was that he wasn't there now. In fact, he was nowhere to be seen.

But the Executioner didn't deceive himself. The hit man wasn't gone. Bolan's mind flew back to the strange words Gregor had said at the end of their earlier conversation. He was trying to *stop* a professional from coming after Bolan, Polyakova, and Johnny Seven.

This was the man.

Bolan glanced at the room down the hall. The door was slightly ajar, and as his brain registered what his eyes had seen it began to swing open farther. The barrel of the PPD appeared in the opening.

The Executioner fired another three rounds of 9 mm and one more double-tap of .44 slugs, then a barrage of full-auto fire drove him rolling back through the doorway. The onslaught went on for another two seconds, the 7.62 rounds perforating the wall just above his head. At almost the same time, a steady stream of fire came through the shattered picture window at the rear of the room. They drilled through the wall next to the Executioner, and then on through the door across the hall, leaving ragged round holes in both plaster and wood.

The Executioner glanced back into the room. Seven was still on the floor behind the bed. He had pulled the M-16 A-2 from the viola case and was struggling to jam a magazine into the receiver in his clumsy position half under the bed.

Bolan turned back to the doorway. He had gone low the last time he fired, so now he sprang to his feet, ignoring the bullets spraying past him. If they got him, they got him, and there was nothing he could do about it. He had long known that the end would someday come, and he had always known it would come in this fashion. If this was the day, if this was his time, then so be it. He had fought the good fight, and he would accept death if that was to be the outcome. But if there was any way possible, he would finish this race first and see that Polyakova and Seven got out of there safe and alive.

Rising to full height, Bolan hooked his left arm around the

barrier, exposing only enough of his body to see the doorway from which the man was firing. He pumped the Beretta's trigger twice, sending six 9 mm hollowpoint rounds humming down the hall into the opening.

But again the hit man had moved. He wasn't in the hall. So he had to be farther back in the room. The Executioner twisted to the side, pulling the Beretta back into his body and angling the powerful Desert Eagle into the hall. He aimed at the doorway, then moved the sights a few inches to his left. Pulling the trigger, he sent a 240-grain .44 Magnum hollowpoint slug raging through the aging plaster into the room, hoping against hope that it might find its way to his unseen target. He repeated the process, emptying the magazine into the wall, moving his sights an inch or so with each shot.

The roar of the Desert Eagle was like thunder in the hallway. When the gun finally clicked on an empty chamber, the Executioner pulled it back and stepped back into the room. Keeping the Beretta ready in his left hand, he dropped the empty magazine from the butt, jammed it into his belt and shoved a fresh load down into the grips.

Sniper fire from across the alley still sailed through the room as Bolan let the Beretta swing out onto his trigger finger. The 93-R hung by the guard as he used his thumb and middle finger to work the Desert Eagle's slide, chambering another Magnum round. As the slug slid home, he heard .223 fire pop behind him and looked briefly over his shoulder to see Seven sending quick bursts back through the broken glass.

Polyakova stuck her head out from the bathroom, her emerald-green eyes wide in shock. A .308 round sailed past her nose. When she didn't seem to notice, Bolan shoved her back through the door and said, "Get down! In the bathtub!"

As soon as the words had escaped his lips, the Executioner tried to bite them back. Polyakova did as he'd ordered, practically diving over the side of the ancient cast-iron tub. But almost immediately, new rounds from the room across the hall sailed through the wall into the bathroom. Whether the man had heard the Executioner or simply figured out for himself that the bathroom was the only logical place to hide, Bolan didn't know.

But it didn't matter. The 7.62 mm rounds penetrated the wall with ease, flying low into the tub to clang off the cast iron before embedding themselves back in the plaster.

White dust filled the air as Bolan leaned around the door and fired the hand cannon. He was driven back once more by return fire. Behind him, he heard the steady release from Seven's M-16 A-2, and the constant pounding of rounds from the roof across the alley hadn't let up since the sniper had climbed the ladder to a better position.

The Executioner took a deep breath. From where he was pinned, the chances of getting a good shot at the man across the hall were a thousand to one. The chances of hitting him blindly through the wall, as he'd tried earlier, were even more slim. And sooner or later, the sniper behind them was going to find his groove. He'd get Seven first, then Bolan.

That would allow the man across the hall to have full access to Polyakova in the bathroom.

Bolan checked his extra ammo. He had enough to keep the stalemate going at least a little longer. And that's all he could do. The bottom line was that if something drastic didn't happen soon to change the situation, they were going to die.

The Executioner leaned around the doorway and fired again.

THE CHECHEN TIGHTENED his finger on the trigger, taking up the slack. Akhmatov found himself smiling when he heard Petrov's following shots from the roof behind the hotel. Akhmatov hesitated for only a split second before readjusting his aim and pulling the trigger. But the American was like a cat. Akhmatov's rounds blew through the empty air where the man had been less than a second earlier. He cursed under his breath, firing again.

A man with reflexes like he'd just seen was highly trained. As he heard Petrov continue to fire from the building across the alley, he ducked back into his room and closed the door. He opened it only enough to peer back out into the hall, and was met with a series of mixed rounds. The first sound he heard was the choking cough of a sound-suppressed pistol. But after that all he could hear was the earth-shaking blast of some tremendously high-caliber weapon. He retreated deeper into the room as the rounds penetrated the door at an angle and drilled through the wall next to where he'd stood.

The Chechen cursed again, louder this time. He knew what was about to happen, and didn't like it. On the other hand, it was the type of battle at which he excelled. Cat and mouse, they called it in America, he had heard. He would shoot, then the American would shoot. Then they would both duck back and start all over again. Neither of them would hit the other until one of them made a mistake, and that would be the one who first lost patience.

Akhmatov's curse turned into a grin. He had been blessed with patience far beyond that of other men. But the Chechen knew he had been blessed in all ways beyond that of mortal men. The writings of Nietzsche had proven that to him. He was what Nietzsche called a "superman."

And it went as he had predicted, back and forth. Fire and retreat. Fire and retreat. The big American showed an unusual amount of skill in both marksmanship and strategy. He was good. Very good. The best Movlid Akhmatov had encountered in a long time, and the Chechen found himself wishing the two of them could sit and compare notes someday.

Of course that would never be possible, Akhmatov realized, as he heard more of Petrov's rounds come from the rear of the hotel. He kicked himself mentally. He hadn't prepared for this contingency, so sure had he been that the shots from the rooftop would drive his prey right into his arms. He should have thought ahead, and if he had, he would have realized that right now the woman would be hidden in the only logical place—the bathroom. If she had any sense at all she would have taken refuge in the bathtub. Which, he would wager, was another cast-iron relic like the one in which he had just bathed.

Akhmatov stepped into the hall and fired a full-auto stream

through the wall next to the door where the bathroom would be. The tub would protect the woman, but the big man with the thunderous pistol had no idea of his plans for Luiza Polyakova, and would be operating on the assumption that Akhmatov was just another man trying to kill them all. He was smart, this big American, so the sudden change of aim to the bathroom would reinforce that idea, remind him of her perilous situation, and in turn should disturb him.

The Chechen grinned to himself. Men who were disturbed lost patience. When they lost patience they made mistakes. And when they made mistakes, men like Movlid Akhmatov killed them and took their women.

More rounds peppered the doorway around Akhmatov's room, but he stepped well back away from them. He had moved forward again, prepared to shoot through the wall at the tub once more, when he heard the police sirens outside. The obnoxious, almost cartoon-like whine of British and Western European sirens had always irritated him, but now his disposition went well beyond irritation. Again his anger was directed at himself for not preparing more efficiently. Not only had he failed to plan for the possible cat and mouse game now ensuing, but he had also charted out only one route for escape.

And from the continually rising sound of the sirens, that route would soon be closed off.

Akhmatov knew he couldn't afford to stay any longer. Hurrying back to the bed, he grabbed both suitcases, then dropped the one holding his clothing and personal items. He would need one arm free to operate the PPD, and there was nothing in the bag through which he could be traced. He could always buy more clothes. But weapons of the quality Petrov had obtained for him were harder to come by.

Several more rounds burst through the doorway as he lifted the weapons bag and turned back toward the hall. Some were the quiet rounds the big man had fired through the sound suppressor; others came with the deafening blast of the Desert Eagle Akhmatov had caught a fleeting glimpse of. It was a big gun, and it took not only a big man but also a well-trained one to control the recoil under combat conditions. That thought brought another smile to the Chechen's face. The American choosing a weapon too powerful for most soldiers was like his own preference for the hard-to-control Stechkin. They were alike, him and this big man, and again he wished he could sit with the man and talk to him—before he killed him.

Akhmatov hurried back to the door, sticking his head through just long enough to glance both ways up and down the hall. The elevators were at one end of the hall—past the American's room. He could get to the stairs without crossing the open doorway.

Another burst of sound-suppressed fire drove him back into the room for a second. But as soon as the shooting stopped, the Chechen darted forth from the room. Triggering the submachine gun, he sent close to thirty rounds from the magazine, firing it dry. Holes appeared all over the hallway, the plaster walls cracking and even giving in at spots, as he sprinted away.

Before the American could return fire, Akhmatov ducked into the stairwell and out of sight. He paused long enough to drop the PPD into his suitcase and draw the Stechkin, then took the steps three at a time until he reached the ground floor.

Movlid Akhmatov was still smiling as he left the hotel through a back entrance and raced down the alley into the darkness. Yes, this American was good, he thought. Certainly good at his trade. But the big man was also good in the sense that he would always try to do the right thing. The laugh that escaped the Chechen's mouth at the thought was sarcastic. Right and wrong. Good and evil. Garbage. Unlike Akhmatov and Nietzsche, the American had not gone beyond, and his shackles would limit his effectiveness, and eventually produce his downfall.

8

The steady pounding of .308 rounds kept up from across the alley, and Johnny Seven continued his sporadic return fire with the M-16. In between the shots the Executioner heard the ever nearing wail of the London Metropolitan Police sirens. Then the man across the hall cut loose with the longest stream of fire yet. Round after round after round hit the front wall of the hotel room, obliterating the few splinters of wooden frame remaining around the door, and blasting several softball-sized holes in the plaster.

But the fire came in bursts, and each time the man let up on the trigger, Bolan heard the sound of footsteps running away from them down the hall.

The hit man had heard the sirens, too.

Suddenly the gunfire both in front and behind the Executioner stopped. Bolan looked over his shoulder to see Seven scowling at the alley. "I think maybe I might have got him," he said. "At least I don't see him."

"You see him fall?" Bolan asked as he raced past the bed to the gaping hole where the picture window had once been.

"No."

The Executioner came to a halt at the window. Across the alley, he could see no one on top of the water tank or the roof below. Which meant nothing. Since Seven hadn't actually seen him go down, the sniper might be lying flat on top of the tank or he might have slipped down the ladder and be hidden behind it. He might also have already left the roof and, like his partner across the hall, be beating feet away from the sirens as fast as he could.

The DEA man still had the M-16 trained out the window when the Executioner hurried back past him. "Get Luiza and our gear," he said. "Stick as much as you can in the guitar and viola cases and leave the rest."

Before Seven could reply the Executioner was out the door into the hall. He hadn't holstered either the Beretta or Desert Eagle. Cautiously he moved across the hallway and slid his back along the wall toward the room the hit man had occupied. He was almost certain he had heard the man running away as the final bombardment of rounds came his way, but being *almost* certain had gotten more than one good man killed.

The room was empty except for a suitcase lying on the bed. Bolan flipped the latches and looked inside. The oncoming sirens grew louder as he foraged through the contents. The suitcase appeared to contain nothing more than clothing, shaving equipment and a few other personal items. He couldn't be sure from such a cursory search but he had no time to be more thorough at the moment. Slamming the lid shut, he holstered the Beretta to free one hand and grabbed the suitcase off the bed.

Seven and Polyakova were waiting at the door to the other room when he returned. The DEA man had done as ordered, abandoning Ontomanov's suitcase and the slender Russian's ill-fitting clothes and stuffing his new wardrobe into the viola case. He had the guitar case strapped across his back, and the woman's heavy bag in one hand. Bolan holstered the Desert Eagle and lifted the viola case. Polyakova was carrying Bolan's light bag.

Bolan led the way to the stairs, mindful of the fact that the man from across the hall had followed the same path only moments earlier and might be waiting in ambush somewhere in the stairwell. It was unlikely. He suspected the man had been intent on leaving before the police arrived. But anything was possible, and Bolan was ready at the first hint of trouble to drop one of the suitcases and draw a gun.

They encountered no one on the stairs, however, and emerged into the lobby a moment later. A dozen or so hotel patrons had been downstairs when the shooting began, and rather than follow common sense and simply escape to the streets, they had huddled nervously together around the couches and chairs in the sitting area. Like a herd of human sheep, they had frozen in fear, neither fighting nor fleeing but simply waiting.

The Executioner led the way to the front door, and turned to the right. He led Johnny and Polyakova casually along the sidewalk as several police cars screeched to a halt. Officers exited the blue-and-white vehicles and ran inside the Durrants lobby. They weren't the average London street bobbies with their wooden truncheons, helmets and gunless belts. These men wore black uniforms, ballistic vests, and carried Glock 17s on their hips. Several also toted Heckler & Koch MP-5 submachine guns.

The Executioner recognized them immediately as SO19—the Force Firearms Unit within the special operations branch of New Scotland Yard. One of the men stopped as he headed toward the door, looking curiously at Bolan and his companions. His eyes moved back and forth from the guitar case to the viola case as the Executioner raised his hand to hail a passing cab. The SO19 man finally decided they must be musicians, gave a slight shrug with his shoulders, then turned back and followed the others inside.

Bolan, Polyakova, and Seven got in the cab.

"Where to, mate?" the red-faced cabbie behind the wheel asked in a thick Irish brogue.

"Le Meridien," Bolan said. "Piccadilly."

"Good choice," the driver said, and a moment later they were rolling away from the scene of the massive gunfight.

LE MERIDIEN PICCADILLY hotel was aptly named, standing only a few yards from Piccadilly Circus. Seven had checked them in and taken the luggage to the room. There, Bolan had carefully gone through the suitcase of the man sent to kill them. But he had found nothing that might lead to the man's identity, and nothing out of the ordinary except two books by the philoso-

pher Nietzsche. By then, it was time for the nine-o'clock meeting with Raymond Smith-Williams at the gallery.

Bolan had originally planned to leave Polyakova and the DEA
man in the room, going to meet the art-and-drug dealer alone.
But after the attack at the previous hotel, he didn't want to leave
the Russian woman alone. Seven was a good man, and had
proved to be a good gunman, as well, but the hard, cold reality
was that both he and the woman would already have been dead
several times over if Bolan hadn't been with them.

Hailing another cab just outside the hotel, Bolan got another
talkative cabbie. The man pointed out sights of interest along the
way. Bolan, Polyakova and Seven rode silently, listening to the
discourse, which sounded as if the man had given it thousands
of times.

All but the lights around the entryway to the art gallery had
been turned off when they arrived. Through the glass, the soldier could see a faint glow coming from the rear of the building.
He remembered that Smith-Williams's office had been located
in that area. He paid the cabdriver as the Russian and Seven got
out of the back seat.

A doorbell that had been invisible behind the doorman when
they'd been there earlier awaited them, and the Executioner rang
it now. A few seconds later, the angular form of Raymond Smith-
Williams came meandering through the shadows to greet them.

"Hello," said the man with the David Niven mustache as he
unlocked the door and then opened it. "Right on time. And I see
you've brought a friend. Fine." Smith-Williams still wore the
ascot he'd had on earlier but had traded his blue blazer for a red
silk smoking jacket. And, as if it might be required when wearing such attire, he held an intricately carved briar pipe in his right
hand. Faint tendrils of smoke, exuding the fragrant odor of some
exotic tobacco mixture, rose from the bowl.

"Let's see," the Briton said as he ushered them inside. "If memory serves me, Fielding and Perez-Riverte were your passions.
Shall we look at them now?" He had moved to the wall and opened
a small door hiding the master light switches for the building.

"In a minute," Bolan replied. "First, let's talk in your office."

Smith-Williams raised a curious eyebrow but said, "Certainly, as you wish," then turned on his heels and led the way back through the gallery.

Bolan had been right about the rear-central area being the office. They entered through a door in the main hall, and he saw more closed doors in all three of the other walls. One, he could tell, led into the rear photography room behind the oil paintings, and another would open to watercolors. Behind the third, in the back wall of the office, might go straight out into the alley or lead to yet another room.

The office itself was spacious, with an ancient oak desk the size of a small swimming pool in the center of the room. Soft cushioned sofas formed conversation areas around three sides of the desk, and a huge skylight made up three-fourths of the ceiling. Through the glass, Bolan could just make out the crescent moon through London's thick fog.

Smith-Williams saw them all look up and smiled. "Yes, the skylight. This was once the studio of Sir Arthur Silversleeves, don't you know. It is said, although it's never been proven, that this is where he painted *The Trumpet of Gideon*."

Bolan had no idea what the man was talking about, but Polyakova seemed to understand. She smiled and said, "Fascinating."

The look on Seven's face said he was as lost as Bolan. But in true undercover expert form, he said, "You know, I'd heard that about Silversleeves myself."

"Yes, it is fascinating," Bolan added. "Want to know another fascinating fact, Mr. Smith-Williams?"

Smith-Williams had walked to the center of the room upon entering and now stood there, as if presenting his office to them. "Certainly, Mr. Cooper," he said. "Do tell."

"We aren't interested in your paintings," Bolan went on. "What I am interested in is your involvement in the heroin trade."

Smith-Williams's face reddened—whether with anger or embarrassment it was impossible to tell. "I have no idea what you're referring to," he spit out.

Bolan smiled. Then he walked forward, grabbed the lapel of the smoking jacket and dragged the man around the side of the desk.

"Hey!" Smith-Williams screeched as the toes of his shoes trailed across the carpet. "You can't just—" The briar pipe fell to the floor but Seven retrieved it, stamping his foot on the glowing cinders that had dumped out.

Bolan roughly shoved the art dealer into a wide armchair, then held a finger to his lips. "Quiet," he said. "For now." Bolan turned to face Polyakova and Seven. "You two might want to go look at some paintings."

The woman had proved to be a good actress, so Bolan had given her yet another part. What he was about to do would involve more psychological than direct warfare, and it would be the cumulation of many tiny mental elements he instilled in Smith-Williams's brain that would make it work. Polyakova's next words were a part of that.

"Oh, darling," she said, shaking her head in distaste. "Not *again*." She paused a second before giving the gallery owner a look of pity, then said, "Why don't you at least give him a chance to tell you what you want to know first?"

Bolan shrugged. "Want to tell me all about your Russian connection?" he asked Smith-Williams.

Already the Briton was beginning to look uncomfortable, but he said, "Sir, as I told you, I haven't the foggiest idea what—"

Bolan looked back at Polyakova and shrugged again. "See?" he said.

The Russian woman rolled her eyes and sighed. "All right," she said in a tone of resignation. That was the end of the lines the Executioner had given her. But like all great actresses, she knew when to ad lib. Walking forward, she grasped the lapel of Bolan's jacket, then tiptoed up to peck him on the lips. Still looking up into his eyes, she rubbed the lapel with her fingers and said, "Try not to ruin your clothes this time, sweetheart. You remember what the dry cleaner said."

In his peripheral vision, the soldier could see Raymond Smith-Williams's eyes darting back and forth between them. The man was thoroughly confused, but he was also thoroughly terrorized.

She turned away from Bolan. "Come on, Johnny," she said, taking his hand and leading him back toward the door. "You don't want to have to watch this any more than I do." Without another word, the two disappeared back into the galleries.

Bolan swept his coat back to the side and reached into the rear pocket of his pants. In doing so, he accomplished two things. He retrieved the two-foot length of black paracord from the pocket, and made sure Raymond Smith-Williams got a good view of the big Desert Eagle on his hip.

The art-and-drug dealer's eyes grew almost as big as the hand cannon.

Without speaking, Bolan reached forward, lifted the man to his feet by the front of the smoking jacket and spun him around. "No, please!" the Briton said but by then his hands were bound behind his back and he'd been thrown back into the chair.

Bolan tied more paracord around Smith-Williams's ankles, binding them together. He stood and looked down at the man, staring into the terrified eyes. Over the years Bolan had found that the threat of torture could be almost as effective as the real thing.

Taking a seat on a couch directly across from the art dealer, Bolan said, "Okay, here's how I see it happening. Feel free to jump right in and correct me if I'm wrong on any of the details. The paintings—both legitimate and stolen—come in from Moscow. You pick them up at the docks, then bring them here. Then somebody—my guess is it's a Russian—comes here and culls out the stolen art, as well as taking the heroin out of the frames."

Smith-Williams started to speak, but Bolan held up a hand. "Let me finish," he said. "This Russian takes the stolen art and the heroin away, and you get your cut. Now, what I need from you are his name and the name of the guy who accompanies the shipments from Russia to England."

The gallery owner had begun squirming. He couldn't stand but was struggling to free his hands behind his back.

Bolan shook his head. "Don't," he said, looking down to where Smith-Williams's hands were. "You'll just make it worse. They're slip knots. Ready to tell me what you know?"

The man quit struggling and slumped back in his chair. Tears began to form in the corners of his eyes. Bolan suppressed a smile. He was going to be easy.

But Smith-Williams wasn't quite ready to give in yet. "Please," he pleaded. "I told you. I don't know." His eyes brightened for a second in hope. "Could you have confused me with someone else?"

The Executioner laughed good-naturedly. "No, I couldn't have." He looked across the room to the desktop where Seven had set the gallery owner's briar pipe, then stood, walked over and picked it up. The bowl was still warm in his hand. "You have a lighter, Ray?" he asked.

As it had so many times in the past several minutes, Raymond Smith-Williams's face contorted into a mask of complete confusion. "You...want to smoke my pipe?" he asked.

"No, I'm not going to smoke your pipe. But I do need a lighter."

"But why—?"

"Where's your lighter!" the Executioner boomed at the top of his lungs.

Another thing experience had taught him was that such sudden, unwarranted outbursts were of tremendous value in such situations. They insinuated a mental imbalance that further intimidated the man being interrogated.

"Top drawer, right!" Smith-Williams shouted back almost as loud. But his voice squealed more than boomed.

Bolan found the lighter. Designed specifically for pipes, it resembled a small black scuba tank. He pushed a button on the end and a long jet-flame shot out. He dropped the pipe back on the desk, and returned to his seat on the couch. The gallery owner's eyes followed his every step.

As soon as he was seated, the Executioner looked at the man across from him. "There's still time for you to tell me what I want to know while I get ready," he said. "Really, this can all be done without pain as easily as with it. The decision's up to you." Then, as the man's fearful eyes opened even farther, Bolan drew the Loner knife from the Kydex sheath under his right arm.

Bolan ignored the gasp that issued forth from the gallery owner's lips as he ignited the flame again and held it to the edge of the blade. The Loner was of top-quality steel and craftsmanship, and the black epoxy coating on the blade wasn't affected. But the silver steel running along the sharpened edges hadn't been blackened. Slowly it began to glow a bright red.

"What...are you doing?" Raymond Smith-Williams choked out.

Again the Executioner ignored him, frowning at the edge of the blade as it grew ever more red in his hand.

"I will tell you!" Smith-Williams suddenly screeched. "Just stop! Stop that! I will tell you what you want to know!"

Bolan knew that as soon as he dowsed the fire from the lighter, half of the psychological advantage would evaporate. "No," he said, refusing to look at the man. "I think I'll go ahead and finish this just in case you try to lie. It takes a while to get it just right, and I don't want to have to start over."

"But I will tell you!" screamed Smith-Williams.

"Then start talking," Bolan said as he continued to heat the blade.

"The man who accompanies the paintings from Moscow is—"

Before the name could leave his mouth, an explosion sounded above the Executioner's head. Out of reflex, he let both the lighter and knife fall from his hand, swept back his coat, drew the Desert Eagle and fired up at the bullet hole that had appeared in the skylight in the ceiling.

A split second later, the entire skylight came crashing down as both a man and a rifle burst through the window. Thousands of tiny, glistening particles of glass rained over the room like a sudden hailstorm. The rifle—a Heckler & Koch 93—hit the carpet and bounced across the room to come to rest against one of the couches. The man fell directly onto the desk, facedown.

Bolan kept the Desert Eagle trained overhead for a second,

half-expecting another attack. He still didn't know whether or not
Seven had killed the sniper on the rooftop. But in the brief second it had taken the man to fall from the skylight, he had seen
that he wore a gray hooded sweatshirt rather than a black coat
like the hit man at the hotel.

Of course that didn't mean he wasn't the same man who had
attacked them from the room across the hall at the Durrants. He
could have changed clothes the same way the Executioner had.

Satisfied that there was no more threat from above, Bolan hurried to the desk. He grabbed the man by the back of the hair and
rolled him over. The bullet had struck squarely in the chest, and
his cold brown eyes stared sightlessly into eternity. He had high,
Slavic cheekbones and a square jaw. Bolan had seen only glimpses
of the man across the hall but he remembered him as taller and
far more muscular than the body on the desk in front of him now.
And the rifle now lying on the carpet was a .308 caliber.

This was not the man. It was his friend, the sniper. But the
man was there, too. Somewhere.

The Executioner got at least a general answer to that question
a second later when a volley of submachine gun fire suddenly
broke out in the gallery outside the office. The shots sounded as
if they had come from the front of the building, on the left-hand
side of the main hall. That would be the oil-painting room.

Bolan sprinted to the closed door to the hallway, reaching up
to flip off the overhead light before he opened the door. He
would already be framed in the doorway from the outside light
filtering into the building, and there was no sense in painting an
even more distinct bull's eye on his forehead. More subgun fire
erupted as he swung the door open, then dived into the hallway.
He hit the floor on his shoulder and rolled to his feet again
against the wall.

Pistol shots followed the autofire this time. They were
.357 Magnum rounds. Seven's namesake Taurus.

The Executioner moved cautiously along the wall toward the
entrance to the photography area. From there, he could cut
through to the oil room. His objective was twofold. He had to

find Polyakova and Seven before they got killed. But it was also time to end the threat the man in the black coat posed, once and for all.

The gallery fell silent. Bolan moved on, his back to the wall, finally reaching the archway into the photo area. He ducked, keeping his eyes up as he rounded the corner. But he encountered no resistance. And whatever was happening in the front of the gallery had stopped momentarily. Silence continued to reign, and the lack of sound was, in its own way, deafening.

Bolan stayed low, the Desert Eagle held tight against his body as he maneuvered between the photographs. Some were small, extending from the tops of easels like flowers at the end of a stalk. Other, larger pictures, blocked his view as he continued toward the oil-painting room. But whether they were large or small, all of the exhibits in the photography room had at least one thing in common. They were framed, and protected by glass. Unlike with the oils and watercolors, that glass picked up and reflected every lumen of light that managed to reach it, and more than once the Executioner swung the barrel of the Desert Eagle at a darkened mirror image of himself.

He had passed the last row of pictures and was nearing the front room when the gunfire erupted once more. Bolan moved to the door, crouching as he peered around the corner into the opening. Through the forest of easeled paintings, he could see automatic muzzle-flashes near the front of the building. They appeared and disappeared with each round fired, partially hidden by the staggered paintings and giving off a strange, kaleidoscope effect. He didn't know where Polyakova and Seven were until he again heard the boom of the Taurus. It had come from the front, from the far left-hand corner of the room. Where, if he remembered correctly, the painting Polyakova had said was by an artist named Fielding had been located.

The hit man was obviously preoccupied with Seven, and Bolan took advantage of that fact, moving quickly but stealthily through the easels. When he had gotten far enough into the maze of canvases to get a decent shot at the muzzle-flashes, he raised the Desert Eagle.

Almost as if he knew what the Executioner was doing, the man with the Soviet PPD quit firing. Bolan froze, listening. He could barely hear the sound of shoes moving quietly near the spot from where the flashes had come. Then they stopped again. The hit man couldn't have moved far. But it was far enough to ruin the Executioner's aim.

Bolan remained still. Shooting now would do nothing but give away his own position. As far as he could tell, it was nothing but bad luck that the subgunner had quit firing and moved when he did. He didn't know Bolan's position, or that the Executioner was even in the room. And Bolan would take advantage of that fact as long as he could.

Slowly, careful to remain silent, Bolan dropped the Desert Eagle back into its holster and drew the sound-suppressed Beretta 93-R.

Thirty seconds, then a minute went by, and Bolan was reminded of the shoot-and-duck game he had played with this same man earlier in the day at the hotel. The temptation in that situation had been to barrel forward, heedless of the danger, and end the threat as soon as possible. There was a similar temptation now, as the tension mounted with each second.

The hit man had patience; the Executioner would have to give him that. Whoever he was, he was a far cry above the gunmen the Russians had sent after Polyakova in New York. This man was a formidable foe. He was well-trained and experienced. But he had something else going for him—Bolan could sense it in the way he fought. It was something no one could be taught or even learn on their own.

The man liked what was going on. No, Bolan corrected himself. The man loved it. It gave him power. It reinforced his personal belief that he was above the laws of man, and that deciding when others should die was his God-given right.

Which meant that the hit man had a form of insanity. And that made him more dangerous.

From where he had heard the gun fire before, Bolan now

heard Seven's .357 Magnum pistol boom again. One of the paintings fell off its easel and crashed to the floor. Almost immediately, the autofire and the muzzle-flashes of the Soviet submachine gun erupted again, this time from a spot roughly ten feet from where Bolan had seen them earlier.

The Executioner swung the Beretta that way and pulled the trigger, sending a trio of all but silent rounds ripping through several canvases toward the lights. The sound suppressor also covered his own muzzle-flashes—at least to a certain extent. But just to be safe, the Executioner took two steps to his right, then dropped to one knee as soon as he'd let up on the trigger.

It was a good thing he did. The fire from the submachine gun stopped, then reappeared a split second later. This time it faced the Executioner, and a steady stream of 7.62 mm rounds sailed over his head to the left—to the exact spot where he'd been a second earlier.

From the other side of the room, Bolan heard muffled whispers. Suddenly the sound of running feet broke the silence that had fallen over the gallery since the last burst of machine-gun fire had died down. Two sets of feet, one heavier than the other. Polyakova and Seven were heading toward the photography room the Executioner had just come from.

A third set of feet now took off in the same direction. Bolan raised the Beretta to fire, started to pull the trigger, then let up. The footsteps had crossed in front and to his side, and now he couldn't be certain that Polyakova and Seven were not in his line of fire. The Executioner knew he had to be close to the front door now, couldn't be far from where he'd seen Smith-Williams start to turn on the lights for the whole building.

For a split second, Bolan considered it. Sudden illumination would startle the hit man and, even more importantly, temporarily blind him. But Bolan knew it would also startle and affect the vision of Polyakova and Seven, so he discarded the idea. Such strategy might make sense if he already had his target in his sights. But he didn't. No, they were better off in the dark.

The Executioner took off running, weaving his way through

the dimly lit art displays. He made the best use he could of the dim light, as he moved back toward the door to the photo area.

When he reached the last row of paintings and could see the door, it became obvious that Polyakova, Seven and the hit man had already entered the rear room. He started to follow, then changed course and headed back toward the doorway to the main hall. From there, he could circle around and enter the photography area from behind them. If any of them tried to leave the room, they would run right into him. He would keep his eyes open, and if he saw his partners, it would afford him an opportunity to move them to safety and get between them and the hit man.

And if he saw the hit man first, he would kill him.

Again Bolan moved down the hall, his back to the wall. When he reached the archway into the photography room again, he paused. Go in after them or wait? He wasn't sure. There were pros and cons both ways. But his hunch was that Seven would try to herd the woman out of the room, and away from the man with the Soviet submachine gun.

He would wait.

A few seconds later, the Executioner heard the footsteps again, but the sound was distant and unclear. And the feet were moving so slowly it was impossible to tell if it was one person or two making them. He took a deep breath and held it, not wanting even the sounds from his own lungs to cloud his hearing. The footsteps continued. He still couldn't decipher whether they were made by friend or foe.

Then came the eerie creak of a door opening near the back of the photography room. It had to be the door to the office. Was it Polyakova and Seven Bolan heard? Or the hit man?

Whoever it was became immaterial as gunfire broke out once more. From where he was, the Executioner could see only the reflection of the flashes in the glass of several pictures. The roars of both the PPD and Seven's SIG-Sauer met his ears. As he turned the corner into the photography room the entire area lit up in fire, the muzzle-flashes multiplied by their reflections in the picture frames.

With only sound to guide him, Bolan picked out the general area from which the 7.62 mm rounds were coming. He triggered a 3-round burst that way, then did it again. Then again, and again, until the Beretta's slide locked open, empty.

In less than two seconds he had dropped the empty box and slammed another magazine up the grips. He thumbed the slide release to chamber a round, then sent another fifteen 9 mm hollowpoint slugs flying after the others. By the time he had reloaded again, he could hear voices across the hall in the watercolor room. Low. Whispering. Unless the hit man was so crazy he talked to himself, it had to be Seven and Polyakova. It had been them at the door to the office, and now they had crossed through the room, past Smith-Williams in the chair and the dead man on the desk, and exited the other door into the other side of the building.

Bolan had started that way to join them when he felt an old familiar pressure against the side of his face. It had happened many times over the years when bullets passed within millimeters of his head. It was strange, like a wall of air pushing against him. And it was always followed a hundredth of a second later by the explosion, proving that bullets traveled faster than sound.

Diving to the ground, the Executioner rolled to his side as more autofire ripped over his head. He looked back into the photography room to see it lit up once again by fire from the barrel of the PPD. The weapon cycled 800 rounds a minute, and that was enough to keep the glass in the picture frames dancing with bizarre strobes of light.

Then, for a brief second, in what looked like hundreds of glass-covered frames, the Executioner saw the face of the hit man.

A smiling demon.

Bolan triggered the Beretta twice, sending six hollowpoint rounds scattering through the easels but with little hope of hitting his man. He was in a carnival house of mirrors, and picking out the real face among the imposters was impossible. The hardman had no such problem—Bolan was still out in the hall, away from the confusing reflections. It was a no-win position, and he rolled to the side, behind the wall, and out of sight.

The gunfire stopped.

The Executioner checked the remaining two magazines for the Beretta, knowing if this kept up he would soon have to switch back to the Desert Eagle. Silence was the only advantage he'd had so far, and as soon as the Eagle screamed out its first thunderous .44 Magnum, even that small edge would be gone. He wondered how many of the 71-round drum magazines the man carried with him. The average man could carry two, even three, before the extra weight became a problem. And the bulky man the Executioner had seen in the hallway at the hotel had been far bigger than average.

Temporarily safe behind the wall and out of sight, Bolan looked across the hall toward the watercolor room. Somewhere inside he knew Seven was trying to get Polyakova to safety. But if the Executioner tried to cross to the door leading directly to them, he would be exposed through the doorway to the photo room again. This time, the hit man would be waiting.

Bolan rose to his feet, quietly walking backward down the hallway, away from the door to the photos. He would again try to circle behind his partners, entering the other side of the building through the sculpture room and then crossing through the adjoining door into the watercolors. With any luck, he might be able to reach them while the hardman still thought Bolan was in the hall.

The Executioner turned sideways, crossing one leg over the other, the Beretta and his eyes still aimed at the door through where the last burst of gunfire had come. When he reached the entrance to the sculpture room, he ducked inside. He had taken only two steps when he saw a sparkle of light suddenly dance off the barrel of a revolver as it rose to his face right in front of him.

The Executioner reached out with his left hand, grabbing the gun by the cylinder and sliding his little finger back over the frame. The hammer had been on its way back, and now it fell on Bolan's flesh, biting into the skin. There was just enough light for him to see the Harris tweed cap perched on top of Seven's head.

"Sorry," the DEA man whispered. He released the grips and Bolan took the Taurus, working his finger out from under the hammer. "Where's Luiza?" he asked in a low voice.

Seven shook his head in the near darkness. "I don't know," he said quietly. "I lost track of her in there." He hooked a thumb over his shoulder at the watercolor room. "I thought she'd come in here so I came after her."

"We've got to find her," the Executioner said. "Now."

The DEA man nodded.

"Take the front half of the room," Bolan ordered. "I'll take the back. Are you sure she came this way?"

Johnny Seven shook his head. "Not sure. I just couldn't find her back there. So I tried here."

The Executioner took off, moving along the rows of statues, busts and other sculptures. The light was a little brighter this close to the street, and it gave the stone heads and faces staring back at him an almost unearthly cast. He was tempted to call out for the Russian woman, but he knew if she could hear him, so could the hit man.

When he had worked all the way back to the common door to the watercolors, Bolan paused. He had thoroughly searched his half of the room, and he had to assume that a DEA agent knew how to search a room, too. He hadn't found the woman, and he had heard no sound behind him to lead him to think the DEA man had any better luck.

The woman wasn't among the sculptures. Somehow Seven had lost track of her in the watercolor room and jumped to the conclusion that she'd come in there.

Then he heard the scream.

"Help me—"

Luiza Polyakova's shrill plea for help, suddenly cut off like that, sent a primitive surge of hatred through the Executioner. He didn't know who the man was, only that in some way he was tied to Gregor and the head Russian in Moscow. Bolan would have traded a year of his life to have the man's throat in his fingers right now. He started to sprint forward, then halted. Anger and hatred would do nothing to assist Polyakova right now. But it could do a lot to blur his judgment, and it almost had.

Forcing himself to relax, he pushed all emotion to the back of his brain. He had to think clearly. His next few moves would be crucial. They would either leave the woman alive or dead.

"You!" A heavily accented voice screamed out in the darkness. "American! Did you hear that?"

Bolan's eyes narrowed, straining to look forward into the murky light through the doorway to the watercolor room, toward the area the voice had come from. Unless the acoustics were playing tricks on his ears, the woman and her captor were to the right of the door, and no more than twenty to thirty feet away. Finally, Bolan shouted out, "I heard." Then he moved two steps to his side and another two forward, crouching behind a giant statue of an ancient Celtic Druid.

The man with the PPD would be keying on his voice, too, hoping to get off a shot. But no shots came. Instead the man holding Polyakova yelled out, "You and the other man! Come forward, then, if you want her to live!"

The Executioner felt a creeping presence behind. He didn't bother to turn—it could only be Johnny Seven. The DEA agent stepped to his side behind the statue, waiting for Bolan to tell him what to do.

The problem was, the Executioner didn't know what to do at this point.

"Did you hear me?" the voice in the watercolor room demanded.

Again Bolan paused. The accent was curious—Eastern European, yes. Similar to Russian, and probably influenced by spending a lot of time in Russia. But not quite Russian. This man was from one of the satellite countries that had once made up the old Soviet Union. "I heard you," the Executioner said. "I can come forward, but my partner's dead. You shot him."

A hideous, satanic-like laugher came from the other room. "You Americans," said the hit man. "I cannot help but love you in a curious way. You lie quite well." There was a pause, then the man said, "I will count to ten. During that time, you will lay down all of your weapons and begin to walk forward. Both of you. If I don't see two men in the doorway by the time I reach ten, I will kill the woman."

"How do I know you haven't already killed her?" the Executioner demanded.

Bolan heard the man whispering. Then Polyakova's trembling voice called out, "Matt! I am here!"

"Are you all right?" Bolan asked, stalling for time, trying to come up with a plan of some kind.

But the woman didn't answer—the man with the Soviet machine gun did. "You have heard her voice. That is enough. Now, put down all weapons and walk forward or she dies!"

"I'll come," Bolan said. Then, trying one last time, he added, "But I told you, my partner is—"

"One!" the man shouted. "Two! Three..."

Bolan turned to his side. "Stay here until you hear shots," he whispered to Seven. "I'll try to move left once I get through the door. He's to the right."

Johnny Seven looked up at him. His face reflected a strange mixture of fear, courage, hope and determination. "How do I keep from hitting *her* in the dark?" he asked.

Bolan shrugged. "Just do your best. At this point, we've got to take the chance. If we don't, she's dead for sure."

"Four!" came the voice from the other room. "Five! I don't hear any movement on your part!"

"I'm getting rid of my weapons!" Bolan shouted. Drawing the Desert Eagle, he let it fall noisily to the floor. "Now, I'm coming forward." He made sure his steps could be heard on the tile as he walked toward the door.

The Executioner held the Beretta in tightly to his side, hoping it would remain invisible in the darkness. What he was about to attempt had a one-in-a-hundred chance of succeeding. But it was the best he could come up with under the circumstances. He would allow himself to be framed in the doorway, and the second he did the man would cut loose with the PPD. Bolan would have to hope he could somehow survive that volley long enough to pinpoint the man's position—again by the flash signature of the subgun. He would also have to pray that there was enough light to discern the man from Polyakova, and that he would have a decent angle to return fire without killing her.

Bolan recalculated his odds. One in a hundred was far too generous. One in a million seemed more on the money.

As he moved the last few steps toward the doorway, the Executioner took a deep breath and prepared himself. He had to assume at least some of the full-auto fire he was about to walk into would hit him. He had to hope there were no head shots or other immediately incapacitating injuries. Even injured, even dying, if he could just live long enough to save Polyakova, he would accept death, and even embrace it.

Suddenly he was at the door. He stepped into the passage between the two rooms with no regrets.

The volley of fire he had anticipated came, but Bolan was surprised to see it hit wide to his left, far along the wall. At almost the same time, he heard the gruff voice of the hit man scream, "Ahh! Bitch! I will kill—"

Bolan turned in the direction of the muzzle-flashes, raising the Beretta. He could just make out a blurry shadow as it staggered to the side of an easel, away from a smaller form. It was a good shot, clean. His finger tightened on the 93-R and the trigger moved rearward.

But a split second before the gun was about to detonate, the smaller silhouette jumped in front of the sight picture. In a flurry of movement, Polyakova appeared to be hammering her balled fist into the larger shadow.

Bolan let up on the trigger and raced toward the two shadows. As he ran, he saw the man push the woman away from him. She reeled into two of the easels, knocking them backward into the oncoming Executioner. One of the watercolors flew off the stand, flying into Bolan's face.

The picture was light and did no damage. He swept it away. But it had blocked his vision for a second, and by the time he could see again, the hit man was gone.

Running footsteps sounded in the main hall. "Johnny!" Bolan yelled. "He's coming your way!" A quick exchange of gunfire sounded.

Bolan knelt quickly next to where Polyakova had fallen. "Are you all right?" he asked.

The woman lay on the floor, furiously wiping her hand back and forth against her mouth. "I am fine," she said.

The Executioner left her where she was and raced after the fleeing man. By the time he reached the front door it was open, and there was no one to be seen on the street.

A low moan came from the sculpture room as Bolan ran back toward the woman. Johnny Seven lay just inside the door. The Executioner cut into the room and dropped to one knee.

"It's just a flesh wound," Seven said. "I think. I hope."

"Can you walk?" Bolan asked.

Seven reached up and grabbed Bolan's arm. "I don't know," he said. "But I'm as anxious to find out as you are."

Polyakova came through the door to the watercolor room as Bolan lifted the man to his feet. She had come across the Desert Eagle on the way, and now she handed it to him as if giving him a poisonous snake. She was obviously shaken by her short stint as a hostage but didn't look to have been physically harmed. But Bolan noticed that she still continued to wipe her lips with her hand.

The bullet that had dropped Seven had missed the bone, and done little more than skim across his thigh. The velocity had knocked him from his feet, but the wound wasn't life-threatening.

As it seemed to happen every five minutes since this mission began, police sirens now sounded, nearing the art gallery. "We've got to get out of here," Bolan said. "I'm going back for Smith-Williams. You two head for the street." He glanced down at the blood on the DEA man's leg. A cab was out of the question. "Luiza, help him. Johnny, you know how to boost a car?"

The DEA man nodded.

"Do it," the Executioner said. "Go back to the hotel. I'll grab the Briton and meet you there."

Polyakova took Seven's arm and he limped out into the hall, then toward the front door.

Bolan sprinted back to the office, knowing every second counted now. He had to get Smith-Williams out of there before the police arrived. Once the boys were there, the gallery owner would shut up tighter than a clam, and Bolan would never learn who the Russian connections were.

Ripping open the door, Bolan switched the light back on and turned to the chair where he'd left the art-and-drug dealer.

Raymond Smith-Williams still sat where the Executioner had left him. But the fear on his face was gone. Instead he wore a moronic-looking grin, and Bolan had to wonder what had crossed his mind in the second before the barrage of bullets ended his life.

The hit man. At some point during the firefight, he had crossed through the office, seen the helpless man and shot him.

The Executioner didn't hesitate. Striding quickly to the desk, he began ripping the drawers open and dumping the contents. Out of the middle drawer fell a large green canvas-backed ledger book. The bottom drawer on the left was locked and, with no time or reason to look for a key, Bolan aimed the Beretta at the key hole, flipped the selector to semiauto and pulled the trigger. Inside he found what he'd been looking for. A small black address book.

By now the sirens had reached the front of the gallery. They still wailed away outside, and the Executioner could hear excited voices already inside the building. Flashlight beams were streaming down the main hall toward him.

Bolan pocketed both the ledger and address book and hurried to the door in the back wall. It opened easily, and he stepped through into a dark storage area and closed it quietly behind him. A second later, the voices reached the office.

"Inspector Robins, you'd better get in here and look at this."

Feeling his way through the darkness, Bolan located another door, which had to lead out of the building. But the knob wouldn't turn, and he felt along the frame until he came to the reason why. A double dead bolt lock secured the rear of the premises. It had to be opened with a key from inside, as well as out.

The Beretta was still in his hand, and Bolan switched it to burst mode. A trio of near silent 9 mm rounds coughed from the gun but made loud clanging noises as they hit the steel lock and door.

"What was that?" asked a voice in the office.

"Our boys breaking down the back, I would imagine," said the officer who had spoken earlier. "I'll go let them in."

Bolan tried the door again. It had loosened but still held. It took another trio of rounds to spring it open.

As it did, the door into the office opened.

Bolan didn't know whether it was Inspector Robins or the man who had called him from the hallway, but the officer who saw the Executioner froze in shock, giving Bolan time to slide through the door, sprint down the alley and disappear into the night.

9

Luiza Polyakova and Johnny Seven had already made it back to Le Meridien Piccadilly, found the first-aid supplies in Bolan's luggage and dressed the shallow wound on the DEA agent's upper leg when Bolan arrived. Seven lay on one of the beds wearing his new corduroy pants. Only a slight bulge was visible above the bandage.

Polyakova was in the bathroom brushing her teeth. As the Executioner walked past he saw her lift a bottle of mouthwash to her lips. As gargling sounds issued forth into the bedroom, Bolan looked over at the DEA man curiously.

"That's the third time with the Listerine," Seven whispered. "The son of a bitch kissed her. Can you believe that?"

Bolan shook his head. Again his suspicion that there was some strange psychosexual thing going on in the brain of the hit man was confirmed. He didn't know exactly what it was but he knew the man's ultimate goal for Polyakova went far beyond a forced kiss.

The television was on, and the program had been interrupted by the breaking news of the shoot-out at the Smith-Williams art gallery. "Metropolitan Police and Scotland Yard are searching for a tall man—" the newscaster said. She then went on to give a moderately accurate description of the Executioner. Bolan knew it had to have come from the brief glimpse the SO19 officer had gotten of him when he'd come face to face with Bolan in the storeroom.

The Russian came out of the bathroom and sat on the bed next to Seven. Her emerald eyes were as lovely as ever, but now they blazed with pure fury. Bolan pulled a chair away from the desk and dropped onto it backward, resting his crossed arms across the backrest. "We haven't had a chance to talk," he said, looking at the woman. "What did you do to make him jerk like he did when I came through the door?"

Her purse was on the floor by the bed. She reached into it and pulled out the familiar nail file. "In the eye," she said, jabbing the file into the air. "A trick my father taught me when I was very young and there was a rapist loose in Moscow."

The soldier looked at the small blade. She had wiped it off, but traces of blood could still be seen. He wondered if the man had lost the sight in that eye. Maybe. Maybe not. But in any case, he was still alive and that presented a problem.

"You heard him speak," the Executioner said. "He wasn't Russian."

Polyakova shook her head. "Chechen," she answered without hesitation.

Bolan nodded. Whether he had one eye left or two, the Executioner didn't get the feeling the Chechen was the sort who would give up. Eventually he and the hit man would meet again.

Bolan pulled the address book and ledger out of his pockets. "I didn't get the names I needed from Smith-Williams," he said. "When I went back, he was dead."

"I noticed he wasn't along for the ride," Seven responded.

Bolan held the books in his hand. "Our best shot now is to go through these and look for anything suspicious. I'll take the ledger and mark all the paintings that have come into the gallery from Russia. Then I'll look for sales going out on the same day or the day after. He may well have coded all this in some way, in which case I'll have to get it to my people back home and have them go over it."

"Your people being the Department of Justice, of course," Seven said with a straight face.

Bolan couldn't tell either of them who "his people" really

were. But he saw no reason to lie to them at this point, either. "Partially," he said. He flipped the address book across the bed so it landed in the DEA agent's lap. "Go through that and see if you can find anything of interest."

Seven leaned forward and opened the book.

Polyakova started to work on her nails, then looked at the file and recoiled slightly in disgust. "I believe I'll get a new one," she said, and dropped it in the trash next to the bed.

Bolan turned around in the chair, placed the ledger on the desk, opened it and turned on the lamp.

Fifteen minutes later, he had marked sixteen shipments of various artworks that had come in from Moscow within the past twelve months. He was no art expert but it seemed like an unusually large amount of business from any one city.

Polyakova, who was an expert, agreed. She moved in to stand behind him and look over his shoulder. Bolan did his best to ignore the enticing scent of her perfume while she said, "Even for a gallery the size of the Smith-Williams, it is too much."

Bolan moved on to the section where the sales were recorded. Paintings and other works had gone out of the Smith-Williams gallery on the same day as all of the imports except one. But there had been a large sale the day after, he noted. The Executioner frowned at the tiny numbers in the boxes. Next to each sale there were letters that might or might not have been initials. The ledger was undoubtedly cross-referenced with other files containing invoices and other information about the buyers. Those files had probably been in the office. He'd had no time to look, and the opportunity was gone now—SO19 would have the gallery sealed off tight while they went about investigating the small war that had gone on inside.

Bolan continued to study the ledger, picking up a pen and piece of scratch paper from the desktop. As he went back and forth from ledger to scratch pad recording dates and initials, a pattern gradually began to take shape. Ten of the sales on the same day as the shipments had gone to someone corresponding to the letters L and N. Were they the buyer's initials? He looked up at Polyakova, who still stood behind him. "The letters *L* and *N* mean anything to you?" he asked.

The beautiful Russian woman shook her head. She had been following what he was doing as he worked. "No," she said. "And any dealer or collector who could afford such large purchases, I would know of them. They would be prominent in the art world."

A fervor began to grow slowly in the Executioner's soul. He turned in the chair to face Johnny Seven. "Look under *N*," he said. "And see if there's a first name that starts with an *L*."

The DEA man flipped through the book, squinting at the page once he'd found it. "Bingo," he said. "Three of them."

Bolan's excitement wavered slightly. He had feared there would be none, but three created its own problems. He had to figure out which one, if any, was the "Ontomanov" of London. That would take time, and each second's delay meant another second in which Gregor and the man in Moscow might figure out what he was actually up to. If that happened, Polyakova's family was as good as dead.

"Read them to me."

"Lawrence Niles," Seven said. "Then—"

Bolan wanted to take it one step at a time. "You have an address for Niles?"

"Yeah. Kensington," the DEA agent replied. "But before we go into all that, I think I can save us some time. The second name is Sir Lambert Neal. But the third one is Leonid Navrozoz."

The Executioner smiled. Three names but only one was Russian. It was the logical place to start. "You're earning your keep, Johnny," he said. "Where does Navrozoz live?"

"No address," the DEA agent answered. "But there's a phone number."

Bolan looked to Polyakova. "You've been a great actress so far," he said. "Want to try it one more time?" When she nodded, he walked to the phone next to Seven on the bed. "Call this Leonid Navrozoz. Tell him it's an emergency. You brought a load of paintings in from Moscow but there was trouble at the gallery tonight." He hooked a thumb at the TV. "He should already know about that from the news. Tell this Navrozoz you've still got the paintings and the heroin but you're scared and you want to get rid of them."

The woman frowned. "But won't there be a regular man who brings the shipments into London?" she asked. "Like Rabashka did in New York?"

"Say you were his girlfriend. He got killed at the gallery."

Luiza still looked worried. "But this Navrozoz," she said. "If they are operating the same way here as they did with me in New York, he will have an emergency number to call. If he has called it already, or if he calls to check after I talk to him—"

Bolan held up his hand to silence her. "It's not a perfect plan, Luiza. It's got some potential flaws in it but it's all we've got. I'm counting on your native command of the Russian language, and the confusion at the gallery, to throw him off stride." He shrugged. "And if it doesn't work, we haven't lost anything."

Polyakova nodded. "I will try it," she said.

Seven still had the address book open. He rolled onto his side, lifted the receiver, dialed the number, then handed the phone to Polyakova. A second later her eyebrows lowered and she held the phone up so the soldier could hear.

A prerecorded voice was explaining that the number they'd just called was not a working number.

The DEA man tried again with the same result.

Bolan took the address book from him and stared at it. Something was wrong. According to the ledger, L.N. had purchased several paintings within the past week. Was the phone number in some kind of code? If so, he suspected it would be simple. Taking the receiver from Seven, he tapped the cutoff button, then called the front desk. "Can you tell me what area the prefix 765 corresponds to?" he asked the woman who answered.

"One moment, sir," she said. When she came back on the line, she said, "Is that in London, sir?"

"Yes."

"I'm sorry, we have no such prefix in the London area."

The Executioner frowned. "How about 567?" he asked, reversing the order.

It took only a second for the woman to reply, "Oh, yes, sir. That's Hyde Park."

Bolan smiled as he hung up. He had a hunch, and his gut told him to play it. Handing the receiver to Polyakova again, he tapped the entire phone number in backward.

The woman nodded as the line connected and began to ring. A moment later, Luiza Polyakova began speaking excitedly in Russian.

Seven looked puzzled but Bolan followed the conversation. The Russian woman hung up a few minutes later. For Seven's benefit, she said, "He's coming here."

The DEA man laughed. "Well, you can't beat curb service." He looked at Bolan. "What do we do when he gets here?"

"We get the name of whoever it is who actually brings the shipments in from Moscow."

"Then we go to Moscow?" Seven asked.

"It looks that way," the Executioner replied. He lifted the phone. He had one more call to make—to Stony Man Farm. Jack Grimaldi had taken the members of Stony Man's Phoenix Force to Madrid but he could be back in London easily by the time they needed him. There was no longer any reason to get bogged down flying commercial airlines. And he would need a pilot unafraid to take chances. That was Grimaldi.

As he dialed the number, Bolan looked at Polyakova and Seven. He saw no reason to remind them that when they had finished in Russia it would still not be over. There was still Gregor back in the U.S.

Not to mention the Chechen hit man.

"THIS IS TERRIBLE," Leonid Navrozoz told Polyakova in Russian as soon as she opened the door. "Did you know that in addition to Stavislav, Raymond Smith-Williams is dead?"

Polyakova led him past the closed bathroom door to the chairs around the small table in front of the bed. "Sit down," she said.

"I will sit," Navrozoz replied, brushing the thick brown hair off his forehead. "But we must hurry. The police will soon know there is more involved here than art, and they will come looking for you and the paintings." He paused a second, then said, "What did you say your name was? And you were Stavislav's wife? Girlfriend?"

From his vantage spot beneath the bed, Bolan watched the conversation take place. He had tugged the bedspread and sheets down almost to the floor, and now peered out from under them. Polyakova had done a great job on the phone, convincing Navrozoz that they were in a tremendously confusing emergency in which the paintings—and particularly the heroin stashed inside them—would be confiscated by police in the next few hours if something wasn't done. She had even manipulated him into letting it slip that the man who accompanied the shipments from Moscow was named Stavislav.

Bolan had hidden beneath the bed, with Seven in the bathroom, and ordered Polyakova to continue her act, learning as much more as she could the easy way before they appeared on the scene.

"He was my fiancé," she said, improvising. "And now he is dead." She fell forward, face in hands, and sobbed softly.

Navrozoz appeared to be a man who knew when to show sympathy even if his face didn't reflect any real feeling of it. "I am sorry," he said. "And I feel your pain. Where did you say the paintings are at the moment?"

The woman looked up from her hands, diverting him from the subject. "I will take you there in a moment," she said. "But first you must tell me who it was who attacked the gallery."

Navrozoz sat back in his chair and slapped his chest. "How would *I* know?" he asked.

"He came posing as a friend," Polyakova stated. "And I even spoke to him briefly before he began to shoot everyone." Now, she leaned forward, reached out and touched Navrozoz on the forearm. The Russian looked half-hypnotized by her intense magnetism as she said, "He was a big scary-looking man. He wore a long black trench coat and spoke Russian. But with an accent."

From beneath the bed, Bolan saw Navrozoz stiffen. "What kind of accent?" he asked anxiously.

"Chechen."

Navrozoz's face turned so white it was hard to distinguish it from the bed sheets in front of the Executioner's face. "Akhmatov," he breathed almost too low for Bolan to hear. "Movlid Akhmatov." He lifted his right hand and crossed himself. "The man is the devil himself," he said. "They even say he is a cannibal. They say he tortures women, then kills them and—" The man stopped talking, as if it upset him too much to go on.

There was other information the Executioner needed from Navrozoz, if the man had it. Stavislav's last name. The identities of Gregor and the head man in Moscow, and anything else he knew about the three men. But he saw no way Polyakova could wheedle these things out of Navrozoz without giving herself away, and that meant there was no reason to carry on the ruse any longer.

The Beretta had been in his hand all along, and now Bolan rolled from under the bed and up to his feet, pressing the sound suppressor against the side of Navrozoz's head. The man practically jumped out of his chair, then turned to face the Executioner.

Bolan rested the suppressor on the bridge of his nose. "Don't move," he ordered. Quickly he shook the man down, finding a Vektor CP-1, two extra magazines, and a short braided leather blackjack. Seven had come in from the bathroom by then, and the Executioner handed the weapons to the DEA man.

"What is going on?" Navrozoz managed to squeak out of a throat that had all but closed off.

"You're going to take us to Stavislav," the Executioner said. "What's his last name?"

Both courage and loyalty come in varying degrees, even among criminals. Some have a lot, others have none. Leonid Navrozoz fell into the latter category. "Nemets," he said without hesitation. "Stavislav Nemets."

"Where was last time you talked to him?" Bolan demanded, grinding the sound-suppressor a little harder into the Russian's forehead.

"Moscow," Navrozoz replied. "He was due in with a shipment tomorrow morning, which is why this incident confused me." He looked at Polyakova for a moment, then said, "I had supposed that since he had brought this woman with him, for some reason he had come to London a day early. Before the paintings arrived."

"There's a shipment due tomorrow?" Bolan asked.

The Russian nodded, then looked at his watch. "In only a few hours now."

The Executioner stepped back but kept the Beretta on the man. Moscow to London wasn't a short trip, but it wasn't a long one, either. "Watch him for me, Johnny," he told the DEA man, then walked to the phone. Five minutes later, Aaron "the Bear" Kurtzman had hacked into the computers at all the cargo airports in Moscow and learned that no flights had left for London since the shooting at the gallery had occurred. Nemets, the paintings and the heroin had to have left before it happened.

Even with the gunfight all over the news, it was unlikely the man knew about it since he was on the plane. Bolan reminded himself that, with Smith-Williams as a willing partner, there were a few differences in the London and New York operations. For one thing, even though they seemed tight-lipped among each other, everyone seemed to know a little more than Polyakova had. "Have you ever met Nemets at the airport before?" the Executioner asked, turning back to Navrozoz.

Navrozoz nodded his head. "A few times I went with Smith-Williams."

"Get up," the Executioner demanded. "We're going to meet him again."

Navrozoz had been cooperative so far but now he shook his head. "No," he said. "I have told you what you wanted to know. But if I do more they will kill me."

"They might," Bolan said. He jammed the Beretta between

Navrozoz's eyes again. "Want to take that chance or have me just kill you now?"

The Russian's eyes told Bolan he had made his decision. But he was a career criminal, and always on the lookout for any way to take advantage of whatever situation arose. "All right," he said. "But how will I be rewarded?"

The Executioner slapped the flat side of the Beretta across the side of the man's face. "With less of that," he said, as an angry red welt began to swell on the Navrozoz's jaw.

A few seconds later, they had collected the equipment they would need and were on their way.

THE CHECHEN HAD CHOSEN the King John Inn near Victoria Station for three reasons. First it was far enough from the gallery that the proprietors wouldn't have heard the gunfire. Second it was still relatively close. He couldn't go long without treating his eye, nor could he parade around London soaked in blood. And last but perhaps most important of all, the King John was not the sort of place that would question such injuries. Knifings, clubbings and brawls of all kinds would be everyday fare in the shoddy pubs surrounding the cheap rooming house.

Under the bare lightbulb above the cracked bathroom mirror, Movlid Akhmatov forced his swollen eyelid up with his finger. With his good eye he surveyed the mutilated tissue inside the socket. He had lost all chance of ever seeing through that eye again—of that he was certain. So there was no reason to seek out professional medical attention now. At this point he could do as much for himself as any doctor.

Akhmatov saturated the blind eye socket with rubbing alcohol, feeling the fire spread from his eye throughout his head, and then the rest of his body. It was painful, yes, but there was a curious satisfaction to the feeling, as well. The apparent conflict of emotions seemed curious to him. He suspected it was somehow akin to the way pain, torture and eventually death itself increased the love his women had for him.

A smile broke on the Chechen's face as he applied a heavy

gauze patch. The woman—Luiza Polyakova—didn't yet understand the relationship between love and injury, pleasure and pain. But she would. Soon.

Akhmatov turned and looked at the tiny red marks on his back. After she had punctured his eye with whatever it was she had used—a small knife, he suspected—she had begun ineffectively stabbing him, over and over, in the back. His coat and shirt had prevented all but several irritatingly shallow wounds, and he would ignore them.

Quickly the Chechen changed clothes, abandoning the blood-soaked coat and other items he had worn earlier. He didn't know exactly what the big American's next step would be, but he had no doubt where the man was eventually headed. He would go there and wait for him. When he arrived, he would kill the man and his partner. And considering the location, it would no longer be necessary to seek out some isolated spot to teach the woman his ways of love. He could simply take her home with him to the mountains. He could love her at his leisure, for as long as she lasted. The Chechen gathered his things and reached out for the doorknob, his mind filled with fantasies featuring Luiza Polyakova.

Yes, he thought as he opened the door. At his home in the Caucasus, they could make love in his special ways until she provided the ultimate proof of her devotion. She was beautiful, and might well turn out to be the best lover he had ever had.

At least he had never heard anyone scream quite as beautifully as she had when he'd taken her in his arms and kissed her.

EAST MIDLANDS AIRPORT, north of London, took less than an hour to reach in the Ford Crown Victoria Seven and Polyakova had "borrowed" when escaping the Smith-Williams gallery. Dawn had broken as Bolan drove, with the woman at his side. The DEA man, who was walking much better now that he knew how superficial his wound had been, sat in the back, guarding Navrozoz.

The soldier turned into the airport. He cruised slowly past the large hotel servicing the airport, then turned left once he'd passed a sign announcing Air Cargo Village. He turned again on the other side of the large warehouses, and drove along the access road next to the runway. He came to a halt in a small parking area near the cargo terminals and left the Ford's engine running.

His plan was simple: get the jump on Stavislav Nemets, who he hoped hadn't yet gotten word that there had been an incident at the gallery. With any luck, Rabashka's London counterpart would escort the shipment in as usual, expecting to be met by Raymond Smith-Williams, to whom he would turn over the cargo after completing the required inspection forms.

Well, the Executioner thought as he sat waiting, the man was in for a surprise. Bolan planned to grab Nemets as soon as the man stepped off the plane. Then he would whisk him across the airport to the private-plane area, where Jack Grimaldi should have already touched down. With any luck, they would be in the air and headed toward Moscow before airport officials figured out what was going on.

During the next half hour or so, two other cargo planes landed, taxiing into the terminals. Men, trucks and other vehicles came and went. Some of the vehicles were marked with the logos of various companies, others were not. It was a good situation, Bolan thought, as a huge four-engine Il-76 finally appeared in the distance. It heightened his chances of getting close to the plane without being noticed.

As the Il-76 neared the ground, Bolan turned to Navrozoz. "Is that it?" he demanded.

The cowardly Russian had shown no resistance to the Executioner's questioning since the beginning, and he didn't start now. He nodded.

The plane landed at the end of the runway and began to slow. The Executioner threw the Crown Victoria into gear but kept his foot on the brake. He couldn't be sure yet into which of the four cargo terminals the plane would taxi, but he intended to be ready to make his move as soon as it stopped.

The Executioner turned and rested his arm over the seat.

Navrozoz had already described Nemets as a big man with blond hair and a matching beard. But a positive ID was imperative on a snatch-and-grab demanding split-second timing like this one, and now he said, "As soon as the doors open, you point him out," he told Navrozoz. "You try to screw us around and make a mistake, you die. Clear?"

Navrozoz nodded again. His face showed less emotion than a wooden ventriloquist's dummy.

"Want me with you?" Seven asked.

Bolan shook his head. "Somebody's got to keep an eye on our friend here." He indicated Navrozoz. He also wanted the DEA man to watch Polakova in case the hit man returned unexpectedly.

The plane arrived at the terminals and headed into number three. Bolan threw the Crown Victoria in gear and began driving that way at a moderate pace. Other vehicles came and went throughout the area as another cargo plane, high in the sky, began to drop toward the runway.

The Il-76's cargo doors swung open as several handlers wearing coveralls walked forward. Bolan halted the car next to a building twenty yards away just as a man fitting Nemets's description stepped down from the cockpit. Bolan turned to Navrozoz, who was staring into space like a zombie again. "That's him?" he asked.

Slowly, as if he were a robot and someone had just tripped one of his switches, Navrozoz's head swivelled to look at the man with the beard. His eyes held a thousand-yard stare but his head bobbed slowly up and down. "Nemets," he said softly.

The Executioner exited the car and walked casually toward the man with the beard. Within the busy area, none of the other men coming and going gave him a second look. When he was ten feet from where the big blond man stood talking to one of the men in coveralls, he drew the Desert Eagle.

Nemets was facing away from the Executioner at an angle. He couldn't see the gun. But the man in the coveralls saw it, and his lower lip dropped open. Then the top lip rose as he prepared to shout a warning.

Before the words could leave his mouth Bolan had stepped forward and clubbed him with the big .44 Magnum, sending the man to the ground.

Before Nemets could react, the Executioner jammed the barrel of the Desert Eagle into his ribs. "Move," he said in a low menacing voice. "Open your mouth and I'll kill you right here."

The Russian's pale blue eyes flickered in surprise. Then they scanned the area for help. But the Executioner had already done the same, and none of the busy men had seen what had transpired under their noses. Grabbing one of Nemets's arms, Bolan pushed him forward.

They were thirty feet from the Ford when the back door suddenly opened and Leonid Navrozoz jumped out. Through the window, Bolan could see Johnny Seven frantically diving across the seat trying to grab the man. The DEA agent was a half second too slow.

Navrozoz had acted strangely in the car, and now he didn't yell or even speak. He just stared at Bolan for a second, then took off in a panic, running in the opposite direction. As he raced away from the Crown Victoria toward the runway, Bolan heard a scream from behind him. "You there! What the hell?" Then another voice shouted, "What's happened to Carpenter?" and yet a third yelled, "You two! By the car! Stop where you are!" The last words were followed by the shrill sound of a whistle being blown.

Bolan pushed Nemets toward the Ford, where Johnny Seven was holding open the back door. He shoved the blond man inside, where the DEA man jammed both his SIG-Sauer and 7-shot Taurus into the Russian's side. As he turned back toward the driver's seat, Bolan heard the roar of the cargo craft he had seen about to touch down. In the distance he could see Navrozoz, still running blind and terrified, about to cross the runway.

The Executioner slid behind the wheel just as the big plane and Leonid Navrozoz crossed paths. Then the aircraft rolled to the end of the runway.

Navrozoz had simply disappeared.

Bolan pulled away from the terminals, speeding along the access road once more. There had been no time to recon the air-port, but he had seen the sign pointing toward the charter area when they'd first arrived. He slowed his pace once he was out of the immediate area, driving moderately—hoping not to draw at-tention—toward the charter terminal. He would leave the stolen artwork and heroin on the Il-76 for the British authorities to take care of. There had been enough commotion around the plane that it should receive a thorough shakedown.

Far ahead, Bolan saw the runway where the private craft landed and took off. What he didn't see was Grimaldi or the Lear-jet. He drove on, hearing a siren go off behind him. In the rearview mirror, he now saw three marked border inspection ve-hicles racing to catch up.

The Executioner neared the runway and finally saw the Lear-jet, its nose poking out behind the corner of the charter terminal. Grimaldi stood next to the plane, talking to a man in uniform. The wild hand gestures of both men made it obvious they were argu-ing. Probably about where Grimaldi had chosen to park the plane.

Bolan grinned, wondering what cock-and-bull story the ace pilot had come up with to stall for time. He would learn all that later. Right now the number-one priority was to get them all on the plane and out of there before security got organized.

As the Ford shot down the access road, the soldier saw Grimaldi suddenly draw back his fist and drive it into the belly of the uniformed man. He grabbed the officer by the back of the neck as he bent over, throwing him away from the plane, then climbed up and into the Lear. A moment later, the plane was taxi-ing onto the runway.

Bolan turned onto the runway himself, racing toward the ap-proaching Learjet. Grimaldi saw him and began to slow. The plane and car halted side by side.

Seven shoved Stavislav Nemets out the back of the car, and the big man hit the tarmac. As sirens wailed, lights flashed and the border inspection vehicles behind them closed the gap, Bolan jerked the bearded man to his feet and shoved him onto the plane. Seven took Polyakova's arm and followed.

They were barely on board when Grimaldi reached forward to the control panel and spun the wheels down the runway. As the Lear picked up speed, Bolan looked out the window and saw border inspection cars racing beside them on both sides. He buckled himself into the seat next to the pilot as Grimaldi looked over and smiled. "They've got pretty fast cars to keep up with us, huh?"

The Executioner didn't answer.

"But let's see if they can do this," Grimaldi said, and the Learjet rose into the sky.

MACK BOLAN WAS A SOLDIER, not a cop. Over the years, however, he had adopted many police techniques to include in his war against evil. Now, as the Learjet neared Moscow, he thought back on how he had decided to approach this mission since the start.

In one way or another, one man had led to the next. Polyakova to Ontomanov, Ontomanov to Gregor. Gregor had put him onto Smith-Williams, and he had followed the Briton's tracks to Navrozoz, who had led him to Nemets. Now Nemets was taking him to the top man in Moscow—a man named Anton Zdorovye. In many ways he had climbed the ladder very much the same as if he'd been working a routine drug investigation. But there were differences, too—differences that no federal, state or city cop could have ever gotten away with. There had been no plea bargaining, and no promises of sentence reduction. In contrast, everyone in the chain had gotten what he deserved. Polyakova, the unwilling pawn, would eventually be cleared. The rest would be dead. But in order to ensure a complete victory, Bolan knew he had to squeeze Gregor's full identity out of Zdorovye before he killed him.

And there was still the hit man, wherever it was he fit into the overall organization. He needed to die, too—maybe worse than any of them.

Bolan looked over his shoulder at Nemets. He had bound the man, hand and foot, as soon as they'd been in the air. He was also belted into his seat. That hadn't been the case during the first part of the trip.

The Russian had been unarmed when the Executioner had shaken him. But he'd been a tougher nut to crack than his cowardly accomplice, Navrozoz. Bolan had been limited in his interrogation techniques on the Learjet so he had gotten creative in a way that thoroughly delighted Grimaldi. Making sure that everyone but Nemets was belted down, he had instructed the pilot to perform an aerial stunt show across the English Channel. It hadn't taken long before Nemets tired of bouncing around the cabin, and began to talk.

The blond Russian had decided he would be more than happy to take them to Zdorovye. And he had confirmed the hit man was Movlid Akhmatov, who had become something of a legend in espionage circles behind the old Iron Curtain. The Chechen was as famous for his perversions as his skills at torture and assassination. Nemets had begun to go into detail, but Bolan had shut him up when Polyakova's eyes began to grow wide with fear.

The soldier didn't need to know any more details than he already did. Movlid Akhmatov needed to die along with the rest. Several times over.

"Ten minutes, Striker," Grimaldi said. Bolan nodded.

The soldier had called Stony Man from the plane, making sure Hal Brognola used his considerable influence to see that they wouldn't be searched by Russian authorities once they landed. And Brognola had called back less than a half hour later to advise them he'd pulled it off. Bolan didn't know exactly how—the Stony Man director's methods of making things happen ran the gamut from political contacts to out-and-out bribery when it was called for.

In any case, they were about to be met by some Russian general who would walk them through customs.

As the Learjet began to descend, Bolan turned back around again. "We're going to rent a car once we're down," he told Nemets. "Then you're going to guide us straight to Zdorovye's office." He drew the Loner knife from under his arm and held it up. "You try anything funny, and they'll find you in more pieces than your buddy Navrozoz. This Movlid Akhmatov will seem like Mother Teresa to you when I'm finished."

As soon as they were on the ground, Bolan cut Nemets's restraints and led him out of the plane, glancing around for the general who was meeting them. He saw no uniform, but he did see a familiar face walking toward him across the tarmac.

Marynka Platinov wore a bright red women's suit and high heels. She had beautiful muscular legs, reminding the Executioner that she had been an Olympic sprinter and hurdle champion before joining Russian intelligence years before. She was every bit as beautiful as her fellow Russian, Luiza Polyakova, but in a very different way. Where Luiza was soft, Marynka was hard. With Polyakova, the desire was to wrap his arms around her and protect her. There was a desire to wrap his arms around Platinov, too. But not for protection. Marynka Platinov was one woman who could take care of herself.

Bolan couldn't keep the smile off his face as she neared, her heels clicking along the tarmac. The years had been good to her. They had worked two missions together in the past, and become close friends. Actually friends might be putting it a little mildly, the soldier thought as he took the hand she extended.

The last time they had seen each other, Platinov had been a colonel. "So they've bumped you up to general now, have they?" Bolan asked.

Platinov stared deep into his eyes and caressed his fingers as she nodded. She kept hold of his hand as she turned to watch Seven and Polyakova step down off the Learjet. She only glanced at the DEA man but gave Polyakova a thorough going-over with eyes that were not particularly friendly. Then, turning back to Bolan, she said, "I see I'll have to change my plans a little." She forced a smile that was anything but happy. "The bottle of vodka in my freezer I can drink myself, but I was counting on you for the other part." Before Bolan could respond, she had turned and was clicking her heels toward the terminal.

Platinov walked them through the formalities as promised, then led them to a Chrysler sedan in the parking lot. "I knew you would need a car," she said as she handed Bolan the keys. "Try not to wreck it—it's in my name." She reached out and took the soldier's arm. "Care to tell me what you are doing?"

"You're better off not knowing," Bolan replied.

The gorgeous Russian intelligence officer smiled seductively at him. "We've broken a few laws together in the past," she said. "Not to mention *all* of the rules." Bolan saw her eyes flicker toward Polyakova to see how the woman had taken the insinuation. The other Russian woman either hadn't heard or pretended she hadn't.

Bolan leaned down and kissed Platinov. "Not in Russia, we haven't. And believe me, what I've got planned could cause you a world of bureaucratic trouble." He pushed Nemets into the back seat and got behind the wheel while Polyakova took the passenger's seat. Marynka Platinov stuck her head through the open window and gave her rival one last look. "Treat him well, my dear," she told Polyakova. Then she unabashedly turned her head to Bolan and kissed him for a good ten seconds. Without another word, she was gone.

"I take it you've bumped into each other before," Johnny Seven said with an innocent face.

Bolan stuck the keys in the ignition and drove away.

Thirty minutes later, the Chrysler was parked along the street in front of the building that housed the Zdorovye Russian Fur Company. They were deep in Moscow now, and when he got out of the car Bolan could see the Kremlin in the distance. He glanced at Polyakova as she and Seven got out. He didn't like taking her with him on what might very well turn into a gunfight. But he liked the idea of leaving her alone in the car even less. The Chechen would show up again, sooner or later. And there was no telling when that would be.

Bolan opened the trunk, lifted the viola case out, and handed it to Seven. He turned to Nemets. "Remember," he said, "you can live or you can die. It all depends on what you do in the next few minutes."

The blond man had been silent most of the time since giving Bolan the information he wanted. Staying true to that form, he just nodded and then led the way into the building. An elderly man—blind if his sunglasses were any indication—stood in front of a snack bar counter just inside the lobby. Bolan noticed Nemets glance his way, then reach up and tug at his ear.

The blind man turned to a telephone.

The Executioner drew the Desert Eagle and grabbed the blond man by the beard, dragging him down the hall to the elevator. No, he thought. They would be expecting that. "Where are the stairs?" he demanded.

Nemets was leaning forward awkwardly as Bolan pulled him along, and the arm he shot out looked just as awkward, but it pointed Bolan toward the corner of the lobby.

Pushing Nemets ahead of him now, Bolan took the stairs two at a time. The blond man was out of breath by the time they reached the second floor, where Zdorovye's offices were. Bolan grabbed him by the back of the hair and waited for Seven to reach the landing behind him. "Open the door, Johnny," he whispered.

The DEA man complied and Bolan shoved Stavislav Nemets though the opening. A burst of automatic gunfire immediately broke out and the blonde danced like a mad puppet before hitting the carpet. Bolan leaned around the corner and triggered a trio of .44 Magnum rounds into a broad-shouldered man with closely cropped hair. The man blew backward into the hall outside the offices, cracking his head loudly on the tile. His AK-74 clattered to the floor.

Bolan stepped through the opening as a man wearing a blue sweater and khaki slacks came out of another of the office doors. He held a short Simonov SKS carbine in his hands and with wild eyes and complete abandonment he sprayed 7.62 mm slugs down the hallway. Bolan dropped him with a well-placed shot just above the nose, decapitating him from the ears up.

Seven had pulled the M-16 A-2 from the instrument case and now stepped through the door behind the Executioner. "Keep an eye on Luiza!" Bolan shouted as the shots still rang in their ears. He sprinted down the hallway to the open door where the second man had just come. Diving forward, he hit the floor rolling, as another burst of gunfire sailed over his head. Coming up to one knee, the Executioner triggered a double-tap of booming Magnums into the chest of a portly man wearing a short-sleeved white shirt and tie. The man turned and fell face forward over a desk.

From behind the desk came a whimpering sound.

Bolan rose to his feet, changing magazines as he walked to the side of the desk. He kept one eye on the only other door in this outer office as he said in Russian, "You! Under the desk! Come out."

A small woman in a skirt and blouse crawled out from the desk looking terrified.

"Who are you?" Bolan demanded.

"Amalia," came the high, screechy voice.

The Executioner pointed to the door in the rear wall with the Desert Eagle. "Zdorovye back there?" he asked.

Amalia's head bobbed up and down quickly.

The Executioner waved at the door behind him with the big hand cannon. "Go, Amalia," he said. "Now."

He didn't have to say it twice. Amalia was gone with a speed that would have rivaled that of former Olympian, General Marynka Platinov.

Bolan waited until she was gone, then moved to the closed door. He heard movement on the other side as he reached down, twisting the knob. Throwing open the door, he dropped to a squat as several rounds exploded over his head. Behind the desk he saw a tall man with black hair turning gray. He held a Heckler & Koch Mark 23 in both hands, and when he saw the Executioner near the floor the barrel began to drop.

The Executioner triggered a lone round that blew upward at an angle through his chest, blowing flesh, bone and a pink mist of blood and other body fluids out through his back. The man screamed and fell to the side of the desk on his back.

Bolan rose to his feet and walked forward. The man on the floor was still alive. Kneeling beside him, he aimed the Desert Eagle down at his nose. "Who is Gregor?" he said.

Slowly, Anton Zdorovye shook his head.

"Tell me," Bolan said. "Do one good thing in your miserable life before you die."

Zdorovye's eyes rose beyond the Executioner then came back. "I am dying?" he said.

Bolan nodded.

"I...will tell you who...Gregor is..." he said. "If you will kill me...the way I want to die." His eyes rose again, to the wall. "And I will tell you...something else as...well."

Bolan looked over his shoulder and saw a Cossack sword hanging on the wall. He turned back. "The sword?" he said.

Zdorovye nodded.

Bolan turned and walked to the wall. Seven, M-16 in hand, suddenly appeared in the doorway. "What—?" the DEA said, looking around.

The Executioner waved him off, not wanting to break whatever strange bond it was that seemed to have sprung up between him and Zdorovye. The sword held some kind of significance to the Moscow drug peddler, and if dying by the sword rather than a bullet meant he'd tell Bolan who Gregor was, that was fine with the Executioner. He took the sword off the hangers and unsheathed it, then stepped back to Zdorovye's side. "Tell me," he said.

"It is...too late for the woman's family," he breathed out, and another pink mist blew out with each word. "I learned of...Smith-Williams." He closed his eyes for a moment as his last strength began to fail. "I have sent men...."

Bolan felt the fury build up in his chest as he raised the sword over his head. He wondered how much head start the men had toward Polyakova's family, and whether or not they were already dead. "Who is Gregor?" he said.

Anton Zdorovye kept his promise and told him. When he heard the name, Bolan nodded. Suddenly many of the odd coincidences began to fall into place.

Bolan kept his promise, too, and Anton Zdorovye died the way he wanted. But even as the sword came down, he heard

Polyakova's bloodcurdling scream from the hall. The Executioner had heard her scream like that only once before at the Smith-Williams gallery—when the Chechen had grabbed her.

10

Both Bolan and Seven moved back into the outer office as Polyakova screamed again. "Matt! Johnny!" She was somewhere down the hall. And the Executioner had no doubt as to what was prompting her outcries. He glanced to the DEA man, who had disobeyed his order to stay with her. But rebuking him now would serve no purpose.

Another voice, low and gruff, with the accent of Chechnya's northern Caucasus Mountains, now replaced the woman's. "You! Americans!" Movlid Akhmatov shouted. "Step out into the hallway now or she dies!"

Johnny Seven's face turned red with anger. He raised the M-16 and started toward the hallway. Bolan reached out and grabbed his shoulder. "No," he whispered softly. "He'll just shoot you as soon as you step through the door."

"But we can't just let him have her," the DEA whispered back.

The Executioner shook his head. "He's not going to kill her. At least not here. Not now. If that was what he wanted he could have done it back at the gallery." Bolan's jaw hardened with his outrage at the monster in the hallway. "He wants her alone."

Seven lowered his rifle, his face a mask of frustration. "Well, what do we do?"

Bolan told him. "But you'll have to be convincing," he said. "We tried a similar scam back at the gallery. It never went far enough to know if it would have worked."

The DEA man nodded, then moved to a position just inside the office by the door. "Let her go!" he yelled through the opening.

"You must come out first, American," the Chechen shouted back. "You and your partner. Then we can discuss the situation."

"My partner's dead," Seven answered. "Zdorovye shot him."

Vicious laughter echoed down the hall. "Again you lie, American pig," Movlid Akhmatov said. "That is what you told me when we were among the paintings and statues. Yet I saw both of you enter the building a few minutes ago." A long dramatic sigh came down the hallway into the office. "But if you are telling the truth, send Zdorovye out to prove it."

Bolan caught himself nodding silently. The Chechen hadn't yet bought the story but he hadn't categorically rejected it, either. It wasn't much, but it was a start.

"Zdorovye's dead, too," yelled Johnny Seven. "I shot him right after he killed my partner."

There was a moment's pause, then Akhmatov said, "Step back into the room. I will come see for myself. The woman will be in front of me, and if you are armed when I enter, she will die first, then you." A few seconds went by, then he spoke again and it was obvious that he had moved closer to the office. "Throw out all of the guns in the room," he ordered.

Seven turned to the Executioner. Bolan nodded. He guarded the doorway while the DEA man hurried back into the other office and grabbed Zdorovye's H&K, then gathered up the guns the other men had used. Seven added his SIG-Sauer to the collection, and moved back to the door. Again he looked to the Executioner as his eyes dropped to the 7-shot Taurus jammed into his belt under the tweed sport coat.

Bolan shook his head.

Seven left the weapon in his waistband and Bolan dropped the Desert Eagle on top of the pile of guns already in the DEA man's arms. Seven turned back to the door. "Here they come," he shouted. One by one, he slid the weapons out the doorway on the tile.

"Is that all?" the Chechen asked.

"That's it."

Once more came the horrendous laugh. "Except for the sound-suppressed one you used at the gallery."

Bolan had expected it. He drew the Beretta and handed it to the DEA man, who slid it out the door.

"And the .357 Magnum someone also fired," Akhmatov said. "It makes a sound like no other firearm."

Johnny Seven was worried when he looked at Bolan this time. But the Executioner nodded yet again. The Taurus, too, went in the hallway.

Another of Bolan's suspicions had just been confirmed—the Chechen wasn't sure who was who, or who was talking to him now. He had caught only glimpses of them both in the dark gallery and at the hotel, and while he had heard Bolan speak he hadn't known from which body the voice came.

That meant they could still switch places for the rest of the Executioner's plan and Movlid Akhmatov wouldn't know.

"Where is your dead partner?" Akhmatov demanded. He sounded as if he was just to the side of the open doorway now. But that meant so was Polyakova.

Bolan hooked a thumb over his shoulder and mouthed the words "Back there."

"He and Zdorovye are both in the back office," shouted Seven.

"Lie down on the floor," the Chechen ordered. "On your stomach, arms spread, your head away from the door."

The DEA man started to kneel but Bolan grabbed him by the shoulders and shoved him toward the rear office. Seven looked confused for a second but understood a moment later when the Executioner dropped to the floor himself. "I hope you know what you're doing," he whispered as he disappeared into the back office.

Bolan drew the Loner knife as he turned and dropped to his knees, then tucked it under his chest as he lay down in the position the Chechen had ordered. He stretched his arms out to his sides and waited.

Akhmatov would come in behind the woman, using her as a

shield. But before he went back to check on the dead men in the rear office, he would put a bullet into the head of the man on the floor. Whether he and Johnny Seven survived the next few minutes, and Polyakova escaped what he suspected would be a hellish experience, would be determined by when and where Akhmatov chose to pull the trigger.

If the Chechen chose to shoot Bolan as soon as he stepped into the room, from a distance, it would all be over. It would be physically impossible for the Executioner to move out of the position he was in and close the gap with the Loner before he was riddled with bullets. But Bolan's instincts told him that Akhmatov—a man who considered himself superior to mere mortals—wouldn't be able to resist moving closer to taunt him first. The odds would still be stacked against the Executioner. But there would at least be a chance.

From the floor, Bolan could see the open door into the rear office. His eyes shot around the room, looking for anything that might act as a mirror, reflecting even a distorted image of what was happening behind him. There was nothing.

A moment later he heard slow, shuffling footsteps enter the room to his rear. "Are there any other guns?" the Chechen demanded. "If you lie and I find them, you will die slowly."

Bolan hesitated to speak. While Akhmatov didn't seem to know which of them was which, he had just heard Seven's voice and might note the difference between the two. Still blind to the man behind him, he shook his head.

Footsteps shuffled toward him, and a few seconds later he could smell Polyakova's perfume. He tensed his muscles, ready to spring. Ready to take the only chance of survival they would get. Polyakova's scent grew stronger, and he knew the Chechen was still holding her in front of him. How close were they now? And how would he know when they were close enough? Bolan needed some kind of cue when they entered striking range or Akhmatov might shoot before he even decided the time to act had come.

Bolan felt a soft hand squeeze the back of his calf—too soft to be any man's. Polyakova. It had to mean the Chechen had forced her downward, still using her for cover as he leaned in to deliver the coup de grâce. She was telling him where they were— by the placement of her hand. She hadn't spoken, which meant that, at this moment, Akhmatov still had the gun jammed into her neck or back.

But to kill Bolan, he would have to take it away and aim it at the Executioner. There would be a split second during which the weapon would be pointed at no one. The Executioner's timing would have to be perfect. He wouldn't get a second chance.

"Like all Americans, you are a fool," the Chechen said. "Say goodbye to the pretty lady. I will take care of her for you."

With those words, Bolan knew the moment of truth was at hand. Without warning, he twisted like a cobra, twirling onto his back, as he swept the Loner from the floor. With his other hand he grabbed Akhmatov's gun hand. The 9 mm Stechkin exploded, the bullet passing harmlessly to the side. At the same time, the Executioner lunged upward and drove the knife past Polyakova's ear and through Movlid Akhmatov's throat.

Sobbing, Polyakova fell forward into his arms, loosening Bolan's grip around the knife. But the Loner had done what it had been designed to do.

The Chechen staggered two steps back, both hands clawing at the blade embedded in his neck. His face drained white as bright red shot from the severed arteries. He dropped hard onto his knees, jarring a paperback book from his back pocket, and mumbling words the Executioner couldn't make out through the blood flooding his throat.

But Bolan had read the man's lips, and Movlid Akhmatov's last words were "She loved me."

The Executioner glanced to the book on the floor. *Beyond Good and Evil* by Friedrich Nietzsche.

THERE WAS NO TIME to rest.

Bolan leaped to his feet, pulling Polyakova up with him as Johnny Seven came barreling out of the rear office. "What happened?" asked the DEA man.

Bolan still held the Stechkin in his hand by the barrel. "I'll tell you on the way," he said.

"The way?" Polyakova said as he hurried her out into the hall. "Where?"

"Your family," Bolan said as he swept the Beretta and Desert Eagle up off the floor. "Zdorovye sent men after them."

Polyakova swore in Russian.

Two minutes later they were down the steps and in the Chrysler. Seven had retrieved the viola case from where he'd left it in the stairwell, and shoved it into the back seat before diving in after it.

Polyakova acted as navigator, telling Bolan when and where to turn. They hurried out of the Red Square-Kremlin area, crossed the Moscow River and turned off the main thoroughfare into an area of long block buildings. Bolan had seen such residences before, many times. They had been built by the Soviet Union as housing units.

Polyakova directed him down the street past at least two dozen of the stark, characterless structures, then pointed him into a building that looked no different than the rest. They parked the car in front, and the Executioner threw the transmission into park. "What numbers?" he asked the woman next to him.

"I'll show you," Polyakova said as she opened the door.

Bolan reached out and grabbed her arm. "There's no reason for you to risk it now," he said. "The Chechen's dead. You can stay here." But before he had finished she had shrugged out of his grip and was racing toward the entrance to the building.

Bolan caught up to her halfway there with Seven a step behind. As the Executioner reached out to open the door to the common entryway, he looked through the glass and saw a tall Russian pulling a shorter man out of a doorway at the end of the hall. The tall man had wavy brown hair and a bushy Joseph Stalin-style mustache. In his hand was some sort of pistol.

The Executioner's hand froze on the door handle and he dropped low, waving the others behind him to do the same as he stared through a corner of the window. A woman, not as beautiful as Polyakova but with the same coloring and bone structure, came awkwardly out the door into the hallway in the grasp of a man with a shaved head. He also carried a gun, and together the two of them began to herd the couple down the hall.

Bolan turned to Polyakova, who had crept up and was looking over his shoulder. "Your sister and her husband?" he whispered.

She nodded. Her face was drained of emotion, as if she had experienced more terror and tension over the past three days than her system could handle, and it had simply shut down.

Bolan turned back to the window in the door. What was happening was painfully clear. The two men were taking the young couple to the apartment of Polyakova's parents so they could kill them all together. "Stay here," Bolan said. "Wait until I wave at you."

Seven and Polyakova both nodded.

Bolan stood and opened the door, whistling as he walked boldly into the hallway. As he'd suspected they would, the two men heard him coming and shoved their guns into their captives' ribs, hiding them from view. They continued to walk toward him as the Executioner whistled his way down the hall, then stopped just as they were about to pass each other.

"Excuse me," he said in Russian. "Could you tell me which one of these apartments belongs to Karl Gellbert?"

Polyakova's sister and her husband's eyes pleaded for help. He pretended not to see them. The two hardmen looked at him blankly, then the one with the mustache said, "We don't know him." They started to walk on but Bolan reached out and grabbed the forearm of the bald man and said, "Wait, I have a picture of him." His hand went under his jacket as he added, "Maybe you'll recognize him from this."

The Executioner's hand came back out from under his jacket holding the Beretta 93-R and flipping the selector switch to semiauto. One 9 mm round went into the head of the bald man and the next hit the other man two inches above the bushy mustache.

And it was all suddenly over.

Except for Gregor.

IT WAS REQUIRED that he be unarmed. But that was no problem for a man of the Executioner's skills.

Bolan entered the office and said hello to the woman whose black hair had white roots. She nodded, and said, "Oh, hello. Go on in. He's expecting you."

Bolan walked toward the door. Luiza Polyakova had decided to stay in Moscow for a few days to visit her parents. It would also give Hal Brognola time to do the behind-the-scenes groundwork that would get her charges dismissed, and publicly clear her name. Bolan had dropped Johnny Seven off at his apartment in Manhattan to get some well-deserved rest. The DEA man had proved to be an able partner during the mission, but Bolan didn't want him involved in this final lap of the race. It was one thing breaking the laws of another country—even for a good cause—but another in the U.S. And Seven was nearing the end of his career. He had served his country well, and didn't need anything coming back to bite him in the rear and cost him his pension.

Bolan smiled inwardly as he thought of the man, still wearing the Harris tweed sport coat and cap when he'd waved goodbye. He had been lucky that Johnny Seven hadn't accompanied him to El Cuchillo Rojo where the Russians had first videotaped the Executioner accepting the heroin. And keeping the DEA man away from the cameras he had known would be at Duane Park had been another reason Bolan had gone alone. Johnny Seven's face wouldn't be on any of the tapes should they surface sometime in the future, and he could end a long and distinguished career with no worries.

As for the Executioner, should the tapes show up, just let them try to figure out who he was.

Bolan opened the door and entered the office, greeted by a smiling face wearing black horned-rim glasses behind the desk. "Ah, Agent Cooper," Rutherford B. Kasparak said. "Good to see you again." He leaned across the desk and extended his hand.

Bolan saw no particular reason not to shake it. So he did, then sat in a chair across from the desk. "I've been looking forward to seeing you again, too," he said.

The New York City Department of Corrections deputy commissioner still had the nervous twitch to his hand, and it fluttered lightly back and forth as he interlaced his fingers on the desktop. But, all in all, he didn't appear to be as skittish as he had been when Bolan had last been in the office. "And how is Luiza Polyakova working out?" Kasparak asked.

"She's done an excellent job," Bolan said. "We've been very pleased with her cooperation."

"I'm delighted to hear it," Kasparak replied. "As you know, I was a little worried about releasing her the way we did. But…well, it all seems to have worked out splendidly, then." He paused and cleared his throat. "Now," he said, wearing a smile that looked like he might be planning to run for governor, "I don't like to sound mercenary, mind you, but you had mentioned that the Department of Justice was grateful…." He let the sentence trail off.

Now Bolan returned the smile as he said, "I spoke with my boss only a few hours ago," he said. "And he instructed me to reward you accordingly."

"Excellent!" Kasparak said. "Now, I know all of the important posts are filled, and that's far more than I expected anyway. What I was thinking was—"

Bolan held up his hand. "Not so fast," he said. "Don't you want to hear about all of the work Luiza did and where it led us?"

The deputy commissioner's face reddened and he said, "Yes, forgive me. I was being rather selfish, wasn't I? Please. Do tell."

Bolan began to run down what had happened over the past three days, telling the man behind the desk about Rabashka, Ontomanov, Smith-Williams, Navrozoz and Nemets. With each name he mentioned, a little more of the color faded from Kasparak's face. The Executioner saved Akhmatov and Zdorovye for last, and watched the deputy commissioner's face finally settle on a pale gray tone. He finished with the story about the sword in Zdorovye's office, and ended it with, "Which of course, led me back here to you, Gregor."

Rutherford B. Kasparak sat stunned for a moment. But like any decent undercover mole, he recovered his composure quickly and tried one last gamble. "Excuse me?" he said, his hand waving back and forth across the desk. "I'm not sure I heard you correctly. Gregory, did you call me? Actually, my first name is Rutherford— Rudy to my friends, and you're certainly welcome to—"

Bolan merely shook his head and that was enough to stop the man in midsentence. "It's over, Gregor," he said. "But I've got to hand it to you, it was a brilliant scam while it lasted. The Soviet Union sets you up in New York City and you rise to a position where you can create havoc within one of the largest correctional systems in the world. You have access to police, and some military and other federal government intelligence, and who knows where you might have gone from here." He kept staring at the man behind the desk and said, "When the Soviet Union went belly up, you simply switched allegiance to the other former Soviet officials who went into the drug-smuggling business." The Executioner looked around the room, taking in the office. "This also explains why the inmates had such good access to Luiza when they tried to kill her, and how the other gunmen knew to hit us so fast at her gallery. In fact, it explains just about everything."

Kasparak started to speak, but Bolan said, "One last thing, then I'll let you have your say." He uncrossed his legs again. "The name, Kasparak. Czech, isn't it?"

The deputy commissioner nodded.

"Nice touch," the Executioner said. "I haven't checked it because there wasn't any need. But I'd guess your phony bio includes escaping Czechoslovakia sometime in your teenage years and coming to the U.S. That would cover the occasional word you accidentally drop with an Eastern European accent. I began to think I'd heard your voice before somewhere when we talked on the phone. Then when Zdorovye gave you up, it all came together." He stopped, then said, "Okay, what was it you wanted to say?"

Kasparak had settled back in his chair, and the shock of being exposed had worn off. He looked confident, even cocky now— not a thing like the nervous bureaucrat he had masqueraded as when Bolan first met him. Now he came out with the gravely chuckle the Executioner had learned to associate with Gregor, and when he spoke his accent was the same he had used as Gregor on the phone. "Why protest it here and now? I will say this once, and never again. You are correct. But you will never prove it in a court of law, Agent Cooper."

Bolan sighed as he stood. "No, Gregor, I won't."

Two steps took him to the edge of the desk where he leaned over and grabbed the mole by the tie. Bolan jerked up and back, pulling the man over the desk. With his other hand, he drew a ballpoint pen from his shirt pocket and drove it up under the man's chin, through the soft palate, and into the brain.

Rutherford B. "Gregor" Kasparak was dead long before Bolan shoved him back into his chair.

The Executioner stepped out of the office, closing the door behind him. The secretary wasn't at her desk. She must be on her lunch break. Good, Bolan thought. He'd be long gone before anyone discovered Gregor's body.

Bolan picked his guns up from the locker, walked to the Highlander and drove out of the parking lot and back over the bridge from Rikers Island. He thought of Polyakova, and smiled. Soon the whole nightmare would be behind her, and she'd reopen her business in Greenwich Village, and never fear for her safety again.

As he drove toward the highway leading south toward Stony Man Farm, Bolan wondered what the rest of the day would bring. He had talked to Hal Brognola by phone right before driving back to Rikers.

All he knew at the moment was that Jack Grimaldi was warming up the plane.

DEATH LANDS®

Separation

*Available June 2004
at your favorite retail outlet.*

The group makes its way to a remote island in hopes of finding brief sanctuary. Instead, they are captured by an isolated tribe of descendants of African slaves from pre–Civil War days. When they declare Mildred Wyeth "free" from her white masters, it is a twist of fate that ultimately leads the battle-hardened medic to question where her true loyalties lie. Will she side with Ryan, J. B. Dix and those with whom she has forged a bond of trust and friendship…or with the people of her own blood?

Or order your copy now by sending your name, address, zip or postal code, along with a check or money order (please do not send cash) for $6.50 for each book ordered ($7.99 in Canada), plus 75¢ postage and handling ($1.00 in Canada), payable to Gold Eagle Books, to:

In the U.S.
Gold Eagle Books
3010 Walden Ave.
P.O. Box 9077
Buffalo, NY 14269-9077

In Canada
Gold Eagle Books
P.O. Box 636
Fort Erie, Ontario
L2A 5X3

Please specify book title with order.
Canadian residents add applicable federal and provincial taxes.

GDL66

THE DESTROYER

POLITICAL PRESSURE

The juggernaut that is the Morals and Ethics Behavior Establishment—MAEBE—is on a roll. Will its ultra-secret enforcement arm, the White Hand, kill enough scumbags to make their guy the uber-boy of the Presidential race? MAEBE! Will Orville Flicker succeed in his murderous, manipulative campaign to win the Oval Office? MAEBE! Can Remo and Chiun stop the bad guys from getting whacked—at least until CURE officially pays them to do it? MAEBE!

Available April 2004 at your favorite retail outlet.

TAKE 'EM FREE
2 action-packed novels plus a mystery bonus

NO RISK
NO OBLIGATION TO BUY

James Axler
Outlanders®

SUN LORD

In a fabled city of the ancient world, the neo-gods of Mexico are locked in a battle for domination. Harnessing the immutable power of alien technology and Earth's pre-Dark secrets, the high priests and whitecoats have hijacked Kane into the resurrected world of the Aztecs. Invested with the power of the great sun god, Kane is a pawn in the brutal struggle and must restore the legendary Quetzalcoatl to his rightful place—or become a human sacrifice....

Available May 2004 at your favorite retail outlet.

Or order your copy now by sending your name, address, zip or postal code, along with a check or money order (please do not send cash) for $6.50 for each book ordered ($7.99 in Canada), plus 75¢ postage and handling ($1.00 in Canada), payable to Gold Eagle Books, to:

In the U.S.	In Canada
Gold Eagle Books	Gold Eagle Books
3010 Walden Avenue	P.O. Box 636
P.O. Box 9077	Fort Erie, Ontario
Buffalo, NY 14269-9077	L2A 5X3

Please specify book title with your order.
Canadian residents add applicable federal and provincial taxes.

GOLD EAGLE®

GOUT29